I'd Wait Forever

Shivani Rana

CONTENT WARNING

Although this is a simple romance story, there are topics in here that may be heavy for some readers.

Possible triggering topics mentioned include:
anxiety, grief revolving around loved one's death, bullying, dysfunctional families/divorce, and general mental health.

There are also explicit scenes throughout the book. The novel is considered low spice but not no spice so please be aware that this is an open door romance.

If all these topics sound okay to you and you continue reading, I hope you enjoy this book and the story of Sonia and Kartik.

Thank you and happy reading!

*for the ones who find themselves wishing to the stars
to finally be someone's first choice,
the ones who stay haunted by the possibilities
of 'what ifs'*

and the artists who yearn to be someone's muse.

this one's for you.

PLAYLIST

How You Get The Girl (Taylor's Version) - Taylor Swift
Somewhere Only We Know - Keane
A Little Death - The Neighbourhood
Meddle About - Chase Atlantic
See You Later (Ten Years) - Jenna Raine
Wrong Time - Clay Newton
Line Without A Hook - Ricky Montgomery
I Miss You, I'm Sorry - Gracie Abrams
Waiting Room - Phoebe Bridgers
Those Eyes - New West
Memories - Conan Gray
Wildest Dreams (Taylor's Version) - Taylor Swift
Yellow - Coldplay
Lovers Rock - TV Girl
Falling In - Lifehouse
Bad Idea Right? - Olivia Rodrigo
Say Don't Go (Taylor's Version) (From The Vault) - Taylor Swift
Maan Meri Jaan - King ft. Nick Jonas
Right Here - Chase Atlantic
Beside You - 5 Seconds Of Summer
We Can't Be Friends (Wait For Your Love) - Ariana Grande
Supercut - Lorde
The Only Exception - Paramore
Look After You - The Fray

CHAPTER 1

Sonia

My hand flew up towards the pendant that remained hidden underneath my shirts every day. No one could see it except me.

And no one would.

I made sure of that.

I didn't like keeping it from my best friends, Jyoti and Addie, but some things were meant to be personal, memories that only we could recount. There were pieces of us that were too broken to share, too special to taint with speculation from other people. So for the past eight years, my secret has been tucked away, hugging my skin and never seeing daylight.

Drifting into the parking lot, I put my car in park, my knuckles growing white from the grip on the steering wheel. The message tone from my phone covered the silence and I glanced over to see Addie's name.

Addie: *Jaymin says Kay is really sweet. Let me know how it goes!*

I had suggested to the girls that I was considering getting my first tattoo, and Addie's new boyfriend, NFL Quarterback Jaymin Mehta, had informed her about his college friend who started tattooing not too long ago and just so happened to come back to New Jersey, making sure the information was conveyed to me through the mouth of my best friend. Apparently, it had been one of his roommates from his freshman year of college, someone who'd been through hell and back alongside him, surviving the toughest of their classes together. Hearing Jaymin say that I'd be in trusting hands was all that mattered, though.

So here I was, crazily sitting in the parking lot of a tattoo shop thirty minutes from my silent neighborhood apartment, still contemplating if I even wanted to go through with having the memorabilia of the biggest heartbreak in my life permanently drawn onto my skin. Pushing aside all doubts, I stepped out of the vehicle with a sigh, my feet dragging me swiftly inside the shop before any repulsing thoughts could pass through and stop me early.

The paper white walls were draped with artificial vines and plants, string lights flowing through every opening possible. Deep green couches lined the sides and an oak desk sat right in front of the door, a cheery woman clicking on the keys on a computer right behind it. "Hi!" Perching up at the sound of the entrance bell attached to the top of the door, she smiled, brightening the room even further.

"Hi." Timidly, I walked over, placing my hands on the cold wood as she grinned. "I have an appointment with Kay." Kaitlyn, as it read along her name tag, went back onto the computer before meeting my gaze again.

Tattoos skirted down both her arms, meeting at the base of her neck, the delicate snakes and flowers making her look exactly as an image of the environment. It was me who was the imposter, constantly debating whether to linger or bolt. Despite any better judgment, my feet stayed rooted there, pushing through all the uncomfortable thoughts that threatened to pull through.

"Got it." Kaitlyn stood up, rounding the desk towards me. "You can follow me." With a nod, I fell in step beside her, climbing up the stairs into what seemed like a hallway full of private rooms. After settling into the one at the farthest end, she signaled for me to take a seat and began setting up the tools. "You're getting a collarbone, correct?" I nodded as she ran a small razor along my skin, preparing it. "Bold choice for the first one!" She placed the disposable blade into the trash can before turning towards me again. "Alright then, Kay will be right with you!"

Taking a step back, she'd almost made it out the door had I not stopped her. "Oh, are you not Kay?" The surprise was evident on my face and she beamed in response.

"No, no. You're not scheduled with me!" I racked my brain, unable to piece any other person in here when I'd walked in. I was sure the shop was barren, the only inhabitants being the two of us. After another moment of confusion, she spoke. "My boyfriend actually. We work here together and you're scheduled with him." The way she was radiating had rubbed off onto me, the slightest smile pulling at my lips. "His name's Kartik."

All movement halted as her words registered in my brain. "What?" That name. I hadn't heard it in years. There was no way, right? But before I could pry further, Kaitlyn disappeared, leaving me all alone on the chair with nothing but a supercut of my life playing through my head. My heart was hammering, thumping out of my slightly exposed chest and goosebumps took residence all over me.

No.

There was absolutely no possible way.

I was overthinking it.

I should have left because after a moment, the door swung open, cold air rushing through the air but all the hairs on my body raised for an entirely different reason. My eyes traveled towards the opening, all breath stopping abruptly in my throat. I was choking on nothing.

I saw him before he could even notice me.

Kaitlyn, who was tangled onto his arm, stood taller and diverted his attention to me, his eyes bulging as realization hit. "Sonia." God, it'd been forever since I heard him say anything, let alone my name. I shut my eyes as all those high school nights manifested in front of me. All those memories. All those moments I was about to draw onto my skin.

Oh my God, what was I doing?

I couldn't get a tattoo anymore.

No matter how hard I tried though, the world was stacked against me, the words struggling to leave my mouth. "You two know each other?" Kaitlyn's brows furrowed as she looked between two seemingly strangers who couldn't stop their eyes from locking onto one another.

"We're old friends." Still, it was him who spoke words that hurt me even when I never wished they hadn't. Despite being a teacher, all vocabulary was wiped from my brain, all traces of the English language disappearing like he once did. It was getting harder to breathe.

I needed to get out.

"Oh small world," the smile was back again. "Well then, I'll leave you to it." He finally glanced at her and she rose on her tiptoes, pressing a peck onto his lips and it was only then I noticed his eyes were still on me. My heart quenched behind my chest and I struggled to move a muscle.

She was out as quick as she'd come and now it was just the two of us, suffocating in these four blank walls. "It's been so long, Sonia." I nodded. "How are you?" His voice entailed that he was just as disoriented as I had been, shifting from one foot to the other.

He was still so handsome, it stole my breath. The same boyish grin was plastered across him but a hint of longing lay beneath it. His droopy hair was carefully pushed back, the waves lining his ear and hairline like they were handcrafted and placed there with reason. The only difference was that he was no longer the kid I tutored in high school, he was all man, wrapped in a white button down and black jeans, the splitting image of a fallen angel covered in ink.

But it was no different than it was all those years ago. "Hi," I managed. "Kartik." I froze as his name left my lips on instinct, something I never thought would ever happen again. It was so far-fetched and I pinched myself to confirm that this was indeed reality. All of a sudden a painful sadness encompassed me as he moved around, readying himself to get to work. We both acknowledged the silence, acknowledged the fact that at this moment we didn't need any words.

We didn't want any.

It was hurtful enough that we were in a position where we no longer had the right to speak.

He moved across the room, glancing every now and then towards me while I stayed simply hypnotized by the ghost before me. What were you expected to do when the only love you've known in your life showed up at your doorstep almost a decade later? Do you pretend like you've always been unfazed, unaffected? Or do you let it know how it's impacted your life to the point of no return?

I decided upon the first one.

And seemingly, so did he.

"Where?" A tick formed in his hard set jaw, the motion indicating that he wanted something else from the moment. "I have to put the stencil on, Sonia."

An unintentional audible sound left me before pulling the v-neck of my shirt off the shoulder, exposing just a slight amount of skin around my chest where Kaitlyn had shaved. His eyes locked onto my neck and it was only then I remembered I still had his necklace around me.

Shit.

Something in him changed as he took a step closer, invading all my space and merging it until it became his own. He never glanced at my face again and I never prompted him to. Was he thinking about that day just as I did every morning? Did he even remember it?

Swiftly, I felt his hands brush along my flesh and instinctively flinched as he rubbed his fingers along the paper that carried remnants of us. The tips of his fingers slid across my collarbone and I shut my eyes reminiscing about how that touch once made me feel. Or still made me feel. Even after all these years, he had a power over me that I was never able to hand over to anyone else.

He was able to make me feel more alive than anyone ever would.

I kept my lids shut as he motioned for me to lay down and pulled a stool close by. One hand rested on my exposed skin as the other gently steadied to pierce the needle into my skin, small gasps escaping me. Whether they were because of the pricking or the man who was now cascading in my bubble, I didn't know. I couldn't look at him.

Goosebumps intensified across my skin as he repeated his motions.

Pierce.

Wipe.

Pierce.

Wipe.

The thirty minutes he'd been at work did nothing to level my breathing. And with each dredged minute, the memories started pouring through my mind again.

"All done." His voice had a rasp that it hadn't before and I opened my eyes to see his face still just a breath away. The fingers that still lay on me twitched against my skin and a chill rushed through my bones. Had he noticed it too? The way the past lingered thick in the air between us? The way we were still frozen there? Or was I the only one who stayed there, right where he left me?

After another minute, he finally moved, letting the coldness of the shop take over in his absence. And I hated it. I hated everything about the coldness, the warmth, the man who simply didn't say a word but managed to say a billion in silence. But then I hadn't either.

Was I wrong for continuously living here—in the past? Whereas he was fully ten steps ahead of it all. He'd moved on all while I strolled into his tattoo shop to get a permanent reminder of him.

He extended a hand, placing a mirror on my lap and I lifted it with a gasp. It was beautiful.

I'd seen the stencil but couldn't imagine how much more stunning it would be once it was all shaded in black. One long wave extended along the hardness of my collarbone, stars lining the entire top. The detailing took my breath away and I couldn't help the praises that left my lips. "This is perfect, thank you, Kartik." At the slip of his name, my hand flew towards my mouth and a pain passed through the entirety of my arm, the hurt doubling as I winced. It all happened so fast and like clockwork, he was in my vicinity for the second time, his eyes scanning my shoulder while his palms lightly caressed the skin. "You're going to want to be a little careful, shona." It was him who stepped away now, awareness coursing through him as the nickname slipped through his tongue. That nickname. The one that helped me survive all those years. And I never thought I'd ever hear it again.

Clearing his throat, he walked towards his tools and placed a sheet of Saniderm protection onto my skin, pressing so slowly that it was enough to reduce the pain that shot through every part of me. "You might feel a little sore because it's a delicate area but it'll heal soon." Did he know why I had picked it? Or was he null of all the memories?

"Okay." It was all I could manage. Quickly pushing off the chair, I safely created some distance between us, walking backwards toward the exit. "Do I pay at the counter?" He still refused to move an inch, as if the moment had trapped us both in closing walls. "With Kaitlyn?" At the reminder of his girlfriend's name, he jerked, snapping back into his body as reality slapped him.

He was a different man now. And I was not the same woman. We'd never meet again. He had his life and I had mine, despite all the ways mine still revolved around his.

Kartik simply nodded and that was all the sign I needed to leave.

CHAPTER 2
Kartik

8 years ago

"Mr. Sharma, you're on the road to failing." I sat back in my chair, my feet bouncing as the only thought in my head revolved around leaving this place as quickly as I could. "Mr. Sharma," my geometry teacher, Mrs. Kate got louder, her voice ringing through my ears, causing my eyes to roll back. "I suggest you take up tutoring if you want to walk with the rest of your peers."

"I don't need tutoring," I barked. How the hell was I supposed to make time for tutoring when I barely had time for any other extracurriculars? What the hell would all my friends say if they knew I had to take up extra help? What would my family say?

School was never supposed to be the main stress but the way my personal life began bleeding into it, I seemed to be blurring the lines between my escape and reality.

"You do if you want to pass this class, Kartik."

"Whatever." I proceeded to lift onto my feet but as Mrs. Kate mimicked my motions, I halted.

"Look, Kartik. I know it's your senior year of high school. All you kids want to do is relax before the real world gets you. But you're two months into the school year and already on track with having to repeat this class. If you don't catch up now, that summer before college won't be yours to keep. So I really suggest that you think about it before you're in a position where you can't save your grades." She took a step forward as I remained voiceless. "I can't force you to go up to tutoring but I will be putting in your name with the department and they'll email you the details. Now if you're not going to show up, at least have the decency to reply back to them so the poor tutor they assign you with won't have to sit there waiting for you."

With another disgruntled sigh, I left her room, running into the same group of boys I always met with. Trevor and Colt. Both of them had grown up in my neighborhood and had the reputation of heartthrobs in this school. All the girls went after them and because of them, me. But none of that interested me as much as it did them.

"What'd Kate hold you up for?" It was Colt who spoke as we dabbed each other up. I shrugged, not wanting to get into it because I knew what they'd say already. "She needs to chill sometimes."

"Yeah." My voice was a whisper, an attempt at putting an end to this particular conversation. "Where are you guys headed?" It was routine for us, every day, after class to go hang at the local diner or park, depending on whether they'd be in the mood to smoke their cigarettes or not. I'd always tried drifting them away but like the hard headed boys they were, they lived to the typical image of a motorcycle bad boy, dwelling in leather and smoke. I, on the other hand, was more of a third wheeler in their activities, only showing up for the sake of friendship. The only time we'd all possibly shared a common interest was when we were on the stage in front of crowds. Other than that, our unspoken bond proved to show that people didn't need to know your core to establish a heavy connection with each other.

"Let's stop by the corner store." Trevor chimed in, tapping both our backs to start the walk to the lot outside. "Gotta grab a few snacks before we head to the park."

"Bet." Colt agreed, following close behind Trevor.

I ran a hand through my hair, pushing it out of my face as a deep breath flowed through me. Tutoring. Fuck. How was I supposed to explain why I was staying long days at school to anyone? Why the fuck did I even need it? I closed my eyes for a second, shaking my head as I caught up with the boys.

They were laughing about something and it only made me feel more distant, not knowing what. Because all I could think about was what would happen if I didn't graduate this year. Lost in my thought, something slammed against my arm, reeling me backwards with the force of the thousand bricks. "What the fuck?" I turned to see nothing in my line of vision but as I drank in the scene, a girl was crouched against the floor, hurriedly grabbing onto the books that spread across the tile. All I could see were her blonde streaks flailing across her shoulders, moving ever so slightly against the movement of her body, making it hard to single out any other part of her.

My breath hitched as I stayed mesmerized in the moment, unable to tear my eyes off of her. She didn't even turn back, didn't pause at the feel of me. Maybe she didn't even notice it. Maybe I wasn't something in her vision. But it didn't stop me from continuously watching as she knelt on the cold ground stacking the books one at a time. Was she not embarrassed? Hell, even I was for her.

The only thing that broke me from the trance was Trevor's voice. Fucking Trevor. "Watch where you're walking next time."

Still, she didn't turn. Her face remained angled away but I didn't miss the way her spine hardened at the remark. Something in me awoke, and I got a feeling she was fired up and as much as it pained me, I had the urge to instigate further on the off chance that she'd finally show herself. "Clutz."

She jolted up at the sound of me, books steady now, wrapped in her arms. But surprise, surprise, she still didn't fucking turn. I wanted to see her. I wanted to see who was so unaffected by the fact that she'd done the damage to herself that it didn't matter how many voices taunted her. But as I kept watching her back, she began shrinking when all she chose to do was walk away.

"Let's go." Colt pressed a hand to the back of my neck, pulling me towards the exit again, all the other high schoolers watching as we stormed off. But my mind still remained dancing around the mysterious girl, thinking about those light streaks that fanned across an unaffected body.

Who the hell was she?

CHAPTER 3

Sonia

8 years ago

I'd allow myself another five minutes to wait before deciding to leave and report it to the tutoring office. Because how careless did someone truly have to be to fall ten minutes late to something that was meant to help them? But then again, why had I expected anything else when I read his name?

Kartik Sharma.

The most irresponsible boy ever known in this school.

The only boy who I avoided at all cost, knowing it would never be beneficial to be in his sights.

The boy who sat at the back of my English class, oblivious to everyone and everything around him.

Just last week, when he'd purposely bumped into me on his way out of class, he and his troublemaking friends had not only made jokes but also just stood there, watching as I picked up the books they'd caused to fall off the ground. Something about him boiled my blood, my normally sane mind filling with rage and anger and it was a feeling I absolutely despised.

On seeing his name on my list of students, I almost begged the department to hand him to another tutor but I knew everyone's schedules were packed and filled, with me being the only one with an open spot. Begrudgingly, I kept my mouth shut and hoped for the best.

But I knew now how wrong I was.

Or, in fact, how right I was about him.

Why had I expected him to care about anyone's inconvenience except his own?

With a sigh, I began gathering my math books and tossing them inside my one shoulder tote bag, tapping on the table in hopes that if I held on for just one more second, he'd show up. Another resigned sigh later, I lifted off the seat but to my surprise, the door swung open, warm air flowing in immediately. I turned, eyes meeting his and as relieved as I was, something inside me had awoken, bringing me to the edge immediately.

As frustrated as he made me, just like every woman in this school, he captivated me. There was no doubt that he was a sight for sore eyes but I knew that was all in the outer layers, there was no depth to his kind and there never would be.

"Sorry." He wasn't serious? Was he?

"What?" The question slipped my lips, the surprise masking every corner.

"I'm sorry." He took slow steps towards me and I suddenly felt consumed in a way I never had before. My hand shot up to my hair, tucking the strands behind my ears, my mouth snapping shut. "I didn't tell anyone I was coming to tutoring and it was kind of hard to slip away. That's why I'm late."

"It's okay," I pushed out. I couldn't look away from his eyes, hypnotizing me with the honesty through them. I didn't think he could ever feel apologetic for someone else's time but as he stood awkwardly, I found myself wanting to believe him.

He began his slow tread towards me, and it was at that moment I realized he had no clue what an asshole he'd been the day when he'd crashed into me. The anger began piling up again, once more wanting to get this session over with. I had no interest in dwelling on him longer than I was required to so I turned around, sitting back down on my extended seat and waited for him to catch up in front of me.

"Can we just get started?" My voice was harsh as he leaned back in his chair, a smug look pulling across his features, as if in some sort of challenge. What for, I had no idea. He crossed his arms and tilted his head towards me, not letting a peep through his sealed lips. I stared at him for a moment longer, waiting for him to drop the cool guy attitude but when he refused, I sat up straighter, gathering all my books again. "You know what, I don't need this. *You* do. And if you're not willing to sit here and act like you *want* to be here, I won't either." His smile only grew, and despite wanting to hate it, I couldn't help but admit it was devastatingly beautiful, only serving to further infuriate me. "Whatever."

I began to stand but his vow of silence finally broke. "If you're leaving, make sure you watch where you walk this time and don't drop all those books you just spent five minutes stacking neatly." His knowing smirk was still wide across his chin and I wanted to grab onto it and wipe it off so harshly that it would leave a mark. My eyes widened, practically glaring at him as he broke into a chuckle. My grip tightened around the textbooks and I pushed them further into my chest, my sight on him unwavering. "You know, I didn't know it was you at first but those highlights are easily recognizable."

"I can just tell Mrs. Kate that you have no intention of staying in tutoring and you can figure out how you're planning on passing your classes all on your own, deal?"

He sat up straighter in his chair, and despite the difference in our positions, I still felt as though he were towering above me. The satisfied look never left him, even as something borderline to fear clouded through. "Okay, okay."

For whatever reason, a guilt-like sensation overtook me and I truly looked at the boy who sat before me. His eyes were sullen, hung like their only source of light were nowhere to be found. His face was dull, all life sucked out. What the hell was going on with him? And why was I suddenly willing to drop everything to make sure whatever it was, was okay?

I sat again, wordlessly, waiting patiently for his eyes to meet mine. A sound escaped my lips, just inaudible enough to not raise any ears, and the red rims finally met me. He was broken. And it hurt me just the same. "Can we start over?" His voice was a whisper, a plea, and I couldn't help but nod my head along with it. Just as quickly as they appeared, all pained appearances vanished and he was back to being the arrogant *bad boy* of the school. "I'm Kartik."

That change alone was enough to confirm in my head that this would be the most life changing school year I was destined to have. And I couldn't figure out whether I should've been scared or excited.

I stared at his outstretched hand for a moment, his mischievous smile alerting all the warning signs in my brain to not indulge. But I was never one to refuse a challenge. Never one to back down. I grabbed onto his open palm and squeezed my fingers tight around his. "Sonia."

CHAPTER 4

Sonia

As the kids dispersed at the sound of the bell, I stayed frozen at my desk, my thoughts still reverberating around the same day two whole weeks ago. The tattoo was healed but all my old scars and wounds were rehashed and reopened, burning as though they were fresh with salt rubbed all within their surface.

His face refused to leave my sight.

Although the image of a younger version of him remained permanent in my head, it was now updated with all the mature features, merging into someone I couldn't recognize.

Those dark eyes pierced through my soul, the memory of the first time I'd looked into them still fresh in my mind. The way they forever hypnotized me, even to this day. It was worse when he was mere inches away from my face. There was no way I could escape him anymore.

Not to mention he was around for God knows how long. And all I could wonder was why.

Why was he here again, after all this time?

Why did he leave in the first place?

Why didn't he reach out?

Why did he move on like there was nothing left to come back to?

Perhaps those answers were no longer my right. Once upon a time they had been. But now, all his justifications belonged to someone else.

Kaitlyn.

The girl looked like she fit right on his arm. Together, they looked like the dream, like nothing could tear them apart. Two halves of a whole. So far off from what we did.

I was always the plain jane, the quiet girl who focused more on other people rather than myself while he was the complete opposite of all that made me. He was equal parts carefree and self absorbed. Hints of everything I had once aspired to be. But it was unattainable. It wasn't real. And neither were we.

"Sonia!" A voice snapped me out of my thoughts and I shook my head to clear the memories before turning towards one of my favorite colleagues in the school, Mortada, or Mr. M as the kids called him. While I taught English to the kindergarteners, he was everyone's favorite math teacher. And one of the most genuine and sweetest staff members in the school. "Are you okay? You look like you're sick."

He came around the desk and leaned against it, with a face full of immense concern. "Yeah, sorry." Pasting a smile across my chin, I glanced up at him, gathering all my papers neatly in front of me. "Just lost in thought."

"One day at a time, Sonia." I nodded along as he got himself comfortable. "You're always running ahead in that brain of yours. Take a breath. Just live in the present." He was right. From anyone else, the advice would have sounded pretentious, but Mortada somehow knew me better than most. He'd become a friend, someone who didn't need much time to establish a strong connection with. He knew I was always the planner, the one with everything borderline figured out. But for the past two weeks, everything I knew had become jumbled into a mess I could not seem to untangle.

"It's okay. I'm okay." I wasn't really but I would be because there was no point in dwelling in the ghosts of my past. Especially not the ones that became strangers whose laughs I'd recognize anywhere. "What'd your day look like?"

"You know how Mondays go. The kids were cranky, loud and sometimes too energetic, but you gotta love them." As high functioning as they were, my job was the one good thing about my life. It was exactly as I had dreamt it'd be. From tutoring high school students to making a difference in a young child's life, I knew it was what I was born for, the only path my life could have taken. It was also the only thing I could see myself indulging in.

Other than the man who plagued my mind these past few days. Years even.

"Yeah, I know exactly what you mean." I chuckled in response, nodding along with him.

"So Sonia, any plans for the big spring break?"

I'd almost forgotten that the week-long spring break was coming close. It was already mid march, which explained why the kids were more excited than normal. "No big plans honestly. My girls wanted to go celebrate Holi. They're having a big celebration out in the city, Central Park and we might just head out there."

"Oh yeah, I saw something about that online. It looks really fun."

I hummed in agreement as I rose with all my papers, placing them in the metal file holder at the corner of my desk. "Yeah every year they do the whole *Festival of Colors* event out there for adults, you know marketing it like that so more non South Asians could show up. It's usually packed and all kinds of people show up." As if remembering an important detail, I placed a hand on his arm excitedly. "You should totally come!"

"I would love to but me and Alyssa are planning on taking a cruise out to Bermuda. She's been looking into it for a while now and I think I want to surprise her with it." Alyssa and Mortada had been together for about three years now, and as far as I knew he was taking it at her pace. Being surrounded by happy couples, including my best friend Addie and her sweetheart of a boyfriend Jaymin, had never bothered me until I ran into my personal Voldemort. Now, I was suddenly in irk of anything that reminded me of him. But that never stopped me from feeling happiness for my loved ones.

"That sounds fun! I guess I'm going to have to wait longer to meet her but I'm sure she's gonna love it!"

"Yeah, I do too." He pushed off the desk as he waited for me to rise. Together, we silently made our way towards the car park, stopping at mine first. "Look, whatever is bothering you Sonia, I hope you figure it out. I haven't seen you this lost since I've met you and it kind of worries me."

I was typically the held-together one. The one who never let her emotions show on her face. Not around others and typically, not even around myself. But the truck hit me so hard mid road that I had no choice but to stop and stare.

"I will, don't worry." I feigned the most genuine smile I could, opening my driver side door to slide in while waving him off as he strolled towards his vehicle. For a moment, I rested my head against my steering wheel, still the same thoughts plaguing me, confusion racking my brain on how I even ended up here.

All I knew was I had to figure it out before I fell back into the empty shell I once had been.

CHAPTER 5
Kartik

Two weeks had passed but it only took two seconds for everything to come rushing back that afternoon. I never expected it. I didn't even think she'd still be here. A billion places in the world and we both landed in the same city at the same time for the second time in our lives. If that wasn't fate, I don't know what was.

No, I was definitely going crazy.

I shook my head slightly, palming it between my hands as they swallowed my frustrated grunt and vanished it into the air. She was still the beautiful girl I once fell in love with. The same highlighted eccentric hair, the same crooked smile, the same soft skin. She was everything dreams were made of. Except she was no longer mine.

Now unattainable.

But I didn't want her to be.

But that wasn't my decision to make. It was always her in the driver's seat, controlling my every move as I continuously handed her the keys to my life. And I didn't even want them back regardless of the fact that we no longer rode together. But

I'd be damned if I didn't try to get her to steer towards my pathway again.

For the entirety of the two weeks, all that ran through my head was the way she was just as beautiful as she had been since the very first day I saw her. And I knew I had to find her again.

When I'd been informed that my appointment had arrived, I'd been in the office, thinking all was right in the world. Her name was unknown to me because I never handled the bookings, that was Kaitlyn's job. And regardless, all I knew was that Jaymin knew her and I trusted him and his friends. But I should have looked. I could have. But if I did, would that have changed anything?

Would I have gotten it canceled?

Would I have attempted to avoid her?

Or would I have pretended like it didn't affect me just as I did when she was holding her breath on my chair. Her eyes were shut for most of it but I was looking nowhere else. She still held my gaze like the very first time. Seeing that necklace around her, the choice of her tattoo, everything took me back to those careless, stupid nights we once shared in secret. In silence.

Eight whole years ago.

We were just kids. But we always knew what it was. We knew we were in love.

But somewhere along the way we screwed it up.

The sound of the door startled me back to the present, away from the fairytales I still thought of and in walked my reality—Kaitlyn.

Seeing Sonia shouldn't have shifted my vision around what was already in front of me. I was comfortable where I was at, maybe not at my potential happiness, but I told myself this was all I could have for years now. And Kaitlyn was just an addition to that. I had met her a year ago through a mutual friend and we instantly hit it off as friends and just two months ago decided to take things a step further.

We were in our own fucked up way a version of happy.

That was until the nickname slipped through my lips at the sight of the only person who could bring me to ruins. My shona. My love.

And I knew then that I couldn't drag along innocent victims under the illusion that nothing had changed.

Her face instantly dropped once she caught sight of what I assumed was a bloodshot look across mine. Wordlessly, she crossed the room to stand in front of me, waiting until I glanced up at her. She wasn't angry, she wasn't mad, but sadness seemed to cross her for just a moment, making the culpability feel all the worse.

"It's her, isn't it?" I nodded, knowing she was smart enough to connect all the dots together. I never shied away from telling her about my history, Sonia included, in hopes that one day maybe I could move past it. Sometimes recounting the details worked towards helping you move forward. Except, in this case, Sonia's memories were adamant on never leaving me. "I could tell. You haven't been the same since that day." With a defeated exhale, she took a seat on the chair beside me, no longer looking my way, her levelheaded gaze following the light bulbs atop our heads. "I don't blame you, she's beautiful."

"She's always been." I knew the careless slip of tongue had pierced Kaitlyn a bit, but she would never say it. "I'm sorry." My voice was a whisper, longing for more than I could attain.

"You don't need to apologize, Kartik." Her dark eyes were still turned towards the ceiling. Reaching over, I placed a soft hand on hers, squeezing for a moment. "That place was never mine to take." She shook her head, finally meeting my eyes. "I'm not mad about it. I'm not even really sad." She appeared to be relieved but my brain still struggled to understand what she was attempting to say. I opened my mouth to speak only to be cut off instantly. "At least not about the fact that she's back in your life. I'm sad it took you so long to realize it."

"I don't understand." I retreated my hand, straightening in my chair.

"Kartik, I saw it the day she walked in here. I knew something was wrong, something was out of place. And I watched you from a distance while you were tattooing her. You and I may look like we're aesthetically fit, but you and her? You two look like you're helplessly strung together, as if the universe itself had broken you off from one piece and left you out to find each other." She let out a breath, this time sounding far more relaxed than earlier. "Go get her, yeah?"

"Why are you not more upset about this?" My forehead wrinkled, my brain remaining muddled.

"Because you were never mine to keep. I knew there was a spot in your heart that was forever reserved for someone else. And when she came back, whenever it would have been, I knew my time would be over." A genuine smile took its place across her face. "I know what it's like losing someone and never getting them back. I've lost someone who I thought I never would and it was the most ravaging year of my life. I wouldn't want to be the reason you go through it too." Half of the reason why we ever platformed into a relationship was because of our twinning histories and tragic endings of love.

"You're amazing, Kaitlyn." I leaned towards her, pulling her into me for a side hug, affection pouring out of me. My eyes were now open. I knew what I had to do.

"Yeah, yeah. Just don't fire me from the shop, okay?" With a shared chuckle she squeezed tighter against me before breaking apart, her hand still casually resting on my arm. "If you do I might just have to hold onto you."

"I won't, don't worry." Rising onto my feet, I pulled her into me again, hugging her as all relief passed through me. "You're an absolute necessity to this place. I don't know what I'd do without you."

"Good." She pulled away, tip toeing just a bit to press a small kiss onto my cheek. "Now go get your girl."

I nodded in response. "I will."

CHAPTER 6
Sonia

8 years ago

He stared at me as if I had been speaking a made up language. "What aren't you understanding?" I placed the pens back down, finally observing his calm demeanor. "Are you intentionally not trying to pass this test?"

"I am." His arms crossed against his chest as he slouched in the chair beside me, an irritated tone covering his words. I turned to face him, the slight brush of our knees causing my body to jerk back a bit. Noticing the movement, a smirk appeared around him, the image of arrogance pouring out of him. "But it's been a week. Naak pe itna gussa kyu hai?" *Why are you carrying this much anger at the tip of your nose?*

"I'm not angry." It was my turn to cross my arms. He stared at the movement for a moment too long and I felt myself shrink under his sights. It'd been happening all week and I managed to avoid it like the plague. His gaze possessed something unnameable that made it far more addicting than it should have been, and I knew if I stayed under it for too long,

I'd find myself disappearing into it, losing sight of everything important.

"Well," he finally sat up, resting his elbows on the desk in front of us. Suddenly, the entire room shrunk, nothing but his dark eyes taking root of the atmosphere. "If it's not anger, it's *definitely* annoyance."

"Yes because I'm sitting here day after day trying to do my job while you sit there acting like your time is more valuable than anyone else's." His smile only grew, making the blood in my veins boil to a temperature I had previously thought impossible. "If you're not keen on passing, let me know and we can both save our breaths and time and be done with this." I waited a moment longer, watching as he watched me, observing, scrutinizing me under his stare. I was growing weaker by the second, feeling as though I was on the losing end of the battle, holding the shorter end of the stick. "Alright then." With a slight nod, I sat up straighter, slowly capping my pen, mentally preparing myself to make my exit.

"You need to loosen up." His direct voice pierced through me, earning a stern look back.

"Excuse me?"

"You heard me, Sonia." His slouch was now gone, all traces of it vanished as he leaned into my personal space, taking my breath along with him. From up close, he was even more deadly, those cheekbones cutting through any resolve I once had about him. I wanted to like him but my brain knew indulging in his nuances could only hinder my life. "Loosen up."

"I don't *need* to do anything." Never backing from a challenge, I remained steady in my place, letting him breathe my air while his eyes traveled from my head to my toes. I found myself wondering exactly what was going through his curious mind, waiting to understand if he had me figured out, if he could see through all the masks I wore for the rest of the world. "What?"

"You need a break." He was so nonchalant, speaking so matter-of-factly as though nothing else was right besides him in the world. His finger came up towards the thin skin of my cheek, the air between us bursting with static before he brought it back down to his side. I found myself releasing a breath I hadn't realized I'd been holding, the anticipation of his touch bursting my sanity.

"And *you* need to study." With another roll of his eyes, he resided back in his space, his knee still extended far enough to lightly brush against mine. "If you want to pass, that is. When we started you were so hell bent on paying attention and doing well, where's all that now?"

"You're all work, and no play. How about we make a bet?" After I hadn't responded, he continued. "A challenge if you want to call it that."

I was sure my eyes were now bulging out my head, shock coming in all ways. However, I was unmistakably curious and my curiosity never sat well when it was buried. "What exactly do you mean?" I moved away from the slight point of contact we had, attempting to gain the upper hand in the situation but just as he towered me when we stood, he did so in the conversation as well.

"If I fail my test, I'll start being a good student in tutoring. I won't waste your time anymore. Maybe I'll even ask the counselor to switch out my tutor because it wasn't working out between us. I won't be in your hair anymore. I'm sure you'd like that." After spending a week with Kartik, somehow I found myself against the idea of his departure. There was something unknown that had me looking forward to my after school nights with him, something I couldn't pinpoint exactly. He was like fresh air, although arrogant, he showed me that sometimes people weren't as obtuse as you think.

Dulling that stab his suggestion gave, I responded. "Okay. And if you somehow pass?"

He imitated a dagger going through his heart, dramatically falling back further into his chair, which unintentionally coaxed a chuckle out of me. "Have you no faith in me?"

"No." I lied. I knew he had it in him if he just applied himself. He was smart, he just needed to believe it too. Throughout the entirety of the week, I saw the changes, the way he cared without actually making it obvious that he did. It was like he was hiding what he really was from the world, not wanting them to think he was just human too. Time and time again, for just small glimpses, I saw that sadness I saw on the first day again but it would escape so quickly, I wondered if I ever saw it at all. But I was drawn to pulling it out again, even if it meant coaxing it out of him.

"Ouch, Sonia. And here I was thinking we were finally getting along." With a slight *tsk* he shook his head, no more words furthering his statements.

"We don't get along." I shook my head, still laser focused on him. "I tolerate you. So now tell me, what if you magically pass?"

"Well," the cockiness was back, "for one, you get bragging rights. Mrs. Kate would love you for making her star student even better than he is."

"Star student my ass," I whispered just loud enough for him to hear, his bold laugh vibrating within my core. It tugged at the corners of my lips, and I found myself fighting hard to dim the way he'd made me smile so easily.

"Second, you do something for me." My brows rose in intrigue. Something *for* him? This wasn't smart. But it excited me just the same. "Something to make you let go of your hard personality for a moment."

"Like what?"

"Anything I say." He was fully grinning now, the joy of control overtaking him. "Take a risk, Sonia." I was never one to gamble with anything, my whole life built around routine. I made to-do lists, I followed a proper schedule in the morning, I set one alarm and woke up with it. There was never a moment in my life where I allowed any sort of mess to concur, but for some reason, this possibility of a mess with Kartik seemed to click something in my brain. He was affecting me too soon, too quick. "Don't think too much." His deep voice pulled me out of my thoughts, bringing my attention back to those mischievous night reminiscent eyes. "You already don't have faith in me passing. So why not just accept? Just for fun."

"You're right, I guess." But was he really if I had to think this much about it? Did I truly believe he couldn't do it? And what was he even going to make me do?

"It won't be anything illegal. Nothing to get you in trouble." Unknowingly, that calmed my nerves, knowing he wouldn't put me in harm's way. But I believed that already. I knew it. "Just agree already, trust me."

"What am I going to have to do? I can't just accept it without knowing."

"Well, Sonia," he was back leaning against the desk, his hands clasped at the nape of his neck, causing the breath to hitch in my throat, "wouldn't that just defeat the purpose of it being a blind challenge?" A lopsided smirk coated his skin and I wanted to wipe it off as easily as it appeared. "So, you in?" He extended a hand towards me and I watched as it steadied, waiting to be filled.

I knew it would bring me nothing but chaos, but I also knew there was absolutely no other choice. I couldn't let him think he had leverage over me. After a moment of deliberation, watching his face contort into giddiness, I lightly grabbed onto the lone hand he held between us, wrapping my fingers around his palm that seemed to engulf me. "Fine. Deal."

CHAPTER 7
Sonia

My life had become a homage to him. The devil in all my nightmares.

Immediately, as I stepped inside my apartment, my feet drove me to the closet door I'd left slightly open. Falling to my knees, my hands scrambled in the darkened area and found the box in the back corner. The one that held all our memories safe.

The black painted shoebox suddenly shined in my face, glassing my eyes. Or maybe that was just the tears coating my pupils that threatened to fall. But I wouldn't let them. Not while looking through this.

Not ever.

This box was everything to me, knowing it was the only thing that kept me stable after that night. The only thing that provided me comfort. It was two weeks after that night where I decided the tears were done and I was only going to bury myself in the happiness of it all because even if it didn't last, at least it happened. But that didn't last long. Making the box was destroying me and I did it all the same, because it was a reflection of my heart which remained shattered and beat for eight years now, only to be carved out of my body once again.

I lifted the lid as a gasp involuntarily left my mouth, all emotions rushing back in. My fingers moved on their own, maneuvering through all the photos and wrappers and letters, all the symbols that once crafted the greatest love story ever written. They'd done this dance about a million times already. I didn't realize when the tears started coating my skin, dropping onto the printed photographers now sitting ruffled inside the cardboard.

One particular shot had caught my attention, my fingers tracing the outline of his figure. His hair was messy and tousled, his sleepy face illuminated under the moonlit sky on my pink and white sheets. He'd always looked like he didn't belong in my life, the black cat in a bed of clouds. But for some reason, the same boy who sat here, vulnerable with his guitar in hand looked like he was at home. It was that night that I knew it had all changed. But it was that night when it all collapsed as well. Neither of us saw it coming, or maybe he did, but I had always been under the impression that we'd make it out alive.

I had never been more wrong in my life.

Kneeling forward, I stuck my head into the dark closet, searching for the one thing I kept deeply tucked away for eight years. My heart stopped for a moment as my hand pressed against the strings of the acoustic, looking just as freshly used as it had been in the picture. For a moment longer, I allowed myself to stare before bringing the shoulder strap around me, placing the guitar firmly in my lap. It was familiar, like an old friend, but the nostalgia of it still pained me like I'd just been scorned in the moment. My gaze still never wavered from the pictures that sat beside me, staring at me in mockery.

Without a thought, I subconsciously began strumming a few notes of *Somewhere Only We Know* by Keane, the song he taught me, as though I'd been playing it daily. I didn't even realize how engraved it was in my brain, along with his name, the lyrics hitting me deeply in the gut.

The tears were now flowing like a river, coming down hard as the weight of the past few weeks took over me. I was stronger than this. I was over it. I convinced myself of it.

So why had I gone so weak so sudden?

I had to move on. I would.

Jerking the strap off my shoulder, I gently placed the instrument back in its spot, covered and tucked away from everyone's eyes, and neatly piled all the memorabilia back into the small cardboard box. I stared at it once more before placing it under my hoodies, hiding it in plain sight. *No more pining, Sonia,* my brain ran a mile a minute but still managed to convince my heart that it wasn't worth the suffering all over again. *You're much better than that.*

I'd been staring at the hollow room for God knows how long, only to be snapped out with the sound of a phone ringing. Without looking, I'd pressed answer, bringing the receiver to my ear solemnly. "Hello?"

"You okay?" Shit, it was Addie. "You sound like you're crying."

Wiping my face with the back of my hands, I silently cleared my throat before proceeding. "Yeah, sorry. Was just cleaning and dust got all over me."

"Acha, teek hai." *Alright, cool.*

From a distance, Jyoti's chipper voice came through. "Sonia!"

"You're both together?" A wave of fake surprise and hurt passed through my voice. "And you didn't even invite me?"

Jyoti's laugh came through before any words did. "No, budhu." *No, dummy.* "I'm driving home right now from campus.

Spring break starts for two weeks now and Addie called me up just now."

"Ah, okay." I nodded on impulse as though they were standing right in front of me.

"Anyways, Sonia, I'm surprised I'm the one calling you regarding all of this now. Can't believe we have to take on your role."

"Literally, she's been too busy for us. Marf kar de na, hum aap ka time le rahe hai." *Forgive us, we're taking your time.*

"Shut up, Jyoti." I was sure she could hear the roll of my eyes through the cell phone. As they both chuckled, I struggled to fight off the way my mind drifted to my shut closet doors. "Is this about Holi?"

"Vah." *Wow.* "You remember." After another round of chuckles, her lacy voice came through again. "I'm sorry Sonia. I'm just giving you shit. I miss you guys."

"Us, too." Addie returned the sentiments, speaking for the both of us. She was right though. We'd all gotten so caught up in our everyday lives that seeing each other wasn't always the easiest thing to plan out. Addie had started freelance photography, traveling around the country with Jaymin during his games, booking her own gigs while he'd practice. Jyoti was in her second semester at The Fashion Institute, tackling her design degree while commuting in and out of New York City. Meanwhile I was still getting comfortable at the school, transitioning from substitute while studying to now a full blown teacher. "But let's talk about next week!"

"Are you both planning on wearing a white kurta or a lehenga?" The best part of going to these cultural events was the coordination between the three of us. It made the whole ordeal a much funner experience. Ever since we'd been kids, our parents had gotten us used to this routine of spending the holidays together, a tradition they'd followed before, and growing up, we made sure we'd never lost sight of it.

"How about a sari?" Addie piped in. "We can probably just order them online and get overnight shipping and it'll be cheap too, getting just a white chiffon sari so we don't have to worry about it getting dirty."

"Addie, you genius." Jyoti's excitement was evident through the phone. "Jaymin clearly is having a positive effect on you." Before Addie could rebuttal, Jyoti spoke through her fit of laughter. "Maaf kar do. Mazak tha." *Forgive me, it was just a joke.* Addie let out a sound while I couldn't contain myself with their banter anymore. "Do you want me to hold my ears and get on my knees to beg for your forgiveness now?"

"No." She tried to sound stern yet we both knew she'd been laughing along just moments ago. "If you guys are done with your teasing, I wanted to let you guys know that Jaymin is gonna join us too this year."

"Oh, that's good." My brain started sending off signals, warning me about what was to come.

"Yeah," she continued. "He also said he's planning on bringing a few friends of his to join so you guys won't feel like you're third wheeling."

"How considerate." While Jyoti indulged in it, my heart began pattering out my chest. "But let him know *he'd* be the one third wheeling." After a moment of silence, she proceeded. "Wait, no. That'd actually be fourth wheeling."

As they continued bickering back and forth, my mind stayed stuck onto the words Addie slipped in the beginning. Jaymin was bringing his friends. That meant there was the possibility that I'd end up coming face to face with the man who has managed to screw up every form of control I had these past two weeks.

"Sonia!" Addie's scream pierced through my ear, my head shaking back to reality. "Where are you lost at?"

"Huh?" My voice was streaked with insincerity and I hoped neither of them could pick up on it through the phone call. "Sorry, I just got distracted with something." It wasn't a complete lie but I couldn't afford telling them yet. I was distracted, but it wasn't by something, instead by someone. Addie and Jyoti both made a sound of approval and on instinct, I let out a silent breath of relief. "You said Jaymin's bringing his friends? Do you know who?"

"I'm not too sure actually." She seemed to think about it for a moment, an *aha* sound slipping as soon as she'd recalled. "I'm sure Kyle's going to come, obviously, and he'll probably even bring Jenna. But I'm not entirely too sure about anyone else that's coming."

"Okay." My voice was barely a whisper, the panic threatening to rise again.

"Why do you ask?"

"She's rishta hunting for herself after Jaymin turned out perfect. His friend group has to be great, too, no?" Jyoti piped in, my heart thudding at her words again. Technically, she wasn't wrong. But I wasn't hunting, I was more so avoiding.

"Yeah, right." I attempted to steady my voice, fearing that the girls would be able to detect any issues instantly. But to my luck, I was always the sheltered one, the one considered the *mom*, so they never thought twice to ask. I knew they cared but they dropped their faith in me opening up when I refused to do so eight years ago and never attempted to do so again. "I was just wondering for you, Jyoti. I'm sure your parents are on your ass after finding out about Addie and Jaymin in their public love declaration. I'm actually surprised aunty hasn't planned your wedding yet, Addie."

"Don't remind me." She snickered, prompting a laugh out of the two of us. "Ma is ready and looking into bridal lehengas. If she thought I barely visited home before, she's shocked at how little she sees my face now." She sighed and although she sounded annoyed, I knew the addition in her life was nothing but good to her. Addie used to run from love but seeing how Jaymin made her break out of her shell, she'd become such a confident and bold woman, the same girl I had met when I was a mere baby. "Your moms haven't tried anything with you both?"

"No, and I'm hoping she doesn't any time soon." Jyoti was the ultimate party girl. Going to school in the city entailed long nights with her classmates and fashion shows every season. Knowing her, she wouldn't be ready to give it up for anyone. "How about you, Sonia?"

"Nah." My response was sudden, knowing my mom hadn't tried to push me towards anyone since she'd witnessed my biggest heartbreak all those years ago. She vouched for my protection and my time, knowing pushing me towards a boy would only push me from her.

"Well maybe one of you could get along with any of Jaymin's friends! And then we can go on double and triple dates!" Addie continued her conversation with Jyoti while I stayed zoned out, focused on the week ahead. I knew if I saw him there, I'd freeze, all strength I built up over the years evaporating into the colors of the night. It was a risk to go but there was no alternate option. It wasn't like I could tell anyone either.

I had to gather my courage before it hit me by surprise and knocked me into dirt, staining me in browns instead of vibrant yellows.

CHAPTER 8
Kartik

8 years ago

I made it to the classroom before her today, excitement racing through every bone. I hadn't been this eager in a while, and I didn't know whether it had to do with her or the paper in my hand.

Perhaps both.

My leg continued bouncing at a skewed rhythm under the wooden table, my fingers making beats on the fabric of my jeans as I willed the door to open. My brain was muddled with thoughts, ranging from songs to fighting to math, which was a surprise. Typically, I consciously shut off every receptor in my head, wanting to shield myself from feeling anything. But not today.

Today, I had a mission.

Today, I would let every emotion run its course in me.

The door swung open as she locked her big brown eyes on me, and I could have sworn a hint of a smile passed her before she shoved it back under that hard snare of hers. She was addicting to look at, her blonde highlights a direct contrast of her golden skin, framing her to be an image so classic it could have been framed in a museum. She was beautiful, there was no denying it.

Sonia carefully placed her books down, all of them organized in a pile like usual, nothing out of the ordinary, her items stacked so perfectly on top of each other. Instantly, my eyes drew towards my things, notebooks scattered across the table already, backpack laying open on the floor. She made me feel inadequate in a way where I wanted to better myself. I think it may have been because she didn't take my shit, told me things exactly how they were. And no one had ever gathered the courage to say how they feel about me to my face. She had surprised me and it only made me want more.

"Hi, Sonia." I grinned wide at her, her brows pulling together in return. "I've been waiting for ten minutes now. You're late."

Her pearly eyes rolled as she settled into her chair. "You're early." She looked at me for a beat longer before sighing. "Why are you early? And you're chirpier than usual. What's wrong with you?"

"Guess." Crossing my arms across my chest, I leaned back, making my chair stand on only its back two legs.

Indecision was on her mind as she scoured her mind for the root of my glee. After a moment, I knew she figured it out but didn't want to admit it. She contemplated before opening her mouth again. "You didn't." With a small *mhm* and nod, I watched her again as her eyes bulged out her head in what seemed like happiness as my grin widened. "Oh my God, you passed?"

"I did." Grabbing the paper off my lap, I placed it on the table, using my index finger to slide it towards her as though it were a discreet business deal. "Look."

She shone as she hurriedly reached for the paper, her eyes moving at record speed, skimming through everything written in my atrocious handwriting. "You got a B Kartik!" If there were no table between us, I was sure she'd reach over and wrap those dainty arms around me. The thought of the possibility had me saddened, for some reason yearning for her touch. I shook it out of my mind as I observed her once again. She was like the rainfall that was needed to survive a drought, showering and saving people who were lost like me. "I'm so proud!"

The sentiment rang through me as a new emotion bubbled up to the surface. It was a sense of self fulfillment, of someone finally acknowledging that I had done something on my own. Albeit it wouldn't have been without her slight push and help. She eyed me for a moment, noticing the smirk I still kept across my chin. "What?" Sonia's grin wiped off her face as recognition hit her.

"You owe me something." I tapped my fingers on the wood like a villain.

"Nuh uh." Placing the test sheet down, she leaned back, angling away from me as if that'd get her out of it, rapidly shaking her head. "Not happening."

"You shook on it." My shoulders lifted in a shrug as she continued denying it in fear. "Are you one to break promises, Sonia?"

"No, but—"

"Then a deal is a deal." Her eyes shut as her breathing slowly leveled, her fingers pinching the bridge of her nose. After a moment of silence, she stared through me with those auburn globes, curious. "Fine." She was afraid for no reason. She hadn't known how coming here was my only escape from the real world, a shelter from the mess. "What do I have to do?"

Coming into the classroom I had already planned beforehand what I wanted her to do. But torturing her was proving to be even more fun. "Don't worry I promised I wasn't gonna make you get arrested. And I'm also a man of my word."

Her eyes rolled back and I couldn't hold in the laughter it prompted. Something about the action was so innocent and I knew I wanted to stitch it into the corners of my brain so that it'd remain in my memory forever. "Can't be too sure about that. You're the poster boy for trouble, Kartik."

With a slight shake of my head, a chuckle escaped me as I leaned forward on my elbows, closing the distance between our faces. I had to commend her for standing on guard, unmoving as I invaded her personal territory despite her eyes bulging out her socket. She gently pulled her bottom lip under her teeth, the movement startling me internally. "Am I *that* wrong for wanting to break you out of your shell, shona?"

"Shona?" The slip of a nickname, simply calling her beautiful, shocked me as much as it did her. My unfiltered emotions towards her were threatening to claw their way out of my bones. Panic sirens were ringing in my head, warning me of the damage I could cause.

"Sonia. Shona." I attempted to fizzle the evident tension that showed through the lines across her forehead. She was unnerved, and it only made my heart palpate faster. "Same thing, right?" I put on a 'cool guy' image while inside I was completely helpless to my devices. How could I let that slip? And more importantly, *why*? She was just a girl who'd somehow become the only balanced part of my life other than my music. That didn't mean anything. Tutoring was just an escape from reality.

"Yeah, okay." Her words dragged out and she nodded once, then twice, slowly coming to terms with the conversation. "What is it you want me to do?"

"Meet me later." A sound of irritation left her soft lips and her face creased under her hands. "Under the bleachers."

Her groan colored the air with indecision. "Why?"

"Why not?" Sitting back, I let my brain observe her. Her delicate fingers were rubbing at her temple, her body slightly shaking while her legs eagerly shook under the table. In the two weeks I'd known her, this was the rawest I'd ever seen her. Sonia wore a black cat's glare, and I knew she was attempting to read me to a filth. But no one who had tried had ever gotten close, and I had no qualms about her either. She was chasing down a path she could never reach the end of.

"When?" She whispered into her hand before twirling those blonde streaks that framed her face between them.

"After school tomorrow. Meet me in the middle of the football ground's bleachers."

"Are you planning on singing and dancing like Heath Ledger did in 10 Things I Hate About You?" Amusingly, she laughed to herself.

"What?" I had known she was referencing a rom-com but I didn't believe in watching unrealistic displays of love. Love was meant to be messy, useless and full of screaming and fighting. All these movies were doing was enforcing a heightened perception of something that never existed. But as I watched her deflect at my dismissal, I unexpectedly found myself wanting to know exactly what she was talking about.

"Nothing," her head shook in embarrassment. "Nevermind." A large inhale later, she met my eyes again, goosebumps rising in a path through my body as I wanted to take that shame away from her. I wanted her to know that I was willing to hear her just as she saw me in my most honest form. "Bleachers, after school. For what?"

"I'll tell you your end of the deal then."

"Why not now?" Glancing at the clock, she began piling her books one atop each other, reenacting the same routine she's kept for the past few weeks.

"Tutoring is over." With a shrug, I lifted off the seat, waiting for her to follow suit. "You've been unintentionally eying the clock for the past five minutes. Your days go by like clockwork and I wouldn't want to mess with that by keeping you longer than you need to." Her face contorted in different expressions before finally settling on skepticism.

"Okay." Her tongue stretched out the two syllables, hanging onto them like her life depended on it. "I guess."

Hurriedly, she packed her bag, silent with words dangling between us. I knew I was messing with her head, making it seem like tomorrow was something that was beneficial for her, but in reality, I just wanted an excuse to keep myself longer on a Friday afternoon when tutoring wasn't in existence. Four extended days a week seemed no longer enough when staying in school was the only thing that made me forget about my loud life.

As I watched her storm out the door without giving a double glance towards me, once again I found myself screaming to her back. "I'll see you tomorrow, shona."

CHAPTER 9
Sonia

8 years ago

The sound of the bell rang through my ears, immediately perching them up like a dog. I knew what that meant. Convincing myself that I wasn't afraid was proving to be a lost cause. I had to go meet him.

Taking longer than usual at my locker, I began stuffing the unnecessary books inside, dragging out the seconds as much as I could. A few of the other tutors passed by, waving their hands in hello as we made eye contact but otherwise walking by. I preferred it that way. I never considered anyone from this school truly a friend, coming here for just my education. My friends were the ones I grew up with, although now cities apart with their parents putting them in different high schools, still the ones I could rely on.

People at this high school were more focused on their reputations, keeping pretentious fake faces and facades while pretending to care about everyone around them. Everything was about cliques and popularity and I learned that my freshman year when I tried to mingle. Quickly, I understood that I was better off than messing with predetermined friend groups. I didn't fit in here. I just wanted to graduate and go back to my friends and family and focus on my future.

My eyes locked onto the little clay horse that sat on the top metal shelf, my heart stopping every time I saw it. The wound was still fresh, still affecting my family like our skins had just been carved with a knife, the cut only getting deeper by the day. It'd been two years now, but I still missed him the same. Especially knowing I was nearing the age he was when it all happened.

The slams of lockers dragged me back to my harsh reality, reminding me of the task I was set out to do. The hallways were clearing up now, and I looked around, hoping for the sight of him so I could finish whatever it was he wanted to do right here, right now, rather than in secrecy. But to my dismay, he must have been waiting at the exact location he had promised because he was nowhere to be found.

The cool air prompted a shiver down my body as I threw open the doors, hesitantly trudging my way towards the football field. It was empty, unlike most days, but I presumed that may have had to do with the fact that I'd been dodging it for time since the school bell rang. Everyone in my vision began appearing smaller as I walked away from the busy street filled with buses and students, all mingling until it was time to leave.

Through the distance, I spotted him in all his glory, wearing that dredged leather jacket as always. Something about it was intriguing, like it was only there to act as a cover, his reality being something completely opposite. The way Kartik was and the way he acted, they both seemed miles apart. It was as though he was hiding something from everyone, but pieces of it had slipped out in my vicinity. I was curious but I also feared I was wrong in my judgment.

He watched as I stepped closer, my hands falling into my pocket to avoid the crisp air. I let out a breath as I approached him, readying myself for whatever task he had prepared for me. Something in my brain flashed, telling me I could trust him and I failed to put my finger on why, ignoring the thoughts to keep my guard up. As trustworthy as he had seemed, I couldn't forget that he was still the biggest rebel of this school.

"Hey, shona." I rolled my eyes at his unironic use of the new nickname. The first time he'd used it, it caught me so by surprise, sensing a hint of affection in the way it slipped out his lips, as though it was meant to be between us. But I knew my mind was weaving stories to latch on to.

"I thought I told you not to call me that." I crossed my hands across my chest, puffing it out to seem bolder. But the truth was, under his scrutiny, I had never felt smaller. He made me want to let it go, to let him take control.

"Did you, now? That's not what I remember." His brow shot up, contorting his face in a way that made him look even more sinful than the whole black getup. "I thought I told you it fits." Scoffing, I turned away as he flashed one of his devilish grins that I'd seemed to somehow enjoy every time. It prompted a smile in return from me, an action I couldn't rebuke. "Glad to see you made it," he glanced at his empty wrist, mimicking what he would have done had there been a watch sitting there, "only fifteen minutes late. I didn't take you as a staller."

"I got caught up with something." I lied. I couldn't have him know how my hairline was dampening with sweat even in the brisk weather.

"Sure you did." It was useless anyway. He could see through me as if I were sheer fabric.

"Get on with it. Why am I here?" I was bouncing on a foot, suddenly looking at the setting around us. There were no more than two feet between us, making me feel claustrophobic under the metal bleachers, a spot that was known notoriously in the school as a makeout area. If anyone had found out that me, the quiet girl who kept to herself, and Kartik, the school's biggest bad boy, were alone in this very spot, the rumors would destroy any sense of respect I had acquired. It would turn me into the world's biggest hypocrite.

"Jeez, give me a moment. You just got here." Kartik took a step towards me, my heart jumping up to my throat.

"What are you doing?" I dropped my hands at my side, readying myself to push and run if the situation called for it.

"Relax, shona. I just have something for you." Confusion flooded my brain as I watched him softly reach into his pocket, searching. Slowly he pulled out of his black denim, holding a chain loosely between us. My brows furrowed as they locked onto the tiny teardrop pendant that mimicked a guitar pick that delicately hung off the golden chain. It was beautiful. But it couldn't have been mine.

"What is that?"

He chuckled, sounding as though the devil incarnate himself. "You ask a lot of questions that don't need an answer. I thought it was obvious that it's a necklace?" He unclasped it, staying exactly where he was.

"Yes but why do you have it?" I swallowed and I was sure the sound it made could have rang through the entire football field beside us. "And why are you showing me it?"

With another step, he was now towering over me, fully utilizing the seven inches he held over my five foot four frame. I craned my neck to watch him as he stared as though he were enamored in something. What it was, though, he gave no indication of. The grin was back, the playfulness of his aura contrasting directly with the way it was making me feel. "You're getting stiff, chill." My eyes would've fallen out of my sockets if it weren't for human anatomy. "I was at an arcade last night with my friends and I won this in a claw machine. It's not something I'd wear, so I thought why not?"

The way he said it was so matter-of-factly, like it was typical and normal to just hand over something towards me. Who even was I to be receiving gifts from someone I was just tutoring? "Why are you giving this to me?"

"Just take it as a token of appreciation for helping me. Don't overthink it, shona." He began saying it as normally as anyone would my name. The scent of his cologne, full of sandalwood and oak, all man packed in a seventeen year old boy, began invading my nostrils, taking over all my senses. His hands came around me and the way his fingers brushed along my hair ever so slightly had me glad that he couldn't see the skin on my neck that was now covered in goosebumps. My vision went black as my lids shut in response, my breath halting as he invaded every last centimeter of my space. The closed necklace fell against my hair and I felt Kartik move his fingers under it, slowly pulling my strands out to let the chain rest against my skin. "Don't say I never gave you anything." The words hit my hair, whispered and low enough to place me in an envelope that was marked with his address.

It was all too intimate, too close, and I couldn't fathom being here for longer.

The rise and fall of my chest did nothing to calm me, the pulse on my neck throbbing against the new jewelry. There was no way he'd won this from a child's arcade game. The edges were too precise, the metal too shiny.

Opening my eyes was my biggest mistake. His desperate face was still so close to my neck, those black eyes of his still hidden behind his lids, making it known that he wasn't unaffected. The closeness was doing nothing but convincing me that things would be different now. And I hadn't signed up for this.

"Kartik." It was a whisper, inaudible, merging with the sounds of the wind and our breaths. But it was enough to snap him out of it.

"Sorry," he murmured, the hard stoney mask back on his vulnerable face. After abruptly clearing his throat once, he began again, "Anyways, that wasn't why I called you here." The sudden change of topic hit me in an instant. "I want you to break out of your shell."

"I'm not in a shell." Apparently, I was nothing if not defensive around him. And being this vocally opposing was not like me.

"If you say so." He was still just inches away, refusing to move. "I'm not sure if you know but I'm in a band." Kartik stated that information like it was foreign, knowing well that the entire school knew of it. It was what apparently added to his appeal. Every girl went crazy over the fact that he could play both the acoustic and the bass. Even I couldn't help but be impressed at the talent he possessed, but that didn't mean I had any interest in wanting to see it when I'd rather be spending my time cuddled in my bed. "I want you to come to my show this weekend."

"Why?" The invitation was too much. Especially after he just delicately wrapped a necklace around my neck.

"Why not?" He dismissed it with a swift shrug, seeming so boyish for the first time. His black eyes got even darker, resembling a night sky under the sunlight above us. "Like I said,

I want you to step out of that head of yours. You're always at school, studying. Plus, you're teaching me math, helping me, so I want to return the favor."

"It's not a favor." I furrowed my brows. "I'm quite literally assigned to help you." Spending more time than required around him would be dangerous and I was in no mood to be risky.

I felt his laugh run through my bloodstream. "Then take it as my assignment to teach you to let loose and have some fun." My mouth opened, readying to speak only to be cut off before anything could be said. "Before you say that you know how to have fun, tutoring and doing homework doesn't make the cut. Come to the show this weekend at The Lokal. They're hosting a local band spotlight set and we're playing at 7." His eyes softened, almost begging as if he couldn't take no for an answer.

And I found myself unable to give it to him either.

"Fine."

In an instant all the worry that harbored his features escaped him and somehow made its way into me. My heart was once again palpating, the thumping ringing through my entire body.

What the hell did I just agree to?

CHAPTER 10
Sonia

"Let me see what jewelry you guys are planning on wearing."

Jyoti rummaged through all our spread out material that lay on my bed, gauging what would catch her eye best. Every holiday and festival, we spent together, getting dressed and ready at one of our houses like it was a whole event. It made the fun of our culture even more exciting, knowing that we would always fall back on the routine of making it a day long event.

I glanced at the clock above our head reading 9:30 am, a yawn escaping me, as I met both the girls at the edge of the bed. Addie ran her hands through her sari, just a plain white chiffon 6 yard fabric that all three of us had ordered, straightening the edges and unfolding it before gently placing it back on the bed. It was traditional for everyone to show up to holi in white, ready to be dosed in colorful powders and water, drenched in a display of happiness. "I don't think I'm wearing much jewelry, honestly." Addie reached for the bangles she kept carefully placed inside their box.

"Except for those, of course." I teased her as she pulled them onto her wrist. They were delicate white bangles, in a beautiful predesigned set with jhumke at the edges, a gift Jaymin had gotten her way before they'd ever fallen in love. Seeing the love he had for my friend was nothing but heartwarming, knowing her past hadn't been good to her, and it made both Jyoti and I love Jaymin even more. He loved her without expectation, without any question and it was what we all wished for.

Well, in my case, I wished for it back.

But I could never find myself admitting that, not when there was a possibility of me running into my history today.

"What are you putting on, Sonia?" Jyoti held two traditional necklaces in her hand, both in a choker style with little beads dangling downwards, but my brain instantly flashed to the tiny pendant that was hidden in my dresser in between my sweats, carefully placed so that no one would find it. But I knew today was not the day to pull it out, the fear of Kartik seeing it for another time terrifying me, so I reached for the ones that lay in Jyoti's hands.

The first one was made of a gold plated material, the full necklace adorned with beading and small gems interwoven within each other. However, my eyes gravitated towards the second one as I ran my finger through the cranes of it. It was a silver oxidized choker, probably around two and a half inches thick, with a black pullable string to wrap around the neck. It was stunning and exactly what I was picturing. "I'll wear this one."

"Yeah that one is stunning, honestly." Addie glanced over my shoulder with a grin, approving my choice. "Are you going to wear the earrings that come with it too?"

My gaze traveled back to the sheets, where the full set lay, my eyes snapping out of my head. Those earrings were huge, looking heavier than the necklace itself. But I was never one to shy away from fully adorning myself in desi jewels. I nodded, reaching for them in my hand and bringing them up to my ears while watching my reflection. They tied the whole look together and I'd be a fool to not look my best knowing my biggest mistake had the possibility of being there.

Passing one of the saris to me, Jyoti found her spot in front of the full size mirror at the corner of my muted room. Addie made her way into the bathroom, doing her everyday makeup under the vanity light. I, however, ran my hand along the edge of my dresser, feeling a heat rush pass through my palms in the exact spot the memorabilia was placed. I shook my head, forcing myself out of that headspace, bringing myself to the picture we were in now.

Dragging the sari around me, I began draping it, tucking it into the skirt after pulling on the white spaghetti strap blouse I had chosen for it. It was innocently sexy, the exact look I was going for. Adjusting the pleats that rested in front of my legs, I threw the extra fabric over my left shoulder, using a safety pin to secure it in its place. My feet led me to where Jyoti stood, watching as her eyes locked onto me, a smile pulling on her face.

Off the table next to the mirror, I grabbed the pack of bindis, picking a small black circle off the paper and sticking it between my brows.

I put my head through the necklace, tightening it around me, watching my reflection change with every step. After the earrings and lipstick, I fluffed my hair, stepping back admiring the person staring back at me. "Damn, you look so hot." Jyoti paused while getting dressed, keeping her eyes locked on mine.

Addie walked over at the statement, watching through the mirror as well. "You really do, Sonia. Wow."

"Stop it, girls." I turned to see them both, realizing how beautiful my best friends were. "You guys are stunning." Jyoti pulled us into a soft group hug, making sure to not mess up our carefully curated looks. "Let's go now before we get late."

A newfound confidence that rang through me and I was finally sure of it. I was done acting like he was destroying me, even after eight long years. I was better than that. If there was anything I'd learned from my mistakes, it was that I could make it through the toughest of moments. Especially when it came to Kartik Sharma. I'd make him regret every choice he made and I'd make him pay for every tear it cost me.

CHAPTER 11
Kartik

Trailing behind Jaymin and Kyle, my eyes wandered the expanse of Central Park for her. When Jaymin had originally invited me, I was unsure of my decision but the moment he mentioned his girlfriend Adhira and her friends, my stance on the choice was final.

I was going even if it was only to see Sonia.

"You've already met Sonia briefly," at the mention of her name, I began paying attention to Jaymin, who was speaking to me over his shoulder, "but Adhira likes being called Addie so just remember that unless you want to be yelled at, and Jyoti is a handful but very, very sweet. I'm sure you'll get along with them both."

Kyle, Jaymin's teammate who was currently clutching on to the hand of the bartender from the bar we frequented at, Jenna, chimed in as well. "Yeah, dude, they're all really sweet, I'm sure you'll get along with them just fine."

I nodded, because it was all I could manage when the only words I had were being saved, strung and woven just for a specific woman. With a small smirk, I treaded forward, following the footsteps while looking over everyone's head to spot her in the crowd. Jaymin spotted his girl first, and immediately after, it was my turn. And the sight of her instantly made me stop in my step.

She was riveting.

With a white sari loosely falling off her shoulder, she turned in giggles with her two friends. I didn't even spare them a glance, my brain taking off in the location of my destiny. If it hadn't been for Jaymin's sharp voice, I would have never remembered that we were in the midst of the world.

The one where she wasn't mine.

Her back was still to me as we approached, Adhira spotting us first with a big grin. With an exaggerated wave and tug, she pulled Jenna into her, yanking her out of the hands of the man she was holding. "Hi Jenna! Hi Kyle!" She was practically screaming over the loud drums and beats of Bollywood music. For the first time, I glanced at the vicinity of the area, the entire park filled with white lehengas and kurtas, men and women all joining together from all over the world in a celebration of a culture that embraced diversity. It was pretty damn cool.

I'd moved around a lot in my life, with a homelife that never allowed me to settle, and with that, loving the heritage I'd grown up with was always tough. I knew the festivals, I knew the holidays, but I was never able to indulge in them, feeling like my only identity was being American. But being here, surrounded by other people who looked like me, it felt like coming home and touching the roots of my soil.

With a slight push through everyone, we were directly next to the rest of the girls, Sonia's back just an inch away from my chest. The way her spine straightened, I knew she felt me there. She always did.

Everyone exchanged pleasantries, my introduction being the last. I waved to Adhira who was still snuggled up with Jaymin, holding a fist full of colored powder up to his cheek. After she successfully doused him in reds, she turned towards me, a friendly smile stretched across her small face. "Kartik, right? Or as Jaymin calls you," she glanced at him from her peripheral vision, "Kay."

Her outstretched hand was like a pebble in mine. "Kartik is fine. It's nice to finally meet you, Addie." Her smile grew as she pointed out her friends.

"This is Jyoti," she called to the tallest of them all, who turned immediately at the sound of her name. Her smile was vibrant, energetic, something that reflected exactly what kind of person she was. "And I believe you already know Sonia?"

My eyes instantly left everyone to watch the object of all my desires slowly turn around, all motion around us stopping the moment our eyes met. The breath caught in my throat, seeing the entirety of her standing beside me. She was what the poets looked to when beginning to craft their sonnets. She was what dreams were crafted of.

She was *my* dream.

Her long hair splayed across her shoulder, all of it pushed on the side without the chiffon fabric. Her makeup was light, the bindi complementing the warm tones of her skin, making her glow in ways I thought impossible. Through the tiny straps of her blouse, her tattoo, the one I so meticulously did, the one that was meant for me, peeked out, just visible to those watching. I wanted to cover it up, let her know it was mine and only mine.

It was about me and her, no matter how much she denied it. I knew it.

This time, however, when I looked in her eyes, I didn't see the timidness that showed itself when she stumbled into my shop. There was challenge, instead. It was the same heat I once fell in love with. The same heat that riled me up all those years ago. In her eyes, today, I saw *my* Sonia.

She was here to play and I couldn't have been happier.

Her shoulders squared as she stared me down, her glare icy. "Kartik, right?" She had a smile that was meant to be a trap, her hand extending between us, but she knew better than anyone, I wasn't one to be messed with. The beauty of us was in the fact that we always walked beside each other, our strengths combating each others like they were made for it.

Swiftly, I grabbed onto her hand, engulfing it into mine like it was meant to be. "Don't pretend you don't remember me, shona." Her eyes widened for a second before she cleared her throat, silently telling me to let go. But I didn't, only gripping tighter at any attempt she made to push back.

"*Shona?*" Jyoti excitedly squealed but all I allowed myself to do was watch the woman in front of me as she tried to piece together an explanation.

But before she could, I took control. "Yeah, the day she came for the tattoo, it was a slip of tongue." I finally let go of her hand, feeling her relax as she released a breath and caught her balance. "Sonia, shona. Same difference, right?" My brow raised, letting her know that I was only playing the game she started, reminding her of the exact words I had said the very first time I'd renamed her as mine.

"Mhm." I could tell neither of the girls believed us and frankly, I didn't care. All that mattered was that I knew now, my Sonia was still in there. And I was going to bring her back to me. "Anyways," Jyoti continued after sparing us a few more back and forth glances, "how do you know Jaymin?"

Thankfully, Jaymin spoke up, getting into our college days, allowing me the time to drink in the sight of Sonia for longer. Everyone's attention was diverted again, giving me the ability to stop her before she could scurry away. My fingers wrapped around her bare arm, feeling her skin burning even with goosebumps polluting it. As quick as I'd reached for her, she turned, standing tall, her chest just an inch from mine. "What are you doing here?"

I smirked, her new found boldness reminding me of the first time I'd met her. "Bhul gayi? Holi hai." *Have you forgotten? It's Holi.* My arms went up in a shrug, the teasing nature of us feeling like we were seventeen again.

On her tiptoes, she looked over my shoulder a couple times, as if waiting for a ghost to appear. "Let me go." Her mouth was telling me the exact opposite of what I was reading in her eyes. She didn't move an inch, didn't back down. And although that could have been her stubbornness, I knew her better than that. She felt the spark just as I always did when I was around her. It was like there was an invisible string between us, shortening every time we were near each other, pulling and reeling us closer. "Where's your girlfriend?"

I leaned down, causing her to crane her neck, and watched as her throat caught the only breath she had taken. "What girlfriend?"

She blinked. Slowly. And then finally, spoke. "What do you mean *'what girlfriend'* Kartik?" She said my name like it belonged to her. She had to know it still did.

"I broke up with her." My sudden statement had her almost stumbling backwards but the grip I kept on her would prevent it.

"Why?" It was almost a question she'd only meant for her ears, but in the noise all I could hear was her. Her downcast eyes were now drowning in confusion.

"Tumhe nahi pata kyu?" *You don't know why?* She snapped her head up again, and I knew then that she knew. She knew it was for her. But there was still a shroud of doubt coated behind her faith.

"No." Sonia shook her head, still in disbelief. "You didn't." Taking a step back, she fell out of my hold, hesitation taking place.

I was losing her and felt the sudden urge to pull her back to me. Her friends were still surrounding us, their attention on themselves, thankfully, as I reached over and grabbed a handful of colored powder off of the tray Adhira had handed to Jaymin. Coming back to a still frozen Sonia, I crouched so our faces would be aligned. "Holi?"

With another slight shake of her head, she excused herself with a smile and ran off into the crowd, but I wouldn't let her escape me.

Following behind, she landed at the table of drinks, and with a glance over her shoulder, I knew she expected me to follow behind. Stopping at one of the vendors, she grabbed a cold glass of thandai, the traditional milky spiked drink that Indians consume on the festival, and downed it like it was water. But I knew what it truly was. It was her liquid courage. Extending another hand, she bought another one, turning towards me and putting it in my hand. Raising her eyebrows, she tilted her head towards the brass glass in my hand, signaling for me to drink it as well.

I reached for the empty cup she had already placed down, dumping the contents of mine into hers, and searched for her lipstick stain sitting on the material. My eyes never left hers as I closed my mouth around the exact spot hers were just a minute ago and a fire lit through her. Her normally brown eyes were now black, and whether it was the alcohol or the movement or the music, I couldn't tell.

Placing the glass on the counter, I silently walked over to the other vendor, grabbing a bag of red color powder and ripping it open before standing in front of her again. Whispering, I leaned into her, reciting the typical phrase most Indians did on this day before staining someone in beautiful colors. "Bura na mano, holi hai." *Don't be offended, it's Holi.* Her lips stayed sealed as she moved her hair away from her face, offering me her cheek.

Grabbing a handful of scarlet, I lifted my hand to stain her already rosy cheeks, the motion nothing short of sensual. As my fingers almost brushed her cheek, a giggle left her, and she took off into the crowd, stumbling as she kept looking over her shoulder for me. She was definitely intoxicated but it made no difference to me. I would've gone after her either way.

A smile broke out on my face as I chased her, watching her head fall back in laughter as I got closer. We lost our friends in the crowd, feeling as though it was only the two of us running to our end. With a sudden movement, I clasped onto her wrist, pulling her flush against me, holding her arm against her lower back, her beating heart thumping hard against mine. Our chests collided, our breaths syncing, and she shut her eyes, feeling the closeness of my fingers. Dragging out the seconds, I slid my hand down her cheek, the golden of her skin turning a deep red, the powder successfully staying in place.

She opened her eyes, a sort of worry harboring them for a second. But as quick as it appeared, it was gone. Tiptoeing, she met my face, and for a moment, I couldn't understand what was going on until she began tilting her face slightly away from mine, her head hovering just above my shoulder. Time stopped as she brought her cheek against mine, all the excess powder transferring onto me, the same motions I did with her glass. She colored me in her colors and I didn't want to be anywhere else.

Just as she began pulling away, her earring caught on my white kurta, snapping off her ear as she got back on her feet. She reached for it the same time I had, our fingers brushing together again. The silence between us had somehow become louder than the joyous screams around us.

I held the silver jewelry in my hand as a pout appeared on her face, her doe eyes pleading at me with the confidence that the thandai provided her. She reached for it again, and I shook my head, concealing the broken item in my fist. With my other hand, I reached to the part of her face that was exposed to me, letting it skirt in her hair for a second before pulling it over her shoulder, covering her now bare ear.

When her brain registered what I'd been doing, she gave me a hint of a smile and one single nod of her head. I returned it with one of my own, watching as she wordlessly mouthed thank you before turning and running towards her friends, leaving me there alone. She disappeared into the crowd like she was never there, leaving behind the trace of her in red and silver.

I gave myself one more minute to look at the earring before I tucked it into my pocket and left to meet the boys as well. I'd keep it with me forever.

CHAPTER 12
Sonia

8 years ago

What the hell was I even doing here?

From the sidewalk, I looked like an outsider dressed in sheep's clothing, not fitting in. Maybe because I didn't.

Glancing down at my white flowy dress, I contemplated turning back, not going into a crowd of leather and chains, but a deal was a deal. I was never one to break promises, no matter how desperately I hadn't wanted to do the task promised.

The bouncer motioned me inside, ID's not being checked on spotlight nights, and the blare of music rang through me. The bass was bouncing off the floors, hitting my body with every step I took. The sound of drums reverberated through my feet, my skin feeling as though it were being struck along with the instrument.

But I couldn't lie, the vibe was enchanting.

That was the thing about music. People connected through sounds, whether they understood them or not. Music was a language everyone spoke.

Pushing through the herd of people, I found myself still unable to clearly see the stage, weaving my head between shoulders to get any glimpse I could. Piecing together the buzzcut and faded beard sitting behind a red drum set, I recognized him as the boy that was with Kartik the day he'd crashed into me. One of his best friends, Trevor.

At the mic stood a tall blonde haired boy who would've looked as out of place as me had it not been for the worn out graphic tee and ripped black jeans. From school politics, I had known that his name was Colt.

The three of them were the heathens of the school, wrecking havoc everywhere, but still the most desirable to all. Everyone was swooning over them, fawning over a crumb of their attention. And this floor was no different.

Screams and shouts plagued my ears and I immediately regretted coming here. I could barely spot the stage and I doubt Kartik would even get anything from my presence, making a bet like such only to see if I had the guts to come alone somewhere. This was pointless.

Giving myself one last shot, I stood as tall as I could, toes digging into my beige flats as I swapped from foot to foot. Regret swarmed through me the moment I spotted him. And he was looking directly at me.

Even in the crowd, his gaze pierced me, pointing towards me as if calling to me. He was carving me, hooking me firmly into my spot.

His fingers navigated through the strings of his brown electric guitar, one hand strumming meticulously while the other marked the notes at the top. The leather jacket he was normally snuggled in sat on the mic stand, drooping just out of reach from the audience. But no one cared to even reach for it, everyone mesmerized by the sight before them. He was jaw droppingly attractive.

Wearing a white tee shirt and black pants, he looked just like a poster boy for West Side Story, rightfully playing any adaptation of an unattainable Romeo wherever he went.

He never stopped looking at me, or in my vicinity, as the song faded out and the claps drowned out the remainder of the music. Had I really come that late or was I just losing track of time under his perusal?

As the ambiance went dark, I turned to walk away, seeing no point in sticking around, only to be pulled back before I could make any further movements. Kartik's fingers were buried on my exposed arm, grasping, almost begging me to stay. His thumb slightly caressed the inside of my forearm, causing goosebumps to strike through everywhere he went. I was surprised how quick he found me after his set, as though he'd run and cut across the mass of people to stop me.

There were curious faces looking our way, seeing how the boy from the stage had already made his way out. Shouts were coming for his name but none of that mattered as he leaned over me, his breath hitting my ear as he spoke. "You're leaving already, shona?" For some reason, his puppy dog eyes were melting me.

"You invited me to see the set and I did." My throat was dry as he took a step closer, leaning into me further to hear me better. "There's nothing else for me to do here."

"Let's go grab some ice cream across the street." He didn't even wait for an answer, his hand falling softly onto the small of my back, leading me towards the door and my deceiving body simply followed like a loyal dog. The crowd opened up for him, their fanfare moments being cut off by his ignorance. Any protest I had stayed behind my closed lips, my thoughts plaguing me. How did I end up here?

Cold breeze smacked my face as Kartik held the door wide open, signaling for me to take a step in. Thankfully, the shop was near empty, the anxiety in my stomach coming to a halt at the prospect of no one seeing us here, together, alone. The quaint dessert shop was small, a strip with the register and ice cream flavors displayed behind a glass, and a few tables lining the big window up front. The entire creamery was full of pretty pastels, pinks and blues making it seem like it was straight out of the 80s.

"Welcome to Delia's! What'll it be?" A brown haired boy, Jake as his name tag read, stood behind the ice cream buckets, wearing the brightest smile I'd ever seen. His gaze trailed me as I walked closer towards him. Smiling back, I took a glance at the menu behind him, lost in the different flavors, until I felt a hand wrap around my shoulders. Kartik was towering beside me, glaring at the boy waiting for our reply. I tried to break free but his hard stare made me stop fidgeting. What the hell had gotten into him?

"I'll just get a cookie dough scoop on a waffle cone with rainbow sprinkles, please." Jake perked up at my order.

"Beautiful girl with great taste." Kartik's hand felt heavier as I watched Jake work the scoop in the frozen delights. With an even chipper mood, he reached over the glass, handing me my sweet treat, his fingers brushing mine. I could feel my hand burning with the way Kartik had stiffened beside me, his glare now directed to my hand. Jake shrunk as he looked over, feeling the same fury I had. "And for you?"

"Same thing." With a wordless nod, Jake got to work.

"Did the mic stand get stuck up your ass?" His angry glare still hadn't dissipated as he looked down on me. "Would it kill you to be nice?" Wriggling under his arm, all my attempts to break free had failed. "What is your problem?"

"Nothing." He refused to look my way the entire time, grabbing his cone wordlessly, before pulling out his credit card.

"I can pay for my own—" I began to move away, my attempts of stopping him failing along with the words that left me.

"I got it." His tone was enough to make me drop the situation. His hand fell against me again, guiding me to a table in the corner, out of sight from most of the other passerbyers outside. Like a gentleman, he pulled the seat out with his free hand, the gesture so innocent it almost looked like it didn't belong on his unholy face. Kartik quietly sat, still indulging in the silence between us.

"What?" Still nothing.

He was watching intently as I took a lick of my sprinkle filled cone, his eyes darkening for a fraction of a second before disappearing all too soon. Still, unspeaking, he took a bite, like the psychopath he was, and winced. "This is so goddamn sweet."

"So why the hell did you get it?" Irritation was prevalent in my tone when all he did was shrug nonchalantly. I still couldn't understand why he'd suddenly turned into an asshole. "What's your usual? A black coffee scoop?"

After another disgusted bite, his face went normal again. "Don't be silly. They don't make that flavor." A chuckle escaped him as I rolled my eyes, despite the ice cream coursing through me. "What did you think?" When I didn't reply, he continued. "The show. You came late but you saw the end. What did you think of it?"

My mind latched onto everything he said, from noticing my entrance to knowing I was there. I didn't understand why my opinion mattered but while I sat here watching his expectant face, I couldn't hold back. "I liked it. You guys sound surprisingly good."

"*Surprisingly?*" His brow crooked in amusement.

"Yeah, you know. Seeing you guys at school, I didn't think you were capable of anything so melodic." He observed me for a moment before nodding and quietly savoring the ice cream he so providently hated. Kartik seemed off, his quiet mannerisms far from his normally playful and mischievous self, as if he were lost somewhere in his brain. Something told me he needed a hand to pull him out, urging me to help despite our clashing personalities. "Why music?"

"It's an escape." He was quick to answer, almost accidentally reactive, like he didn't mean to say it, but he didn't refrain from it. Instead, he continued. "You know that feeling where life feels like it's too heavy, like the physical weight manifested onto you and you're being crushed under it, with no way out?" I nodded because I understood him. I felt that weight two years ago. I felt it in the form of loneliness and grief. I felt it to the point of it becoming my best friend. And I couldn't escape it. "That's music to me. The rope I latch on to when I'm drowning."

"When did you start playing?" For some reason, my interest was piqued, my curiosity urging me to continue asking.

"I was put in piano lessons when I was around seven." For someone who hated it, Kartik was eating the cone like he'd been starving. "But since we moved around a lot, I only did them for a year and a half but I fell in love with the feeling." A sullen sadness took over his pupils and I immediately fought the urge to reach over and grab onto the hand that rested on the wood table between us. "So on my ninth birthday, we had just moved to some small town in Texas and like usual, my parents didn't really plan anything so they just decided to get me whatever I wanted. And all I asked for was an acoustic and I've been playing since then. At least until I was able to upgrade to an electric on my own recently. So that was that."

"You didn't celebrate your birthday?" For some reason, it was the only part of the story that circulated in my brain, feeling like there was something he still wasn't saying. It saddened me, knowing he never had the chance to celebrate the day that put him into this world, capable of bringing magic into it.

"We're not a big celebrating family, honestly. I've never celebrated my birthday actually." He simply shrugged but the heaviness of his shoulders was evident all around him, tainting his aura like a stain. "Honestly, I'm not big on it either. It's all so superficial."

"I like my birthday." It was only a whisper, the fear of judgment from him stopping my heart. I didn't know why I suddenly cared what he thought about me. Yet, when the words left my lips, he was watching me with empathy, as if he understood me. But I knew he didn't. We were part of two different worlds. Birthdays were special in our house, knowing that even if we didn't have much, we had the closeness of family. Kartik would never get it. He was part of the families who threw money at their kids at their disposal.

After a moment of reserve later, he finally spoke, his tone shy of any sensitivity that was there before. "Makes sense." My brows furrowed, knowing there was no way he meant in any way other than condescending. And all of a sudden, it hit me that I was still sitting here, facing the most ruthless guy I had known. He wasn't my friend, he was nothing but the troublesome kid I was tutoring. The sadness he conjured in his eyes had to have been a facade.

"This was fun, Kartik, but I should get going." He opened his mouth to speak but I pretended I didn't see the movement as I glanced at the time on my phone, knowing it didn't matter. Jumping out of my seat, I gave him as friendly of a smile as I could, storming out, before he could stop me. *I knew it was a mistake to come.*

CHAPTER 13
Kartik

8 years ago

She left almost as quickly as she came.

But the way she lifted off the seat, almost knocking it behind her, I saw no point in stopping her. She'd already made up her mind.

Racking my brain, I tried to figure out what exactly made the soft smile she had disappear, whether it was something I had said and how I could rectify it. But she was gone like the wind, all traces of her leaving beside her.

With a resigned sigh, I got off the wooden chair, dreading where the night always ended up, alone in my room with nothing but my thoughts and my guitar. The boys might still be at the bar, and with their fakes, I'm sure if I wanted, I could've snuck in a few drinks. But I didn't want anything to replace the memories I made tonight with the only peace in this life.

Swiping a napkin across the table, I cleaned up any of the remainder of the dessert that had spilled. At first, I had planned to get my usual plain vanilla scoop, but I couldn't resist ordering what Sonia had, despite it sounding like it'd send me straight to the hospital after having two of them. But there was a nagging feeling inside of me telling me that I wanted to know everything about her, and if that meant slurping on the sweetest ice cream cone I'd ever had, so be it. I'd suffer through it.

Something on the floor caught my eye as I passed the chair once occupied by Sonia and bent down to pick up a white scrunchie, the same one that I saw wrapped around her delicate wrist every day. She must have not realized it slipped off.

Twirling it between my fingers, I exited the shop, walking towards the bike I kept parked outside. Throwing my leg over the seat, I rested for a moment, the scrunchie still pressed against my palm. I'd return it to her eventually, but not today.

Today, it was meant for my wrist as a reminder that things didn't need to be masked in sadness and pain at all times. The hurt could be overcome, it could be forgotten, even for just an hour, if only there were someone by your side to offer a gentle ear.

The satin felt cool against my thin skin, breaking the warmth of the night with its feel. It was the same effect she had on me, causing a mixture of emotions to contradict within me, making me question everything I had once been sure of.

Shifting the ignition on my bike, I set off, drifting in the wind while I let my thoughts roam free, stopping only when I pulled into the driveway of my house. It was different every year, but this time we were here for longer. Four years, staying dormant in one spot for the first time in my life. My parents claimed it was so my high school education wouldn't waver, but it always shocked me when they'd mention it. It had been the only time they were willingly considerate towards me. Unless, there was a hidden agenda, which I wouldn't put past them, their selfish ways altering my life since my birth.

The house was beautiful, and to an outsider, it almost looked perfect, blue with a white picket fence and huge lawn equipped with beautiful growing plants and trees, a poster for a perfect family.

But the inside couldn't be more broken.

Shoving the key in the lock, I began wishing for headphones to manifest onto my ears so I could block out the immediate noise and head straight into my room. But unfortunately, I'd left them inside my school bag which still lay on the floor against my bed, so there was no denying what would come next.

The door had only opened a smidge, before the voices made themselves prevalent in my ears. I knew now that there was no changing it or escaping from it. Not until I moved away to college.

Just a couple more months, I thought. *Then I'll be gone. Away from this all.*

It was the only reason I woke up every morning, eager to head to school, looking forward to that graduation date. I couldn't take it anymore. I was sick of it.

Today, they seemed to be fighting about the television, my mother yelling about a show she'd put on while my father possessed the remote control. They didn't notice when I walked in, they never did, always remaining too preoccupied in their own arguments to ever pay attention to their only child. But it was okay, I preferred it this way. It was comfortable.

Tiptoeing, I climbed the stairs, carefully shutting my door so no one could hear me. It was fairly unlikely that they would, seeing the way their voices traveled through the walls and into the foundation of this very house.

Yanking my shoes off, I lay on my black comforter, reaching for the acoustic I kept close by. Strumming a few notes, I made sure to keep quiet, avoiding any chance of making myself known. My eyes continuously locked onto the scrunchie that sat on my wrist like it always belonged there. My thoughts kept circling around that sullen smile she wore, like she was hiding something too, something sadder, deeper, than she'd ever let out. I figured that's what drew me towards her.

It was a pull, an urge to lean further into the trench with her.

But I refused to drag her down alongside me.

I didn't know what exactly I felt towards her. But I knew it was just a need to protect her. She wasn't as hard as she showed herself to be and I could see through her disguise easily. I wore the same one. Those bright eyes dampened sometimes, those firm hands began quivering. I noticed it when she spoke of her birthday. There was something she was hiding. But I had no right to push her for it so I didn't.

The walls were shaking so heavily with the screams, I feared all the vinyl records that hung around my black walls would tip over. Letting out a sigh, I placed the guitar back in its spot, walking across the room towards my cluttered desk. I was never here anyways so I never bothered to keep it tidy.

Grabbing my laptop, I threw on the headphones, jumping back into my bed.

Just a few more months.

It'd become my mantra, something I repeated everyday to keep myself going.

As I pressed play on my computer, The Scientist by Coldplay began thrumming through me, silencing everything on the outside with its beautiful conception of a deceptive love. It was never real. As a child, I believed my parents were in this soul crushing devotional love, but I quickly realized it was nothing but a lie. All their displays of affection, all their portrayals of a perfect family were all a carefully crafted fabrication.

It did nothing but convince me that I would never want it for myself.

Life was better when you were alone, without the fear of jumping off a cliff with someone to hold your hand.

All it convinced me of was that I would never want to fall in love.

With the melodious music in my ears, I shielded my brain from everything and let myself drift into sleep, hoping that the next morning would bring nothing but quietness.

CHAPTER 14

Sonia

"Aunty," Jyoti perched from the doorway, "thank you for the food. It was really good to see you again."

"Please come over soon," Addie added. "My mom misses you."

Our parents' relationships were what we aspired to be and carrying on traditions like dinner at each other's respective homes at least once or twice every month was our way to honor that. We had always grown up watching the way our moms had been best friends from youth, never losing their friendship to ill factors like distance or lack of time or even marriage. In fact, it gave a platform for all our fathers to become best friends as well. Sure, there had been moments and years in our past where we hadn't been as accessible to each other as we were now, but it never wavered from the love we had for each other. These girls were the biggest constant in my life and they will remain forever.

Girlhood was the foundation of a beautiful life.

"Tell both your moms that I'll see them soon." My mother walked over, pulling both of my best friends into her embrace, pressing a kiss on their temples. "It was lovely seeing you girls again."

The Indian way of leaving homes was staying at the doorway having an extra hour of conversation before actually leaving. After exchanging a few more goodbyes and hugs, I shut the door behind them, going back into the kitchen to help finish cleaning up.

"Is dad still working on his case?" My father was a lawyer, one with a great reputation which meant busy hours and days, and, to compensate, my mother retired from her life as a teacher to become a full time stay at home wife. Yet, she never complained, happily giving up a part of her for her love. It was partially why I was so drawn towards her life goals, following through with everything she once wanted so she could see her dreams play out through her daughter. But she loved her new life, and I loved what they had, never doubting that either of them were unhappy with their choices. It was exactly what I aspired to have in my life.

A great love that would keep me satisfied no matter where I was or what I was doing.

I thought I had it once, but life was funny like that, causing it all to be thrown away for a reason I had no intention of figuring out.

"You know how it is for him, Sonu," my mother had always opted for the shortened version of my name, claiming that it was her way of showering her love to me. "He's probably still locked away in his office."

A message tone lit up the silence and my heart somersaulted reading the name. I hadn't realized I still had his number saved, never realized he'd never change it. But mine had, multiple times, and reading *Kartik* above *one new message* had me wondering how he even got to it.

Quickly, I flipped my phone around, hiding the screen from my mother's prying eyes, but the beeping never stopped, messages coming in like repeatedly and it wasn't until my phone began buzzing that my mom finally spoke up. "Who keeps calling you? Is it important?"

"No." My voice was hurried, immediately striking concern in her eyes. "Sorry, I'll just go see."

Pressing the phone to my chest, I climbed the stairs into my childhood bedroom which remained untouched, full of little plushies and teddy bears and a sage green wall with fairy lights in every corner.

My phone rang again as I pressed my entire weight against the dresser for support before swiping towards the answer button. "Why are you calling me?"

He chuckled and I was immediately reminded of the nights we spent in this very room, curled up against each other. This was a terrible idea. "No hi or hello, shona?"

I let out an irritated breath, preparing myself to go through this conversation. "Where did you get my number?" I had no intention of letting this drag out, knowing the longer it took, the more I'd reminisce. "And why are you calling me?"

"You still have mine saved." It was a murmur, as though he tried to silence it hoping I wouldn't hear him but accidentally spoke too loud. But hearing it warmed my cheeks, ruby red rising and making a path up my skin. "I'll get straight to the point then. Your number was in the forms you filled out when you got your tattoo and I'm calling you because I want to see you again."

"The forms?" I could almost hear his obnoxious smile through the phone and I wanted to reach through and wipe it off. "Isn't that like a breach of client privacy or something? That's illegal."

"Not if the client is you and the tattooist is me." I knew what he meant. We were never strangers, we never could be. No matter how much time passes, you can never wipe away any trace of a beautiful history you share with someone.

"My dad's a lawyer."

"I remember." Two words that shook my world and I couldn't place why. An agitating voice in my head wanted to ask what else he remembered but the sensible part of my brain knew it was better to never dive into that information. I was better off not knowing, not opening the Pandora's box full of memories of a life we no longer lived. "See me again."

"No, Kartik." I already knew I was screwed with the way his name once again slipped through my lips so easily, as if it were never wiped from them. As if he'd always been someone I called to. "Why are you really calling?"

"Shona," he let out an audible breath of frustration, stopping my arguments over the nickname. It still made my insides bubble, holding a weight over me. "I just want to see you again. After Holi, I know you still—"

"Don't, Kartik." There was no way he was going to say what I thought he was. I didn't *still* feel anything. I don't. He was misunderstanding the fact that I let him play Holi with me because that's all it was.

A festival.

However, now I was struggling to pinpoint whether I recited it in my head to convince myself or him.

My heart began pounding out of my chest with the memories of what really happened that night. I wanted to prove that I was over him, that I was bigger than the past but I ended up almost kissing him. I had almost forgotten how far I'd taken my '*be bold*' initiative.

"Okay, okay. But—"

I cut him off once again, feeling defeated and conflicted. "I have to go." Kartik began speaking but I ended the call before any words could come through again.

My hands instinctively gripped the furniture behind me, holding me up when my weight simply wanted to fall into a puddle on the floor. "Sonu," my mom's voice startled me, causing me to snap my head towards the door.

All the air in me hitched and I waited. *How much did she hear?*

As if hearing my thoughts, she moved into the room, wrapping her arms around me. "Maine suna." *I heard.* I immediately gripped her, tightening my hold on her, just as I did all those years ago. "Was that him? Is he here again?" I nodded into her shoulder, feeling like I was seventeen all over again. She sighed in return, gathering her thoughts before speaking again. "Tum badi ho gayi ho." *You've grown up now.* "I won't tell you anything except just be careful, okay? I don't want to see you go through the same thing you did with him after all these years."

"I know, ma. I don't want to."

"Shh." Her hands caressed my hair as involuntary tears fell, all the pain making its way up my skin again. She was right. I couldn't do that to her, and especially not to myself. She'd seen me broken, unable to piece myself together, losing every bit of sanity over this guy. The pain I felt then, I vowed to never feel again. From this point on, I would stay as far away from Kartik Sharma as I possibly could.

CHAPTER 15
Kartik

The overhead bell rang as the door to the shop swung open and I stepped out of the office to see Jaymin and Kyle making their way inside. "What's up?" Kaitlyn still sat at the front desk but at my voice, indicating that I'd already known them, she decided against greeting the boys, opting for a friendly smile instead. Although I didn't miss the starstruck look that showered her face as she stared at the two football players as they strolled towards me.

"Kartik," Jaymin started, "you do walk-ins?"

Kaitlyn eyed me concerningly, waiting for a response. Typically, our shop didn't accept people coming in at the moment for their tattoos, operating strictly on an appointment basis, unless on special holidays. However, for friends, I figured the policy could be vetoed.

"For you, yeah." Jaymin grinned and I faced Kaitlyn. "They're old friends and we're clear for two hours, right?"

After browsing through the computer that sat in front of her, she perked up again. "Yeah, *you* are. My next client is coming in two hours. Yours isn't until 5pm, Kay."

I glanced at the clock above the door which read 1pm, giving me four hours for whatever the boys needed. Tapping my fist atop the desk, I offered Kaitlyn a sweet smile. "Thanks." I gave them a 'bro hug,' consisting of a dap and hand slap on the back, then started the walk to my tattoo chair on the second floor of the shop. "Follow me." I swiftly set up the chair for a new guest, placing the plastic covers on the arm rest just in case. "Are both of you getting tattoos?"

Kyle made an exasperated sound, his face morphing into something nearing fear. "Nah, just here for some moral support. Needles and me, we don't get along."

"This coming from a man who plays a sport that's ranked one of the most dangerous?" I immediately laughed at the mockery that left me, Jaymin joining me with no time to spare.

"You rather get a torn ACL than get your skin stabbed once for some ink?" Jaymin spoke in between his laughs.

"*Once?*" Kyle was fully shaking his head in disbelief, no humor on his face. "A tattoo needle stabs you a million little times constantly. Not to mention you have to be so careful with it."

"Okay, okay no one's coming near you with a needle." I held up the capped tattoo gun, inching it closer to him to get a rise out of his paranoia, watching as he looked as though he'd seen a ghost.

"I'm out." He turned to leave, only stopping when Jaymin apologized profusely. It was sweet seeing their friendship in real life, knowing how Jaymin used to talk about Kyle all throughout college. He swore I would love him if I met him and he wasn't wrong. The only thing that pained me was the yearning I had for what they possessed. A real friend. I've only had one in my life and I went and lost her too.

"Dude," Jaymin tapped my shoulder, "you okay? You zoned out."

"I'm fine." I shook my head, ridding my head of the thoughts of a particular blonde streaked beauty and focused on the situation in front of me. "So what are we getting today? I'll have to draw out the stencil."

"I'm trying to surprise Adhira." There was pride in his features, as he explained that he'd been talking about a tattoo to his girlfriend for a while and since it was off season, thought it'd be best to shock her. It was a sweet gesture, warming me but also making me colder than I'd ever been. I took a glance at my arms, seeing the tattoos that filled them and thought back to every moment I had gotten them, the memories plaguing me.

Washing them out of my brain, I began working the design on my tablet, getting the approval from Jaymin, who sat himself on the chair, and printed it out. "Where do you want it placed?" I held the sticker out, making sure the size and drawing was up to par as he'd imagined it would be.

"On my chest," taking his shirt off, he pointed towards the left with his finger, "right above my heart."

"Damn, that's kinda cute." Kyle retorted with a pout.

"Shut up, asshole." Jaymin attempted to stay still while I pressed the paper onto him, moving around the room to gather my equipment.

Dragging the stool under me, I filled my gun with ink and began to carve into Jaymin. He didn't flinch at all, as expected of one of the best NFL players as of right now. The buzzing of the needle was the only sound in the room, until Jaymin spoke from under it. "It's been really good to see you again, Kartik." Turning to his best friend, he pointed at me with his other hand. "You know, Kartik used to go by Kay in college and one time the dorm advisors thought they paired me with a girl and almost got him kicked out."

Under a fit of laughter, I gathered my voice. "Don't forget I'm the one with the needle in my hand." He shot his hands up in surrender, mimicking a zipper being closed across his lips and threw the imaginary key behind his shoulder. "It's nice to see you like this though. With Addie, given college frat boy Jaymin was totally looking for a new thrill every day."

"It's Adhira, you know." He looked completely smitten, gazing off into the distance as if he could see her manifesting in front of his eyes. "She's amazing. It's like everything I'd ever done or gone through in my life was just so I could end up with her. Ethereal was what I thought of when I first saw her." I knew the feeling. It was exactly what I felt eight years ago, when I had accidentally fallen for the girl who fell in front of me. With my mind constantly going to her, I knew I had to ask.

"Yeah," I maneuvered the conversation as fluently as I could. "Her and her friends all seem like good people."

"They are," this time, Kyle rose in favor of them. "Addie's great but Jyoti and Sonia are also equally fantastic. They're all like sisters, you'll find them joined at the hip almost all the time."

"And if you ever say anything about either of the other two, the third will always come to bite." Jaymin and Kyle both shared knowing laughs, something that made me feel like even more of an outsider in the group. "But I'm sure, once you get to know them, you'll love them too." Jaymin looked as though he'd been piecing together his words, crafting them carefully as to not offend me with what came next. "That is, if you're planning on staying a while. You know, with everything you told me about your life."

Jaymin was one of the only people I'd opened up to in my life. Even Sonia didn't know half as much as he did, and the only reason for that was the fact that he was the agonizingly annoying roommate in college who would never give you peace of mind unless you told him everything about yourself. Despite my annoyance with him, I was always grateful to finally have someone who would listen. "I'm staying."

"Good." The smile he gave me in return was genuine, making me feel like I could build a home here once again. "You have got to start hanging with us more. Adhira wanted to meet you again as well."

Butterflies swarmed my stomach as I thought of the possibility of seeing Sonia more often. "I'd love to." Out of fear that my smile may have come off too eager, I focused my attention back onto his chest. "So tell me more about everyone." The only thing I truly wanted to know was about Sonia. "What do Sonia and Jyoti do? I know Addie since your little love declaration was so public and televised." I remembered seeing Addie show up during the super bowl celebration and that was partly what encouraged me to come back further, hoping that I'd run into my girl somehow.

I never planned to want her back. I had only just wanted to catch a glimpse of her. But that damn necklace was dangling in my brain constantly ever since I pierced her skin.

"Jyoti's in fashion school in New York City, but she still lives at home, I believe." After mulling it over for a moment, Jaymin continued again. "Yeah, she commutes from home. And Sonia, she works at the elementary school as a teacher." *Bingo.* "I think she's been teaching there for a couple months now."

"Mhm." I tried to contain the grin that involuntarily manifested across my face, remembering all those tutoring nights and conversations about the future. She really did it. The men began talking about something else, the words passing through my ears like they hadn't even been spoken, the only thing truly registering in my head was her.

Finishing the piece, I stepped away from Jaymin, rubbing ointment on his skin before handing him a handheld mirror to more closely inspect the design.

"It's amazing." I looked at it once again. Moon phases, for the meaning of her name, tattooed right above his heart in a horizontal line. "She's going to love it."

"Damn man. Maybe it's time I get one for my girl." Kyle appreciated the art as well. Both the men were lovestruck and I knew it far too well.

Love was so insanely powerful it made you do crazy things.

And I could only relate, knowing what I had planned next.

CHAPTER 16
Sonia

8 years ago

My headphones were blasting *A Little Death* by The Neighbourhood and I assumed that's what contributed to my emotions seeing Kartik prompting Layla, the blonde haired cheerleader who'd been sitting beside me everyday in her unspoken unassigned seat, to move so he could occupy it himself. His eyes were glued onto me, like they were made only for seeing me.

What the hell was I even thinking?

Knocking my fist on my head internally, I pulled out my iPod, scrounging my music library for a song, any song, that wasn't remotely sensually pulling me towards him, but alas, I came up short.

"Hi." He wore a boyish grin, toothy like he'd just won the biggest prize at a carnival.

I didn't want to humor him, but I knew ignoring him would only make it worse so I gave him a quick half-smirk before looking away, back into the direction of the door where our teacher, Mr. Hemly, finally appeared. Swiftly, I yanked my headphones out my ear, tucking them into my hoodie's pocket so no one could see. I'd gotten called out for them just a week ago and it was my first disciplinary issue and I didn't plan to get another one any time soon.

"Good morning, class." He began his daily lecture on Shakespeare's sonnets, Mr. Hemly's words getting swallowed by the hand sliding across my desk.

I promptly ignored it, thinking if I pretended that I was paying more attention to our teacher's projected voice asking everyone to pull out their book of sonnets, it would be as if it hadn't existed. But Kartik wouldn't stop that easily.

He loudly cleared his throat, bringing everyone's attention to him except mine. I could almost hear his smirk from a foot away as I grabbed the piece of paper he so meticulously lay on my table before anyone else could spot it.

"Is there a problem Mr Sharma?" Mr. Hemly turned with the rest of us, his eyes zeroing in on the troublemaker that sat next to me.

"Not at all, sir." A couple of the other students, particularly the football players and cheerleaders, chuckled along with him, partaking in whatever domino effect was rippling from it. They were all pick-me students who'd go home and talk crap about each other anyway, their unity only running deep until class bells rang.

Unfolding the paper under the desk, I peered a look inside to see his messy handwriting scribbled all over it.

Why aren't you wearing the necklace? -K

With daggers in my eyes, I glared at him, silently, as if having a whole wordless conversation.

Seriously?, my eyes questioned.

Yes, shona, his said back.

Even in my imagination he was using the stupid nickname. There was something clinically wrong with me, whatever condition it was only worsening the more time I spent with him. I needed to do something about that and I needed to do it quickly before it started bleeding into my everyday life.

Marking my ignorance, he repeated the whole scene again, reaching over to place a folded paper again on my desk. And it wasn't until then that I realized what sat wrapped around his wrist. I glanced at my own first, for confirmation, before locking my eyes on him again, then his wrist. He had my white satin scrunchie on his arm.

What the hell?

My eyes were bulging out my head at his knowing smirk, his head tilting just a smidge as if mockingly questioning me. He even annoyingly twisted his wrist, cracking the bones there. But before I could make any remark, Mr. Hemly strategically called my name.

"Sonia, how does Sonnet 116 contradict today's beliefs in society and what is he trying to convey in his words? And do you agree?" He was deeply glaring towards me, as if he'd known that I hadn't been paying attention. But to his surprise, he'd called me out on my favorite one of Shakespeare's writings, a sonnet I knew like the back of my hand.

"Simply put, Shakespeare tries to talk of how true love is a constant." The entire classrooms' eyes had been glued onto me, but nothing compared to the burn I felt from the gaze on my right. "How if two people are in love, nothing and no one can stop it. He states 'Love is not love, which alters when it alteration finds, or bends with the remover to remove' in which he points that if whatever love you're feeling can mend itself and change because of outside forces, it isn't as pure as you thought it to be. Then, he continues to compare it to a star, something else that is *always* present, like love should be, not everchanging." The whole class was silent, but it never bothered me. This is where I thrived. "I do agree with Shakespeare. I believe real, true love is something that doesn't just disappear and if it does, it never was."

Instead of commending me as usual, he turned to the side. "Yes, Mr. Sharma."

I turned to find the arrogant annoying boy with a full grin and his hand thrown into the air. "But people are bound to change." His eyes met mine in provocation, something they did often. "How can you say it wasn't love if two people did feel it once? Just because it changes doesn't mean it didn't exist, correct? Shakespeare himself was unhappy with his wife so can we really trust his explanation of true love?" He crossed his arms on the desk in front of him, leaning forward.

"Good point, Kartik." Mr. Hemly nodded along. "Good to finally see your participation."

"People change. But real feelings shouldn't." My eyes were unmoving, stilling on him as he watched me in return. "Change in life is inevitable, people grow and adapt to their environment but what is the point of love if it's conditional in its way to stay constant. That would be unrealistic in itself."

"Then how do you explain why he was unhappy in his marriage? What credibility does Shakespeare even have? For all we know Sonnet 116 was inspired by someone else, not his wife Anne Hathaway." I knew he was doing it just to get a rise out of me, and I hated to admit that it was working. But if it wasn't for the darkness radiating off him, I would've never wanted to prove him wrong as much as I did in the moment.

"You're basing your take on love and Shakespeare on assumptions. We don't know for sure that he was unhappy or whether his sonnets were based on life or fiction. And Mr.

Hemly is not talking about Shakespeare. This discussion is solely on the content of the sonnet and what it means in regards to love. And the sonnet is saying that love does not change no matter what happens. It remains when it's real, it never fades and it overcomes every obstacle. Not that Shakespeare partook in infidelity or that he was unhappy. Clearly he had to have known something right about love to write all the epic romances he did."

My chest was heaving watching his smile grow by the second, the only interruption being Mr. Hemly and the sound he let out from his throat. "Alright then." His hands pressed in a small clap. "Sonia, Kartik, let's take a breath." I was sure the whole class could see the hot fumes escaping my ears and nose as I turned back to face the blackboard, a few chuckles going off around me.

"Geez, nerd," Layla, who now sat directly behind me, whispered into the back of my head. "Take a pause now, would you?"

I rolled my eyes, still feeling heat radiating through me. I couldn't believe I let Kartik rile me up like that in front of everyone, despite my mind telling me he wasn't worth the second glance. Through my peripheral vision, I noticed him high fiving some of the other guys around him, as if rejoicing in his asshole-ery, like it was something to congratulate. Suddenly, his hand appeared atop my desk again, leaving behind another sheet of folded paper and I decided against opening it, until he started making noises, drawing more attention towards us. I had no choice.

Lifting the edges apart, I read the single sentence scribbled on it with messy handwriting I now recognized as Kartik's.

I'm Sorry.

I must have been caught in the apology because I heard Mr. Hemly a second too late. "Miss Sonia, care to share with the class what you're looking at?"

I frantically tucked the paper between my thighs, hiding it like it was never there to begin with. "Nothing, sir." A few giggles went off behind me and I cursed myself knowing if it continued, I would get stuck in the crossfire.

"If I hear one more interruption, I'm sending you all to the principal's office."

I nodded, vowing to keep my mouth shut the rest of the period and avoid looking at the distraction stealing glances at me on my right.

CHAPTER 17
Sonia

Bailey's was always packed, as usual, except the crowd today had nothing to do with NFL and everything to do with a local elementary school. With the final weekend of spring break left, the teachers had all decided to go out for one night of fun and drinks, and eagerly, I agreed to go as well.

I desperately needed a diversion from the way my phone had been blowing up and staying drunk amongst co-workers whose company I typically enjoyed seemed like the perfect idea. Turning the phone face down again, I pasted on a smile as Mortada placed a hand atop my shoulder. "Sonia." Behind him trailed a petite woman, with glass skin and brown waves. "This is Alyssa."

Her smile was bright, growing as she leaned into me, wrapping her arms around my shoulders. "Oh my God." She nearly shrieked into my ear and I chuckled, knowing this was exactly the kind of woman that would attract Mortada. "I have heard so much about you. I'm so glad we're finally meeting."

"Me too." I returned her embrace as best I could in my drunken state. Pulling apart, I scooted in my spot, making space for her beside me. "The way Mortada describes you does no justice." I winked at him as he shyly walked away, making his rounds as he greeted the rest of the teachers. "It's so good to finally put a voice to the face."

She ordered a cranberry vodka for the both of us, grabbing them from the new bartender and handing one to me. Eagerly, I accepted the poison, anything to take my mind away from the constantly loudening vibration of my phone. I couldn't escape the thoughts of the last time I reluctantly picked up, consciously making sure I hadn't made that mistake again.

The eagerness of his voice when he spoke to me, urging me to see him once more, kept replaying in my head like a song you couldn't get out. He was crazy. And what sane man looks through tattoo forms to find someone's number? Without noticing, I angrily chugged down half of my drink, earning a surprised gasp from Alyssa. "Clearly someone needed that." She giggled and I couldn't have it in me to be embarrassed at the act.

I groaned instantly. "Sorry." The phone vibrated again, my eyes zeroing in on the slight bounce the device did against the hard counter. The buzzing was somehow getting louder, or was it just the way it urged my mind to pay attention? The alcohol from my fourth drink hit almost instantly, hazing out the rest of the world just slightly, enough for me to wear my concern on my face.

"Is that important?" Alyssa was looking directly in my line of vision, at the device shifting its position with every movement. "Sorry, I don't mean to pry."

I shook my head, hoping it came off genuine. I couldn't tell when every single one of my thoughts revolved around the problem at hand. "It's okay. It's just someone who thinks I owe them my time when they don't deserve it."

"Is it a guy?" I didn't need to respond for her to figure out the answer by how hard I cringed. "I don't know if I'm overstepping or sticking my nose where it doesn't belong but it seems like he's persistent and if it wasn't for persistence, I would've never given Mortada a chance." She looked at him longingly, the love shining through her eyes. "Did you know he used to send flowers to my house ever since the day we met? We ran into each other at a mutual friend's party and immediately felt attracted to each other but honestly, I had recently gotten out of a long term relationship that was really draining and toxic so I wasn't looking to find anyone. But even then, I reluctantly gave him my number and he dropped me home too. And since then, every week he started sending me flowers with notes asking to take me out until I finally agreed. And even now, he sends them but the notes now consist of the different feelings he has for me. It was easily the best decision of my life." She smiled at him again, their eyes locking as he began walking over. "All I'm saying is, sometimes you need to give yourself a shot, even when you think you don't want it."

Mortada wrapped his arms around Alyssa, placing a soft kiss on the back of her head. The gesture was all too sweet, taking me back to those nights eight years ago. With a defeated sigh, I downed the rest of my drink and snatched my now silent phone off the surface. Alyssa was somewhat right. Kartik didn't deserve my time but that didn't mean I didn't deserve to tell him exactly how I felt. "Excuse me guys."

I stumbled towards the back of the bar near the empty bathrooms before leaning against the wall and with a deep breath, scrolled through all the notifications. The entire screen was full of missed calls and voicemails, along with texts that continually asked me to pick up.

Who the hell did he think he was?

Without another thought, I clicked onto his name and dialed the number, the phone only ringing once before silence met me on the receiving end. He was just as shocked as I had been that I had performatively returned his calls. "What do you want?"

"To see you." He was direct, as opposed to the last time I answered, hitting me by surprise. "I told you this already."

For whatever reason, my heart could not stop clambering out my chest, thundering like a winter's storm. My anger was bubbling but all I heard was his slight breaths through the phone, passing a wave of nostalgia through me. I was suddenly seventeen again, sitting on rooftops next to a boy who had a heart of stone that melted only for me. "Fine." My drunk words slurred, and I knew he understood the state I was in. "Where?"

CHAPTER 18
Kartik

8 years ago

She shuffled through her books, following the same pattern as always, stuffing them in the oversized shoulder bag she lugged around everyday. Sonia began warming up to me and I could tell by the way she lingered every day until I was ready to leave too, walking beside me despite how much her face was covered in a scowl. When we first began these sessions, neither of us wanted to be here longer than we needed to. But now, somehow, we both found comfort in each other's company.

A piece of paper slid out of her anatomy textbook, and as she bent down, I caught just a glimpse of it. The necklace I had given her.

I sheepishly told her it was arcade jewelry and I knew she hadn't believed me, rightfully so. The pendant was far more intricate than any claw machine could've produced. Truthfully, I had spotted that necklace, a teardrop mimicking a guitar pick, when I was looking at new instruments at the store, the shopkeeper telling me that they were newly in stock. And the moment my eyes caught onto it, I knew I wanted her to have it. And she was finally wearing it.

An involuntary smile appeared on my face, my face contorting as she watched me questioningly. Her brows twisted in confusion. "What are you looking at?" She crossed her arms across her chest defensively and pressed her lips together. She was adorable.

"Nothing, shona." She winced, only enticing an even greater grin on me. With anyone else, I would've cut the nickname out a long time ago. But something about the way her eyes glimmered every time it slipped out my mouth had me excitedly scurrying to say it every time.

"Whatever." She rolled her eyes in exasperation and gathered the remainder of her items together, turning towards the door in speed. My chair almost fell back as I stood up, rushing to meet her steps. "What are you doing?" She called from over her shoulder.

"Wait for me."

"No." I picked up my pace, meeting her finally right outside the door. A couple other students lingered around, the cheerleaders and football players getting out of practice and dispersing around the school buses that waited for after school activities. A few of the girls looked my way, attempting to call my name as I wrapped my fingers around Sonia's arm. "What are you doing?"

A few whispers went off around us and she squirmed under my touch, attempting to break free. Her eyes were pleading as they shuffled around, an emotion I hadn't seen in her before. What was wrong?

"Let me go." Sonia's voice hushed, as if shielding it from everyone around us. I could feel the stares burning me, the same way they had in the classroom the other day. Was she afraid of people talking? Of them seeing us together? "Kartik." It was more of a request, a hurried one too.

I released her arm, not wanting to make her even more uncomfortable than she already was. "Let me drop you home."

She snickered and let out a breath. "No."

"Come on." She looked around at the crowd that had weirdly gone silent. It had to be what was holding her back. I took a step closer, lowering my voice so that only she could hear it. "Hey, don't worry about anyone else."

Anger bubbled over her as her expression hardened and she no longer was softly entreating. "I don't." She was lying but I had no intention of proving that now.

"Okay then let me drop you home since you don't care."

The hard headed Sonia I'd grown used to was back. Her chest puffed out, her eyes bulging as she spoke. "Why do you want to drop me home so bad? What's the catch?"

Both my hands shot up in surrender. "No catch." I pinched the skin of my throat, the Indian way of making a promise. "I shapath." *I swear.*

"Then what is it?" Her arms remained crossed, defiance all over that soft face.

I shook my head, piecing together the words before they left me. "I know you take the bus home and most seniors drive. I don't want to ask why you don't but it's after school hours and I know the buses make a billion stops, cramming everyone in. So I thought I'd make it easier for you to get home sooner." I shrugged hoping it sounded like a good enough reason. To be honest, I couldn't place why my brain was so adamant on wanting more time with her but it was my only driving force.

"How do you even know that I don't drive everyday?" She was attempting to make sense of the information I had just dropped like I hadn't just revealed that I observed her daily.

"I've seen you take the bus after tutoring." And every day other than that as well, I wanted to say, but decided against it. "Just an innocent ride home."

"I don't know."

"Come on, Sonia." I thought using her actual name would be beneficial but the short second of pain that passed through her made me feel as though there was comfort in the nickname. Like we were raw in front of each other, showing sides that we had kept sheltered from everyone else.

After a long moment, as she realized I was not going to budge, she finally agreed with a sigh. "Fine."

With a smile, I crossed the parking lot, making sure she was following steadily behind while her eyes trailed to everyone around us. She held tightly onto the strap that weighed on her shoulder and when we got to my vehicle, she gripped it even harder. "You're joking." I couldn't help the laugh that left at her immediate response, which I had already prematurely expected.

"It's not that bad."

"You come to school on a bike!" She was practically yelling, shock and fear both residing in her. Shock I could understand but the fear seemed to prick at me, leering me towards her to know more.

Glancing at my matte black Kawasaki Ninja, pride washed through me. When we had first moved to this town, I had taken up a job at the local record store as cashier as well as played a few gigs with my guitar at parties and saved up enough to purchase it. My parents couldn't even be bothered to notice the job, the bike coming as a surprise to them. But I managed to brush them aside. After all, they'd always been more entwined in their own lives to focus on their only kid. "What's the problem?"

"I am *not* getting on that, Kartik." I couldn't help but grin in response, a chuckle following suit. "You psychopath, you're doing this to taunt me right? Punish me?"

"Now what the hell would I punish you for?" She took a step back, and I knew she was thinking of all the ways she could escape. "Shona, trust me. It'll be fun."

"I can't get on a bike, Kartik." Her eyes were pleading and she shook her head, remaining rooted in place. My hands worked to unlock the helmet I kept strapped across the seat, unclasping it while walking over to her. "Plus, you only have one helmet. I'll take the bus."

"Shh." At my command, her lips clasped shut and I placed the helmet over her head, dropping it slowly. Through the eye band, I could tell her lids had shut, her breathing coming in small huffs as her chest stayed close to mine. There was something so intimate about the way we were standing right now, compromising everything. Her lashes fluttered as she took in a deep breath, meeting my gaze and craning her neck to better view me through the helmet. Fuck, it looked great on her.

My hands still hovered over the strap, prolonging the moment as long as I could. There was a pull between us drawing us further and further into each other's lives, no matter how much we tried to stray from it. Breaking out of the spell, I brought myself to stand at the foot of the bike, my hand roaming the smooth exterior. She was watching my every move, following every inch my finger trailed and for a moment, I found myself wishing it were her under my touch.

I met her eyes again, now shielded by the lightly tinted black cover. "I'm going to hop on first so I can adjust the position and then you're gonna sit on this elevated part. Okay?" She nodded in understanding and watched as I threw my leg over the bent bike, undoing the kickstand and balancing it between my limbs. I touched my feet on the ground, straightening the bike, making it easier for Sonia to hop on when she was ready to. "Just step on these foot pegs and throw your leg over, shona."

She straightened her back and I knew it was terror that she felt. I needed to make her feel protected.

"Trust me, shona." I held out my hand, palm facing up, urging her to latch on. "I got you."

After a deep inhale, she took a cautious step towards me, lightly placing her hand in mine, disappearing with the way mine engulfed hers. With slow steps, she was standing beside me, glancing at the seat before looking back at me. Another breath later, she placed her left foot on the stand, her free hand shooting up to my shoulder, as she hoisted herself onto the seat with a gasp. The hand that was once in mine desperately clutched onto my other shoulder. "Shona, I think it'd be better if you placed your hands around my waist."

She reluctantly placed her hands on my stomach, flat against the jacket, her debating thoughts loud in my ears. Even through the leather I could feel the warmth that radiated from her, warming me as if she were the definition of comfort. She made it her mission to hold me as light as possible, probably thinking I had only told her to grip me like this to get tease her. Although I had been enjoying it as well, she would soon realize it was for her safety more than anything. And I had the perfect way to expedite it.

Prepping the bike, I started it up, moving forward just a bit before break checking it. Just like that, she slammed into me, her hands clasping together at my midsection, holding me like it was the only source of salvation. I smirked at her playful smack, her voice ringing through me again. "Asshole."

"I needed you to see that this is the safest way to backpack me." An annoyed grunt left her lips but she didn't move from her position, her chest pressing deep into my back and her head resting just at the crane of my neck. It made my pulse throb, the closeness enticing feelings I'd never felt before. "I'm gonna start driving. When I'm making turns, I'm going to need you to turn with me and follow my body so the bike can be smooth. Just hold onto me and if you want me to slow down just tap my stomach twice, alright?"

"Got it."

I twisted the handles with a smile, for the first time feeling excited to drive home. And it had everything to do with the girl clutching me, her lavender scent making its way through my unmasked veins.

I made a mental note to offer her a ride home every day, tutoring or not, right before driving to the direction of her house.

CHAPTER 19
Kartik

The moment she'd called me back, I knew she was inebriated. Sober Sonia wanted nothing to do with me. And I originally hadn't planned on meeting an intoxicated one but as soon as I heard the immense slurring of her words, I couldn't resist.

So here I was, standing outside Bailey's looking through the big window like some kind of stalker.

She was draped in a crimson red satin dress, falling at her mid thigh, a small slit drawing up her left leg making anyone want to commit heinous crimes for her. The straps were barely there, thin and pressed loosely against her golden shoulders, her hair moving with the wind as she swayed around. She looked like the object of my wildest dreams.

She reached into the crowd and grabbed another glass, holding it to her lips before taking three large gulps, nearly downing half of it. Her smile grew as she placed it back down and joined another girl who was moving around in the empty space. Just then, a set of hands landed on her shoulder, and a man dipped down into her ear whispering something that brought out a pout from Sonia.

What the hell?

Anger bubbling, I decided that was enough watching. The cold air from the bar hit my face as I stormed inside, my stride sure. She saw me before I reached her, her eyes bulging out her head as she realized that she had truly called me over. I met her in less than ten seconds, standing above her as she bobbled in her stance, unable to keep her spine steady. "Come on. Time to go." It was the only thing I said before gripping her wrist, leading us towards the door.

"What the hell do you think you're doing?" She began calling behind me, struggling to get her words loud enough to make a difference. But suddenly, she stopped moving and I had no interest in hurting her so I turned to face her again.

"Is this—" I glared at the man who was touching my girl just minutes ago. His words were directed to Sonia but I cut him off before he could finish whatever question he was getting at.

"I'd keep quiet if you want your hands still on your body."

"Kartik!" Sonia was damn near yelling and I realized then how much I missed that side of her. It was wrong of me to find her so attractive right now but the way her eyes darkened and her cherry lips moved had me wishing I could run my hands along her skin. "I am so sorry, Mortada, don't mind this jerk." Her eyes rolled at the last word, dragging it out in an attempt to ridicule me. She was back to calling me the same names she did in high school and my lips twinged with a smile, despite wanting to be angry for her misdirected apology. Sonia turned to the girl she was dancing with, finally accepting that I was here to take her away. "It was great to meet you, Alyssa."

"Likewise." They both embraced and pulled back with smiles.

"You and Mortada are adorable together. But we have to hang out some more."

Her and the man that was talking to my girl? Sonia glared at me as the facts dwelled in me. "Apologize."

"No need," the guy, Mortada, spoke up. "I know how things get hazy when you're in love." Sonia angrily glanced at him as my grin only widened at her discomfort while he chuckled, throwing his hands up. "Sorry, sorry. But I'll see you on Monday."

"Remember what I said though," the girl winked to Sonia, and she nodded in a secret conversation they shared.

Sonia made her rounds, saying goodbye to everyone that occupied the bar, before standing wordlessly before me. It was her turn to clutch onto my wrist, lighting igniting at the exact spot she let her fingers rest. Once the door closed behind us, she put both her hands on her hips, looking up at me with a fire in her eyes.

"What the *hell* was that?" Her words were still broken, coming slower than usual.

"I'm taking you home." I reached for her again, only to be met with an empty spot as she took a step backwards.

"You have no right." Her lids were betraying her, shutting at a snail like pace as she still struggled to stand tall. "You can't just come into town all these years later acting like everything is the same! It's not!" I was stunned, bewildered, at what she was going on about. "You walked in here like you owned this place. Like you owned *me*." She pressed a hard finger to her chest, her dress tightening in just the right places. I cleared my throat, willing to hear what she had to say. "What?"

I shook my head but as she continued prompting, I refused to tell her, knowing it would only agitate her up more. "Nothing."

"Bolo, Kartik." *Talk, Kartik.*

"You look good like this." I drank in the sight of her from head to toe, her roused hair all the way to the black pumps she wore. She was always pretty but now, when I looked at her, all I thought about was how dazzling she truly was.

"Shut the hell up." Sonia rolled her eyes, stepping into my territory, closing the space between us. It was my turn to hold my breath, to watch and wait for her to make her move. My fingers were twitching, feeling the loss of her, wanting to touch her and hold her like she was mine. "You have no right to talk about me like that anymore. Not after *you* left me eight years ago."

They were drunk words but they shattered my world like bullets firing through my heart. My face hardened and I was no longer playful. "What do you mean, shona?"

"Stop calling me that!" Her eyes were lined with tears, the alcohol reaching into all the hidden parts of her and clawing it dry. "You know what I mean."

This had to be wrong. "I didn't leave you, shona." I reached up to hold onto her arms, to shake her from this misconception she's seemed to carry with her for ages. But the moment my hands went up, hers shot out, pushing them back down.

"I hate you." She spat the words like they were meant to hurt and I'd be lying if I said they didn't.

But the way she was exposing herself in front of me, I knew I couldn't believe them. "That's why you're gripping my hand like it's the only thing keeping you up."

Her eyes shot to the point of contact, when she finally saw the way her fingers hardly intertwined between mine when she attempted to push me away. The stern look was back, all traces of vulnerability wiped from her features and she released me with the force of a thousand trucks. The lack of her did nothing to cure me of the sting it left behind.

A crowd was beginning to form, watching our exchange as they passed by us suspiciously. "Come on, shona. Let's get you home." She finally noticed the people around us, her fuzzy brain coming to terms with the fact that we were no longer in the confinement of four walls, but, in fact, out on the sidewalk screaming to the world. Whether she gave up the fight or just wanted to leave the place I couldn't figure out as she wordlessly nodded, mouth shutting like her lips were stitched together.

My fingers curled around her wrist again, and this time, she allowed it, following behind as I led us to the secluded parking lot. Her eyes roamed around when we stopped in front of my car, her brows furrowing as she examined the black range rover that was parked. "What happened?" She met my eyes, and I could tell she was lost somewhere far.

"Where's your bike?"

The question pained me, the same thing circling in my head day in and day out. It was at home, sitting in my garage untouched. I couldn't find the courage to use it when all it did was remind me of a time I was unable to get back. "This is my car."

It almost seemed like she was grieving the absence of us and the vehicle that tied us together, just as I was for all these years. She nodded in sadness, head dropping to her shoulders, her gaze on the charcoal gravel never wavering. Walking over to her side, I opened the door, urging her inside with a hand to the small of her back. She stiffened, a hiss passing through her clamped teeth, the touch scorning the delicate skin under the thin fabric.

Sonia stepped inside with grace, no longer hesitating in her steps, and after she didn't move, I grabbed onto the seatbelt, wrapping it around her. Her back got straighter as she allowed me space, albeit there wasn't any to begin with.

My hands brushed hers as I pulled the seatbelt to the opposite side of her waist, currents making the car hotter than it had actually been.

Sonia had angled her head to follow the path of my hand and when I looked up to watch her, my breath halted, her face just an inch from mine. My mind went into overdrive, thinking how badly I wanted to just lean into her and make her mine again. But the words she spoke kept going through my head like a broken record.

What the hell did she mean *I* left her?

She sucked a harsh breath in, breaking me out of the spell and I retracted, moving back and shutting the door in an instant. As soon as I settled into the driver seat, I saw her eyes latch onto the thing I kept wrapped around my gear stick, its spot more permanent than anything.

Sonia opened her mouth to say something but I let out a relieved breath when she decided against it. Because there was no way I could sound sane while explaining why I still kept her scrunchie in my car everyday for the past eight years. There was no way to tell her how I never forgot her. And if I did tell her, today confirmed that she wouldn't even believe me.

I just hoped she'd end up forgetting about it once she was out of her drunken haze.

CHAPTER 20

Sonia

My head was pounding. Or was that just the door? The grunt that left my mouth confirmed that it was both.

Feeling the entire weight of my body, I sat up on my bed, wishing to bang my head on the wall as someone continued their assault on my door. "I'm coming," I shouted to no one in particular, pretty sure in my hungover state, the voice barely left my scratchy throat in anything more than a whisper. I pressed a palm into my head, slapping it just a smidge before hopping off the bed barefoot and dragging my feet towards the living room.

As I twisted the lock open, the knocking finally stopped and I was met directly with an iced coffee and folded brown bag. The smile that had appeared at the immediate sight began vanishing as I took in the person who was delivering it. "Kartik." All of a sudden I was aware of everything around me, the satin blue shorts and tank top that were attached to my body leaving almost nothing to the imagination, the mess of an apartment behind me, and the man who was very clearly a nightmare dressed like a daydream. "What are you doing here?"

He smirked and took a step inside like he owned the place, his broad shoulders bouncing as he made his way to my kitchen counter and placed the goodies down. "You told me I could come yesterday."

"What?" A rush of memories began flashing through my mind like a slideshow, my hands shooting up to my mouth when I realized he was right. After he had strapped me into his car, I couldn't help but reminisce, thinking about all the moments we once shared in the confinement of my bedroom, especially after seeing *my* scrunchie still in his car. Of course, it was just a simple white hair tie but the delusional, drunk version of me wanted to believe it was mine. And like a hormonal teenager, when he asked if he could come bring me food the next morning, I pounced on the opportunity, saying yes before he even finished the question.

The sound of his devilish chuckles brought me back to reality.

"Dammit, Kartik. I was drunk." I crossed my arms in a form of defiance but when I watched his eyes darken at the sight of my chest being practically visible, I immediately dropped them to my side, feeling more vulnerable and naked than ever.

"I know." He was finally looking at my face again, but it was no better. I still fell apart under his gaze, wondering what he was thinking when he looked at me now. "But who could say no to some coffee and breakfast after a night like you had?"

I so badly wanted to kick him out of my apartment right now but the headache was messing with my ability to make smart choices. "Alright."

"I also got something else. Can I put it in the freezer?" He didn't wait for an answer, picking at whatever was in his bags naturally.

"What is it?" Pulling out a stool, I sat at the island, watching him move around in my home. My heart yearned, seeing him maneuver the area like it was his, the picture feeling so domestic. Turning around, he slid me the coffee, knowing I was never one to care about coasters or being careful. A home was meant to look worn in, cozy and like it was loved, not like it was a museum of perfection. "Thank you." There was no energy in my body to be tense so I flashed him a small smile as he turned back around.

He ruffled through the brown bag, pulling out two things I couldn't quite make out. When he held them up, I was at a loss of words. "I brought you cookie dough ice cream and sprinkles. Somewhat to comfort you with that headache I knew you'd have." He proudly held the two tubs containing both of my favorite sweet treats, my brain aching for all the wrong reasons now. I was still at the restaurant, transported to the creamery again.

I was at a loss for words.

He remembered.

"What?" His tone was so nonchalant, acting as though he didn't just provoke old memories in my mind. Like it was just his normal.

He stood there, so unbothered, while I sat watching him, trying my hardest to not let the giddy teenager in me resurface and show Kartik that I was internally freaking out about a boy bringing me my favorite dessert.

"Nothing."

After examining my face, he solemnly shrugged, sliding across what I presumed was a bagel wrapped in white parchment paper. "Sesame with extra cream cheese." My jaw dropped as he recited the exact thing I normally get, an order I never shared with him through the course of my life. At my speculation, he provided an explanation. "I just guessed but you seem like a sesame with extra cream cheese kinda gal."

"What the hell does that even mean?" The grumble of my stomach made the shock wear out, my fingers carefully unwrapping the delicacy before bringing one half of it to my mouth and letting out a very unladylike moan. An amused look passed over him as his eyebrows shot up. "Can't a girl enjoy her food without getting looks?"

Kartik's eyes darkened while the smile he wore grew with every second. He shrugged again, shaking his head as an involuntary chuckle left him. Revealing his bagel, Kartik bit into the poppy seed toasted bread, the butter slightly falling onto his finger. He popped his tongue out slightly, tracing the path that the butter made. I hadn't realized how intently I was watching him until he cleared his throat. "You're drooling, shona."

Instantly looking away, I chose not to acknowledge the fact that I most definitely was, not understanding why. It had enticed emotions in me that had been dormant for ages, reserved only for the man standing tall in front of me. Crossing my legs tight on the stool, I sat up straighter, making sure to avoid looking at Kartik who was knowingly smiling now. It was weird sitting here, pretending none of the history between us was ever sour. "You never answered me."

"About?" He shuffled around the kitchen, getting closer, before pulling out a stool beside me and getting comfortable on it. The sudden closeness felt suffocating yet all the memories were anything but. For whatever reason, the dumbest part of my brain was nagging me to stay exactly where I was, and my body followed suit, letting him invade my space in my own home.

A strangled cough later, words finally left me. "The bagel. How does a bagel look like me?"

He laughed, the walls vibrating in his joy, and despite how desperately I wanted to look over, I resisted, knowing that it would make me swoon the moment my eyes lay on that devilish face. "The bagel doesn't *look* like you." My brows scrunched and I looked him over, almost demanding that he tell me but his finger shot up, halting me where I was. "I don't know shona, you're just very vibrant, and colorful, and I thought your bagel choice would be just that. A little extra but delectable all the same."

A mixture of emotions passed through me and I didn't know which to latch onto first. Was I to show the way that nickname still made my heart stop every time? Was I meant to make it obvious how him calling me delectable made me clench my stomach, and thighs, in response, holding in any and every pathetic cry I wanted to wrap around his skin? Was I to show him that I still felt an insane amount of weakness dazed in the form of attraction any time he was around?

So instead of saying anything, I nodded, focusing my attention back onto my food, attempting to cure the remainder of the headache that still bugged me.

Once Kartik had finished his breakfast, he wordlessly lifted from the chair, walking around like he'd been here before. His eyes roamed everywhere with him, observing the memorabilia I had hung in various picture frames that sat carefully organized in a collage on one of my walls. He stood there for a moment, and I couldn't help envisioning how it would look if he was in those photos, amidst all my friends and family, permanently a reminder any time I stepped into my house. But all pictures of him remained in the forbidden box that would never see daylight.

He walked around some more, stopping at the coffee table, his face locking in direct vision of the seashells and crystals I kept in a small bowl above two specific books. One was a book of Shakespeare sonnets, the other Pride and Prejudice. And I wondered if he remembered the significance of them all.

Everything led back to him.

As he ran his fingers through the bowl, the sleeve of his shirt slightly lifted, exposing his wrist which remained adorned in the same object I saw in his car. A scrunchie. Supposedly *my* scrunchie.

No. What was I thinking?

Why the hell would he still keep the same one from all those years ago?

But for any reason, the possibility of it not being mine halted me, scaring me away from ever questioning it. I didn't want to know.

Finally, he made his way to the edge of the couch, smiling at the Stitch plushie that lay in front of one of the decorative pillows. It was none other than the one he knew and cuddled with for years. It no longer smelled like him, the love we shared washing off as the years passed but I knew he recognized it.

A knot formed in my throat and I suddenly felt strangled by an abundance of memories I didn't want to have. "Are you done peeping?" His eyes were glassy as he looked back at me, a hint of an old version of him morphing into his face for just a moment before it was gone, disappearing like it had all the times before. I reminded myself of what had happened all those years ago, remembering that he was no longer that boy.

I couldn't afford to get entangled in him anymore.

"Yeah," Kartik's voice was hushed, a murmur that was meant for only the silence. "Sorry."

My heartbreak was written all over his face.

I knew we both felt the same way and to save us both from the suffering, I chose to be the bad guy. "Thank you for breakfast, but I think it's time for you to go."

"Okay." He nodded once, grabbing his keys off the counter, and stood at the door for just a moment. Countless times, I thought he'd turn around, maybe say bye, or perhaps say anything.

But here I was, eight years later, watching the same man who was once the love of my life walk away from me for the second time in my life.

CHAPTER 21
Kartik

8 years ago

Shutting the door, I repeated the same practice that was now my life.

Get home.

Lock my bedroom door.

Sit on my bed.

Write songs.

Sleep.

It was all I could do when the shouting never stopped.

Except lately, I found myself finding solitude in what accompanied my brain.

Sonia.

I was drawn to her like a moth to a flame and for whatever reason, I hadn't yet felt the need to run.

Sonia was the only person who didn't shy away from me, never letting me feel like I was expected to act a certain way to be accepted. Even though all she ever did was complain about me, it felt real, like she was unafraid of what I would say or do. Like she was the only person who could tell me the truth unfiltered.

She was becoming an integral part of me, her marks becoming permanent against my soul. She'd become my muse.

Everything was now about her.

I started looking forward to tutoring, keeping it hidden as our little secret out of the fear of anyone tainting it with their conjecture.

Unknowingly, I began strumming out the chords for Meddle About by Chase Atlantic, but I couldn't get any farther than thirty seconds before a pounding came through my door. "We allow you to play in your little band, now stop being so loud in the house. You're disturbing the rest of us." My mother's voice traveled through the shut door, vibrating off the walls as I sighed and placed the guitar down.

If only they knew the real noise was them, constantly bickering at any and every thing they can.

If only they knew the damage they've already caused.

Growing up had been slightly different, when my parents somehow actually loved each other. Or so I thought.

I understood now, they pretended and put on a face for everyone else, declaring *I love you's* for the rest of friends and family to see. But if that was what love was, I felt bad for anyone who was in it. And I made up my mind that no matter what happened, I no longer wanted any part in it.

The chime of my phone broke through my thoughts and Trevor's voice loudly came through as I answered.

"Dude, I can't hear you." Screams sounded behind him and he seemed to be getting even more distant. "Hello?"

"Sorry, gimme a minute." A moment of shuffling later, he put the phone back to his ear. "Good now?"

"Yeah. What's up? Where are you?" I leaned further into the bed, an arm under my head, sighing.

"Nah dude, where the hell are *you*?"

"Home?" I thought back to my day, wondering if I had made promises to be somewhere that I seemingly had forgotten. "What do you mean? Was I supposed to show up somewhere?"

"Casey's party!"

"Shit." Casey was the head cheerleader at our school, and everyone 'important' was expected to show up when she threw parties, which were frankly pretty often considering how often her parents were away from home on business. No one really knew what her parents did, and no one questioned it either, the answer unimportant as long as it meant free booze and music. And like I had expected, I had completely forgotten that I had told her I'd show up for her birthday bash, despite her birthday being a month from now.

"Shit is right, Kay. Get your ass here now. She's been asking for you."

I rolled my eyes at the sentiment. "You know I don't care about her like that. Tell her to get over it."

"Yeah but she's been going around complaining that a bunch of people she didn't personally invite showed up and you didn't. She's a little drunk talking about a promise you made her?"

That was before I was so engrossed in thoughts of Sonia, before tutoring, when all I wanted was to stay busy in a crowd. I was always in every social scene but that quickly got old as soon as I started loving the privacy I could have with someone who much more deserves it. "I don't know."

"Alright, if not for anything, just show up to have a good time. You've been so busy, I feel like we don't even see you anymore unless it's for a show."

"You coming, Kartik?" Colt screamed from beside Trevor.

A groan left me as I contemplated answering. Maybe I could just pretend like I lost service in my own damn house and it'll make them stop asking me to come out.

"Don't even think about saying no." Trevor taunted again.

Breaking resolve, I finally answered, knowing they wouldn't stop bugging me until I got my ass out of bed. They would go to any extent and might even show up at my house to drag me along with them. "Fine." They both cheered and I instantly smiled. "I'll be there soon."

"That's what I thought!" The joy of being around a group was back, my mind desperately needing an escape from all the shouting in my house. "I'm texting you the address now."

"Alright." Pleasantries were quickly exchanged and I placed the phone against my chest, wondering if I truly even wanted to go.

But the thought was gone as soon as it appeared when I remembered Casey threw parties for the entire world. Anyone could come.

And that meant I could take Sonia with me.

CHAPTER 22
Kartik

"Yo, where did you go?" Jaymin lightly smacked my arm, drawing me out of my fantasies. "You okay?"

The blur of that night, the one eight years ago where I realized all the atoms in my world shifted, faded away and I was transported back to the now, sitting in a booth pressed in the back of the same bar I had picked Sonia up from, except this time, it was with company I would leave for her any day. "I just zoned out." It was a cop out answer but it would stop them from asking questions.

My fingers curved around the whiskey glass, swiveling it before taking a sip.

"It feels great to be able to hang out again." Jaymin spoke again, shifting the conversation to only include us two as Kyle engrossed himself in his girlfriend. "I don't think I ever asked but what brought you back here?"

The question hit me by surprise since I'd been avoiding my real reason for as long as I could. But I knew it was time I faced the actuality of it all. "I'm selling my parents' old house." The shock of the sentiment had Kyle turning back towards us too. "I haven't gone back yet." Jaymin knew bits and pieces of my childhood life, told in just segments, but the major parts nonetheless. "I've kind of just been avoiding it."

"Selling it? But why?"

"Well, no one really lives here anymore." I shrugged, drifting my attention back to my drink.

"Wait a minute." Kyle chimed in, putting the pieces together. "Jaymin said you've been here for like two months now. Where the hell have you been staying?"

"I rented an AirBNB on an extended stay."

"What the hell, Kartik?" Jaymin's voice prompted me to divert my attention back to the men. "Why didn't you tell me? You could have just stayed with me. There's more than enough room at my place. It could've just been like college all over again."

"Nah, don't stress about it." I shrugged, emptying my glass. "I wasn't planning on staying long anyway."

"*Wasn't?*" It was Kyle again who picked up on my undertone and I cursed myself for accidentally revealing my intentions. "So you are now?"

"Wait, are you staying here long?"

Following my silence, both men shared a look that scared me. I knew I should have never agreed to come hang out.

"He is!"

"Oh my God."

They both began murmuring their accusations and predictions, assuming that I had changed my original plan of only arriving for three months. My only motive to come back to my hometown was to replenish my memories of the shitty childhood I had grown to hate. But the day Sonia walked into the shop, everything changed.

Everything always changed when she was involved.

Even the shop was meant to be temporary, my business only working where I was. I spent years trying to build up my name through social media, developing a reputation as Kay, the tattoo artist who went around the country setting base in random towns for a few months at a time. And in the midst of building a business around my name, I met Kaitlyn, a girl who was running from the same things I had been, and began traveling around with her.

And for the first time in eight years, I found myself wishing to stay rooted to the ground in one town and it was for the same reason as senior year of high school—Sonia.

"It's a girl!" Jaymin once again pulled me out of my daydreams. "Look at the way he's smiling." I wiped the unintentional smirk off my face, not realizing how obvious I had been.

Sonia was always the death of me.

But I'd be damned if I were to tell them that.

"I don't know what you're talking about."

My attempt to distract them was going through dead ears and I was sure of it once Kyle pointed a finger into my face. "Oh you're not denying it. I can sense it. I have a knack for these things." As I raised my brows in amusement, he explained. "When Jaymin first liked Addie, he tried to deny it to my face. But you see this look you have?" As his finger pushed forward, running circles in the air, I was risen with the urge to bite the damn thing off. "That's the same one he did."

"What look?" I looked over at Jaymin who just bemusedly shrugged.

"Like your heart is now no longer in your hold."

"You know, Kyle," I grabbed his finger and threw it down, "for someone who's so carefree, you say the most extravagant things."

"Yeah, apparently only with you." Jaymin chimed in to bicker towards his friend. "With me, he said we were like Romeo and Juliet. You know, the ones who *die*." The emphasis he placed on the final word had us all laughing.

"Let's not get distracted from the matter at hand." Kyle was back to speculating, watching as if he could see through me. And I feared he did. He kept examining me, and I kept slouching away in an attempt to throw him off. "Is it that girl from the shop? What was her name?" He tapped his finger on his chin, feigning thoughts. "Kaitlyn?"

"No."

"Jesus, the immediate reply." I rolled my eyes and attempted to look around the crowded bar to distract them, but all my efforts were going in vain. "Okay if it's not her then…" He trailed off, looking up to the ceiling as both Jaymin and I watched him expectantly. "It's Sonia."

God I wanted to wipe that stupid grin off his face.

"No," I simply stated, except this time, it was far less convincing as it came out more choked than anything and I knew neither of them believed it.

Jaymin, who was still unsure, turned to his best pal. "What makes you say that?"

"Well, I don't think anyone else noticed but it was at that Holi festival." *Fuck.* Kyle was now looking towards me again, like he knowingly caught me in a web of lies. "Jenna was looking for Sonia and asked me if I'd seen her so we went around looking for her because what if she was lost in the crowd, you know? But surprise, surprise. We saw her walking away from a corner where this man was standing tall, with that weird longing look on his face." His hand was in my face again and I swear the urge to bite it off was only growing stronger by the second.

He retracted his finger but only when Jaymin stuck his up. "It *is* Sonia?"

I groaned, unwilling to indulge in their questions but knew there was no avoiding it anymore. With a simple nod, I hoped it would stop them, but I realized how wrong I was when they both slammed their hands on the table, causing a few heads to casually turn towards the commotion. "Jeez, y'all are almost worse than middle schoolers."

"Kartik," Jaymin shook his head as if rattling through all the files he kept stored in it. "Why Sonia?" Once I didn't reply, he decided to rack through the past days a bit longer. "Wait. She has been a little off since you came to town. Wait." I swear he looked like he was about to pass out from the new information. "No, this doesn't make any sense. *Sonia?*"

The constant use of her name had me panicking, worried that somehow someone would hear it and word of this conversation would get back to her. And knowing her, she'd assume I was sharing private information with the boys, the conclusion being birthed from the lack of trust she'd grown to have towards me. And before I could ever admit it to the world, I needed to find out what she meant when she claimed that I left her, which meant the only thing I could do was answer Jaymin and Kyle's questions as quickly as I could to end the topic. "I've known her for a long time."

"What?" Both Kyle and Jaymin exclaimed at the same time.

"Yeah, we went to high school together. She was my tutor senior year and that's when I met her."

"Oh my God. This adds up." Jaymin was profusely nodding his head, to the point where it was concerning how his head wasn't falling off. "Adhira had said that all three of them went to different high schools because they lived in different counties." Finally bringing his voice down a few octaves, he leaned in, "So you really just know her since then?"

I nodded, wishing we were done but I knew that was already too much to ask for when we were this deep into it. These boys were no better than the gossip aunties.

"So what happened?" Kyle was now resting his head on his palms, elbows pressed against the table, prepared for a long storytime.

"Nothing. We had a thing and then we didn't. And now eight years later, here we are." My shoulders slumped as I downed the rest of my bourbon. "I didn't realize she'd still be here when I came back and then she showed up to the shop because you told her to."

"It's fate." I stared at Jaymin, unsure of what he was getting at. "It's like a second meet-cute."

"What are you yapping about? A *meet-cute*?"

Kyle stepped in to answer. "He's been reading those books Addie reads and talking like some romance novelist."

"They're actually pretty good to be honest. And a meet-cute is the way you run into someone through destiny and they're usually really weird and uncommon ways and are the start of your relationship. You met her for the first time after what, eight years, coincidentally in your tattoo shop? Nothing is a coincidence. The universe is constantly working to place you exactly where you need to be at the exact moment."

"That was some of the most philosophical things I've heard out of your football playing mouth and it's all because of those books."

Jaymin glared at Kyle, who then mimicked a zipper across his lips, tossing the imaginary key far behind his shoulder.

"Those books are actually great guidelines and honestly made me understand Adhira even more after reading them. The men are doing nothing but the bare minimum and us guys in real life can't even match up to that. We need to do better and that means groveling." I furrowed my brows, skepticism settling within me. "Whatever happened eight years ago doesn't matter."

"It *does* matter, though." I shook my head, piecing together my thoughts. "As much as I don't care for it and want to start over, she thinks I left her."

"Whether you did or didn't is beside the point. What really matters is what you do with that information. When it came to Adhira, I wasn't giving up so easily despite her pushing me away any chance she got. That's what you need to do with Sonia. Maybe you didn't leave her but that's what she thinks. And that's important."

"What exactly do you mean?"

"I mean," he sighed as if he were being forced to explain the obvious, "it's what she believed for eight years. You can't just tell her she's wrong and expect her to believe you when she hasn't had any reason to for all this time. All you can do is try to convince her now by showing her you didn't."

Jaymin was right. Sonia has been under this impression for God knows how long and I had no power to change that. She didn't even want me around, let alone hear me out with an explanation she didn't care to change her thoughts about.

"You need to show her you're not leaving *now*. Convince her of it." He sat back, slouching as though he'd just dropped the most valuable piece of information he could have, and in a way, he did. "When I met Adhira, she ran from me any chance she got but I was adamant on staying around her to a point where she was lowkey annoyed by my presence but started to trust me. That's what you need to do."

I took everything he said and mulled over it for a second, coming up with ways to show her that this version of me would do anything to stick around her. He wasn't wrong. But I also knew that I would need their help for what I had planned.

"Alright but I need you to do something for me."

CHAPTER 23
Sonia

8 years ago

I pressed the leather cover back down, sliding the strap of my journal to the front to close it before even getting a word out of my pen, too distracted by the sporadic buzzing of my phone. Irritatedly, I placed the book down under my blanket and reached towards my nightstand to grab the device, my jaw dropping at the notification.

There were ten unread messages from Kartik.

We had exchanged numbers a while ago, under the pretense that if he ever needed help while studying, I could be available to him but we'd never used it until now. I opened the thread and the urgency scared me a bit.

Half of the texts just read variations of *Sonia* and *Shona* while the other half were prompting me to call him.

Was he okay?

With an erratic chest, I pressed call on his contact, only one ring playing before a second of silence met me.

"Are you okay?" A chuckle sounded on the other end and I had no idea what was going on. "Is this some kind of stupid prank?"

"Look outside your window."

"What?" My legs remained crossed on my bed, his words not registering in the panicked rush I was still coming down from.

"Shona, open your curtains."

At his command, my head snapped to the right, my chiffon curtains slightly swaying with the heater vent under it. It was ominous and I knew, for some reason, opening my curtains would mean inviting trouble. But I couldn't resist.

Stepping off my bed, I walked over to the white fabric, my fingers lightly grazing it before grabbing a small piece and pushing them aside. The darkness of the night contradicted the shine that came from the moon and for a second I was lost in the starry sky, only to be reminded of the ground when Kartik spoke.

"Look down."

I heeded his request, my eyes landing directly across the street in perfect view under the moonlight. Kartik was leaning against his bike, blending in with the mystery of the night. If this were a film, it would be the perfect *Sixteen Candles*-esque moment.

"What the hell are you doing here?" The panic was back, but this time for a whole new reason. Looking over my shoulder, I glanced at my door, making sure it was locked before pressing myself against the cold window. "Kartik, go away. Koi dekh lega." *Someone will see you.*

"No one can see me." He spread his arms wide, almost mimicking the Shah Rukh Khan pose, and brought the phone back to his ear. "I'm in all black and no one is here. You live on a dead street."

My heart was thumping so hard it must have been audible through the phone. I examined him, as much as I could in the dim environment, noticing that he was indeed dressed in his signature black. The leather jacket and black pants coupled with the black boots and black tee, a combination that still raised goosebumps in me for a very unknown reason that I was trying my hardest to convince myself had nothing to do with him. "Still. Go." I turned to walk away only to be stopped by his voice.

"Wait." It was then that I realized he could see the entirety of my room, including me. Scanning my clothes, I suddenly felt exposed, wanting to reach for the bed sheets to cover the exposed parts of me, which were plenty. The pink shorts and cropped tank sleep set I had on was a direct contrast to what I normally wore to school and I suddenly felt his eyes burning through my skin. I heard him clear his throat and refused to look back in his direction for the fear of drowning in the currents he radiated.

"What is it?" My voice was no longer smooth, more huskier knowing he could see me better than I could him.

"There's a party and I want you to come with me."

"When?"

"Tonight."

"What?" I was practically hugging the window again, eyes bulging out of their sockets. "Have you lost it?" A laugh sounded from me, nerves pricking my skin. I didn't need him to answer to know that he was utterly and completely insane. There was no way he expected that I'd come out at this hour with *him*. "Not happening."

"Come on." He took a step closer, his face now illuminated by the single streetlight above him, making all the harsh lines of his face cast shadows on the softer parts of him.

"If my mom sees me leaving the house, she'll kill me." I shook my head, afraid that if he asked a couple more times, I'd fall weak to his demands. "You need to go Kartik."

"Shona," I swore I saw his eyes turn glassy for a second before they were covered in darkness again, "live a little. When was the last time you did something that gave you a thrill?"

He was right but I couldn't risk being caught. It was too dangerous. But I was on the way to being convinced. "What if my mom sees me leave?"

"Your window is big enough for you to climb out of. I can practically see everything."

"You're joking." I stepped away, looking at all my options. My window was not that high up, although on the second floor, there was an extension on the roof that I've spent countless nights stargazing on. It wasn't death provokingly high but climbing down was something I'd never thought to do.

"Just jump down, I'll catch you."

"No fucking way."

A chuckle sounded from him as he took another step, bemused. "Little miss good girl Sonia Desai has a mouth on her. Who would've known?"

"You're insane."

"I know. You've said it about ten times already. So are you jumping or no?"

"Why do you want me to come so bad?" He was practically right under my roof now, the exact place he claimed he'd catch me.

"I don't really know, shona. I just want you to. Is that not enough?"

Something about how he worded it compelled me enough to trust him. Trust him to jump out my window. Trust him to keep me safe.

Trust him to catch me when I fall.

"Fine." I could practically hear the smile he displayed through the phone. "But I have to change."

Snapping the curtains shut, I exhaled, attempting to keep my beating heart hushed. What was I doing?

The old Sonia would have never agreed to this.

The Sonia before Kartik would have never even picked up the phone.

But the urgency sparked something in me and seeing how pushy he'd been, I felt it was something I needed to do.

Navigating through my room, I put on a pair of comfortable black jeans and a black cropped tee, topped with a gray corduroy jacket. I'd almost forgotten the phone was still running until I heard Kartik whisper my name in an attempt to garner my attention.

One last glance in the mirror later, I picked up the phone, bringing it to my ear, before saying two words that would be the downfall of me.

"I'm ready."

CHAPTER 24
Kartik

8 years ago

Thank God Sonia lived on a quiet street because if not, I would've already had the cops called on me had anyone seen a boy in all black lurking around under a girl's house. But I couldn't resist. Not when I could see her fingers reaching for the curtain once more, opening it to reveal a nervous Sonia.

No longer in a baby pink pajama set, she was adorned in the same colors as myself, and whether that was intentional or not, it prompted me to grin.

One hand still gripping her phone, she used the other to lift the window then the netted screen, providing me with an unfiltered view of her. Standing up there, she looked almost majestic, a vision of an angel falling straight down from heaven, preparing to fall right into my arms.

"Are you sure you'll catch me?" Her voice pulled me out of my trance but still left me speechless, only coaxing a nod in response. "I don't know."

She began climbing down the incline, despite her hesitancy, and it sparked something in me. She was doing this only because I'd asked her to. I positioned myself directly under her, angling my head to watch her take a deep breath before shutting her eyes. "Trust me."

One nod later, her feet left the roof, gravity dragging her all the way down, right where she belonged. Right into my extended arms.

She let out a squeal as she fell, immediately clutching onto my shoulders, squeezing until the blood stopped circulating. But it didn't matter to me. Something about seeing her like this, her normally fighting spirit was now squandered and completely at my mercy. There was something soft about her like this, and my hand instantly twitched, pulling her into me further, my fingers wishing to run across her forehead to brush away the hair that spread onto it.

Slowly, she opened her eyes, pushing herself out of my grip, greeting me with an emptiness I never thought I'd feel. But now that I had, I knew I never wanted to feel it again.

Lost in the haze of her, I didn't realize when she'd begun speaking.

"Kartik." Her voice was a hushed whisper but loud enough to be considered an almost-yell. "Can we go before my mom notices someone's outside?"

I nodded, and with an aching urge to touch her again, grabbed onto her wrist as I lightly pulled her towards my bike, noticing how she didn't resist against me, instead, falling into step like it was what she was made for.

Made for me.

She hopped onto my bike like she did almost everyday, except this time, it felt more private than most, like we were in a getaway car, making our grand escape. Her hands clasped shut at my stomach and I let myself stare at them for a second before pulling away from her street.

"Wait." Over the rumble, her voice was barely audible but due to the silence of the night, it was the only sound I willed myself to focus on. My heart picked up pace, the fear of her being hurt taking plight and immediately pulled the bike to a halt. At the sudden stop, her chest crashed even deeper into my back, clutching onto me like a safety net.

"What is it, shona?" Intertwining my fingers with hers, I held them in their spot, rubbing my thumb across the ridges of her knuckles. "Are you hurt? Did something happen?" A lump in my throat made it hard to swallow as I struggled to understand what was going on. "Kya hua?" *What is it?*

"I'm scared."

"Huh?" Pressing the button on the side of my helmet, I lifted the eye visor, making sure she could see that my attention was now solely on her. She followed suit, her auburn eyes glowing under the whites of the moon and stars. But even moonlight was dull when placed beside her radiant skin. She was the only light that was needed to guide me home in the dark.

"I'm scared, Kartik." Her brows pinched together, lifting slightly as if she were begging to be understood. "What if my mom finds out? I don't do this. I don't sneak out like this." She was barely breathing between her words. "I'm not supposed to be the black sheep. If something happens, my mom—"

"Shhh." Her eyes widened as I lightly bumped our helmets together, mouth shutting reflexively. It felt like there was something else she was worried about, something she was treading the line of and refusing to admit openly. But it didn't matter to me. The only thing that concerned me was making sure she was comfortable. "Take a breath, shona." Unlike most times, she heeded my request, stopping her wandering mind exactly where it was and inhaling with all she had in her. "Good girl. Now I have an idea."

"What?"

She couldn't see it but my happiness was uncontainable. "Do you trust me?" Sonia didn't move, no indication of an answer until I lifted my head in question and watched as she reluctantly nodded twice. A warmth passed through me knowing that for the second time tonight, she admitted that she'd put her life in my hands knowing I'd keep it safe. And because of that, it was all I wanted to do.

Her hands were still on me, my fingers working to break them apart. "What are you doing?" She was watching my every movement, watching how my fingers remained on hers for a moment longer than they needed to be, holding her for a second longer than necessary. But she never objected.

"You're not gonna hold onto me any more."

"What?"

I nodded, waiting for her to process what I had stated. I knew it would freak her out for a moment but all I wanted was for her to experience the exhilarating feeling that coupled with it. "The party isn't that far from here, maybe a five minute ride. Don't hold me, okay?" She shook her head, looking about ready to hop off and run right back to her room. "Trust me shona." I didn't wait for her reply, turning back to the front of the road while turning the bike handles. "Just put your arms out. And if at any moment you feel unsafe, just hold onto me again, okay? I won't stop you."

Still feeling her tense behind me, I put a reassuring hand on her thigh, feeling the muscles relax under the thumb that brushed her lightly. Under the helmet, I smiled, knowing I was about to make her feel as if she were flying.

Starting off slow, I let her get secure with the movement, hands out with no grip. Her hands snaked around my back, lightly brushing the jacket before finally, after picking up speed just a smidge, she let go, throwing her arms straight out next to her. In no time, she was fully giggling, her laugh taking over the rumble of the bike.

Her head was thrown back as she screamed into the night, feeling fearless.

The entirety of the ride, I couldn't stop laughing along with her, shaking my head every time she yelled at the top of her lungs.

Her excitement curbed alongside the speed of the motorcycle and before either of us knew it, we turned onto a street packed with parked cars. "Who's party is it?" Her voice was robotic through the screen.

"Casey." She stiffened again for just a breath of a moment, an action that would have gone unnoticed had someone not been paying attention. But I always did when it came to her. "What?"

She hopped off the bike as I parked it, crossing her arms across her chest. "This was fun, Kartik, but I don't fit in here. I should go home."

Placing a hand on the small of her back, I began leading her to the door. "Casey invites everyone to these things and I already told my friends I wouldn't come alone. If you leave, I leave, too."

"Kartik." Her teeth clamped as she whined, stopping in place, but when she noticed my eagerness to keep going, she dropped the front and followed behind. With a tolerant sigh, she entered the house behind me, the loud music blaring through the overhead speakers.

Casey's house was filled to the brim, almost all the students of our graduating class crowding it. She was notoriously rich, something she never failed to bring into her conversations and status on the social standings in school. It was all a bunch of bogus.

Pushing through, I located Travis and Colt, standing off to the side, and gave them one of those bro-hugs that resulted in us slapping each other's backs. "And you are?" Travis extended a hand to Sonia who was observing the whole interaction.

"Sonia." She stared at his palm for a second, keeping her hands tucked across her chest. It made me laugh, knowing this was the first time anyone has dismissed Trevor as though he were nothing. Trevor shrugged with a smirk and I knew he approved of her company when he passed her an unopened spiked seltzer can. "Thank you." She timidly grabbed it, opening it quickly and took a swig.

My eyes were still glued on her and I failed to realize when Casey had sidled up beside me, wrapping her arm around mine. "What the hell?" My voice was barely heard.

Casey was so visibly drunk but her eyes were focused hard on Sonia, who was avoiding all attention by keeping hers on the ground.

"Who invited the *nerd?*" Sonia's head snapped up at the comment at the same time as mine, and I yanked my arm out of Casey's hold. Casey innocently looked at my furious face and if she weren't drunk I'd easily give her an earful about it, but I knew there'd be no point as she wouldn't remember it tomorrow. "What?"

"Shut up, Casey." Colt spoke before I could and I was sure he could see the rage coloring my face in shades of maroon.

"Whatever." She was still watching me as she shrugged, finally dragging the scent of beer away.

But none of that mattered when I noticed Sonia take a step back.

And then another.

And before I knew it, she had turned in the direction of the door.

Rushing to catch up, I reached for her arm, pulling her into me so there'd be no space between us. But the closeness didn't help. I was immediately possessed by her, the rose spray she must have used taking every residence in every atom of mine. We were in the same air and I never wanted to escape it.

"Let me go, Kartik." I couldn't speak, still intoxicated by her, so I stayed still, hoping she'd stop wincing. "I told you, I don't fit in. This was a bad idea. You go have fun with your friends and I'll find my way home."

My finger flew to her lips, which was definitely a bad idea because now I found myself wishing I'd stopped her with my own. What the hell was going on with me?

Was it possible to get second hand drunk off the smell of cheap tequila?

Her soft lips shut under my touch, her eyes widening as she simply watched me. What was this woman doing to me?

"How about this? Stay with me for a bit, if you enjoy yourself we can stay. If you don't we'll both leave." She almost opened her mouth to talk, only to be cut off again. "I brought you here, so I'm staying or leaving as per your request. And don't think I'll be upset if you wanna leave." I leaned down to her ear, my eyes shutting as her hair brushed my face lightly. Inhaling her scent proved how pathetically she was affecting me. "Between you and me, this isn't really my scene either." Her eyes still remained locked on my face, and if I were a sailor, no map could have prevented me from getting lost in their depth. "Deal?"

I waited another moment, feeling defeated, until her head moved just the slightest bit. "Okay."

CHAPTER 25

Sonia

I was staring directly at the tub of ice cream I refused to touch. The temptation to devour it was strong but I resisted every time his face popped into my face. I couldn't give imaginary Kartik the satisfaction of my pleasure induced by eating the ice cream, even when real-life him would remain clueless. It still felt like he was constantly watching over my shoulder, observing my life to the littlest detail.

For the past three days, although he hadn't visited again, the remnants of him remained in the air. I couldn't escape him. He was in everything, his fingerprints tainting my home claiming everything here as his to mess with. And somehow, it didn't bother me as much as I intended it to.

Instead, I found myself looking to the door every time I heard footsteps in the hallway in the hopes that they'd stop at my doorstep. But they never did. And maybe that was for the best.

It wasn't safe around him.

I wasn't safe around him.

He had the power to bring me to my knees, in more ways than one. I couldn't think about him without wanting to be wrapped in his embrace like I once was. It was once my birthright, but he no longer was mine.

I was fully convincing myself that any chemistry we had now was only because we ended things so abruptly that all the remainders we left behind were pouring themselves into reality, leaking through the edges of the bottle. But it would eventually end and drain anything that brought itself to life from the dead and when it happened, I would no longer fear his presence. But for now, I was better off keeping as much distance as I could.

The ringtone sounded and I shut my freezer door, letting a chill pass through me at the sudden reminder of the cold air. Reading *Jaymin* across the screen, I rushingly swiped towards the receiving button.

"Hello?" A mild worry laced my tone because despite our friend group being tight knit, he would never call me unless it were extremely important.

"Sonia!" His tone gave no hints of urgency, instead, masked with excitement and it served to frighten me further. "I'm so glad you picked up."

"What's going on Jaymin?" He seemed to be distracted, his attention being split in multiple places which confused me even more. "Is everything alright?"

"Yeah, yeah! Just give me a second!"

"Okay." His voice drifted again and I presumed he was excusing himself from wherever he was occupied. Rustling sounded and all of a sudden the extra noises were shut out.

"Sorry about that, there was too much commotion. What's up?"

"You're the one who called *me*."

He immediately laughed and I imagined him smacking his forehead. "Oh my God, I'm so dumb. So sorry, I've just been so swamped with all this."

"What's going on?" His vague answers were doing nothing to cure my anxiety, my emotions now borderlining confusion and worry. Jaymin was always someone who made sure everything was under control yet the only time he lost his composure was when it had to do with Addie. "Is Addie okay?"

"Yeah she's fine!" I let out a breath of relief at his confession.

"To what do I owe this pleasure to then?"

"Well I'm sure you haven't forgotten but if you have, I just wanted to remind you that Adhira's birthday is next week." His voice was a whisper, silent and alert on the off chance of someone walking in with their nosy ears.

"How could I forget? Of course I remember!" The three of us girls had always planned everything together, including birthdays, but this year, we held off on plans since it fell on a weekend and Addie was newly in a very happy relationship. Jyoti and I hadn't wanted to take her big day from her in case she wanted to spend it with her man.

"Well I'm planning a surprise party on the day of and I expect you to be there."

"Neki aur puch puch?" *You don't have to ask me twice.* I'd almost shrieked, knowing even this year, our traditions of being together wouldn't be broken. "Of course I'll be there. Just tell me when and where and if you want me to bring anything or even help set anything up."

"No, no. I've got it all covered. You just need to show up!" Jaymin continued to explain how he had planned on taking Addie to her parents house in the morning and wanted the rest of us to be ready at her apartment by 4pm. He also explained how he'd be setting up the decorations by excusing himself when Addie was tangled into conversation with her family, maneuvering out the house like a sly criminal. "Sounds good?"

"Yeah, of course." I couldn't help but smile at the effort the man was putting into keeping one of my closest friends happy. After her tortured past, she deserved it most. "I don't think I've ever said this but thank you for everything you do for her, Jaymin. I'm so glad she has someone like you in her life."

"She deserves nothing but the best." I could imagine the exact goofy smile he always crafted when he was speaking about his girlfriend. "She's everything, you know. I didn't know what real happiness was until I ran into her." He went silent for a moment as if contemplating what words to string together. "You know, you and Jyoti are actually really amazing and I really appreciate you guys for always being there for Adhira. And I truly hope you both eventually stumble upon something beautiful too."

"Not on my radar Jaymin." I chuckled but it suddenly felt like he was still somewhere in his mind. It felt almost diabolic, like he was plotting something. "I'm too focused on everything else in my life for all that."

"Yeah, we'll see." Before I could ask what he meant, he rushed to end the conversation, worrying me. "Well I should get going, I still have to go buy some stuff for the party. I can't wait to see you!"

"Yeah, you too!" I placed the phone back onto the counter, my eyes still facing the now closed refrigerator door. With a shake of my head, I allowed myself one more moment to think of the man who had cursed all my memories before running to my closet to pick out my outfit for the party.

CHAPTER 26
Sonia

8 years ago

"Come on, let's go somewhere." Kartik began piling all the books I had spread out on the table, readying them for himself. "I've been passing my classes thanks to you and I want to show you something."

"No way." I attempted to grab my books from his grip but it was no use. There was no way my weaker strength would prevail against him. "Just because you've been passing doesn't mean we can slack now. I think, if anything, this is when we should be picking up pace even more so we can get through more material."

"No, chalo na, shona." *Come on.* We locked eyes for a moment, the silence looming between us before we snatched ourselves back. "It's a Thursday. That's enough studying for a week."

He didn't seem to budge and it was beginning to feel like he wouldn't stop until I agreed. "Okay." I reluctantly agreed, causing Kartik to immediately throw his fist in the air to announce his victory.

*

The bike stopped right at the entrance of what looked like the woods, equally barren and eerie. Hesitantly, I hopped off, shaking my head and taking a step away. "Are you planning on murdering me here? Nuh uh. I'm leaving."

With a laugh he placed the stand bar on the ground and hung his helmet onto the handles. "Don't worry, I won't kill you. Not today, at least." Kartik's teasing voice was followed by a playful wink as he began walking down the path into the trees before looking over his shoulder at my frozen body. "Follow me."

Glancing around, it seemed like an abandoned highway, and I figured the better option was to stay together just in case something creepy decided to show face. Hesitantly, I took the same path he did, following downhill for a couple minutes before he stopped in front of me, his back blocking my vision. I took a step to the left and couldn't resist the gasp that left my mouth.

"This is beautiful." It was a secluded harbor, the wood that led to an open grand lake almost falling apart. But it was nothing short of a painting.

"It is." Craning my neck, I looked up at him to see he was already watching me.

"I'm talking about the view."

"So am I." His response was so sudden it made goosebumps crawl up my skin, my brain trying its hardest to convince itself that it was just because of the slight breeze passing in the air. "I come here sometimes when I need to escape from the world. When I need a place that doesn't care about who I am."

I wondered what someone like Kartik Sharma was hiding from. He was the boy who had it all figured out. The boy who everyone wanted to be, the one who quite literally could get anything and anyone he wanted. Yet, he was here, telling me, a random girl from his class who happened to be thrown into his life, that he was no anomaly. He was just like the rest of us, in need of a hideaway.

Leaving him there, my feet prodded me forward, allowing myself to truly take in what was in front of me. Nature surrounded us, with big green trees on all sides of the lake, safe for ours. Our side had a flat surface full of dirt, as if it were dug just for ongoers to sit and bask in the sun. I closed my eyes, letting the heat warm my face in contrast to the chilly lake, a smile forming against my lips. "How did you find it?"

His voice grew closer and I knew he was right behind me, but I didn't dare shift, staying still in my position. "I went on a drive when we first moved here to clear my head and wanted to scream into the world." Kartik's breath was hitting my hair and I knew he had leaned down a bit, lowering his voice as if keeping caution as to not disturb the serenity this place had offered. "Then, just by chance, I decided to park my bike right where I had today and take a walk. And then this is where my feet led me. Guess I was meant to find it."

"You had your bike then?" He must have been fifteen.

"Yeah, I know what you're thinking. But it's too depressing of a story to get into right now. It's not important. I've just had my bike for years now." I wanted to pry more but decided against it, his tone indicating that perhaps I had nudged a bruise that hadn't yet found a remedy. "Come, let's sit."

I opened my eyes, as Kartik sat against a rock big enough to host at least four people. He tilted his head to the empty spot beside him, my legs moving towards it on their own accord. I sat beside him, our knees brushing slightly but neither of us shifted to tow a line between us. "Why'd you bring me here?"

He shrugged solemnly. "It's my secret and I wanted you in on it."

"Does anyone else know?" A pigeon flew across the surface of the water, the sounds of the ripples it left permeating the air.

"Well then it wouldn't be a secret now, would it?" I wanted to ask why he brought me but something stopped the words, feeling like it would've been too intimate for me, unknowing where it would lead from here. We were better when there were strict boundaries between us, despite how many times we'd teetered along nearly breaking them. "I never thought about bringing anyone here but I thought you'd enjoy it and keep my hidden spot between us."

"You have my word." It felt like more than a promise but I didn't dare focus on that even the slightest bit. "So why did we come here today?"

"We see each other this often but I still don't know much about you."

"You don't need to know about me. I'm your tutor."

"But I want to." His somber eyes were glued onto me, as if the world around him disappeared. "Tell me something about you. Like tell me," he tapped his fingers against his chin. "Oh, I know! What's your favorite animal?" When I didn't respond, he continued to urge an answer out of me. I couldn't understand why he was trying so hard to blur the lines that we had between us at school. "How will we ever be friends if you don't tell me these things about you?"

"We're not friends." The admission sounded as false as it was. There was definitely something grander than being just a student and his tutor but it couldn't manifest into reality. The reality was that we were too different, too unlike each other, to ever find common ground, no matter how much we pretended we weren't. But as I watched his face overcome with a hidden sadness, I couldn't stop myself. "A lion," I declared. His brows rose as a look of surprise passed him. "Kya?" *What?*

"I didn't take you for someone with such a bold animal choice."

"Well, female lions are the main hunters and male lions protect their territory which makes them some of the most romantic animals to exist despite everyone fearing them." There was something about an animal that was supposedly one of the scariest animals in the wild yet softest to its lovers. It was exactly the kind of love I'd dreamed of and wanted.

"That's interesting." He said it like he truly meant it and I heard him like I truly believed him. "You didn't ask but mine is a husky. There's just something about them that comforts me. The way they look like they're dangerous wolves but are actually some of the kindest and most protective animals." His gaze wandered in the distance, his reasoning somewhat similar to mine, and suddenly it felt like he was no longer talking about the dogs and more about himself.

I decided against probing for more and let my eyes focus on the water and the unreal ripples that kept forming under the light breeze. They almost began looking like small waves, a sight I had never seen in such a small body of water before. Feeling heat burn through me, I turned to Kartik again, freezing as I realized how close we were. He was smiling at me, his lips curved just a little, like it was an unspoken language.

Perhaps it was.

This thing between us, it was just an understanding.

We knew each other but neither of us would dare say those words.

We were too unalike to speak it into existence.

I was grateful he snapped out of it to continue his interview. "Favorite movie?"

"If you're talking about Bollywood, I'd have to say Kabhi Khushi Kabhi Gham." He nodded in agreement with the classic as I continued. If we're talking Hollywood, Corpse Bride." His brows raised in question, prompting me to explain. "Have you never seen it?" Kartik shook his head immediately and my jaw dropped. "You are so missing out. It's so relatable."

"How so?" With a straightened spine, he fully turned to watch me while I spoke.

"It's such a common story about a girl who just wants to be loved the way she loves but somehow always turns out to be the second choice. The other woman." I shook my head, stopping myself from getting too into why I felt represented by Corpse Bride, knowing it would only prompt more questions I didn't want to get into. "Always the lover, never the loved." My voice was a whisper and I thought he didn't hear it until he let out a hushed *hm*. "What about yours?"

He simply shrugged. "I don't know. I'm not much of a film watcher. But maybe I could watch this Corpse Bride movie." I scoffed, unbelievingly. "What? You don't think I'd enjoy it?" The laugh that left me was uncontrollable, slipping through my lips like sand. He followed immediately, the sound that left him radiating through the world around us. It was almost like a song, and it was then that I realized I'd never seen him laugh like this in the four years I've seen him around. It was different. Personal. Intimate. And I wanted to grab it and lock it away in my box of memories.

Breaking out of my spell, the darkening sky finally came into view and I glanced at my phone, panicking. "It's getting late, Kartik." His laugh subsided and for a moment it almost made me sad. "We should get going."

But he didn't move a bit.

"Watch the sunset with me." I really needed to get home. But the way his eyes pleaded with me, everything I once thought right began to seem wrong. "Please?"

"Okay." Placing my phone down, I relaxed again on the tree stump, still slightly panicking.

Except this time, the panic was fully over the fact that Kartik was starting to become someone who could deter me from everything I should be doing.

CHAPTER 27
Kartik

8 years ago

She clung to me like glue on the entire ride home, knowing we now knew each other on a deeper level. Something had shifted today, whether in the universe or between us, and it had impacted the way we reacted to each other entirely. There was a strung out silence that loomed between us as we watched the stars, all the way to here, as I stood watching her rush through her front door.

I knew she didn't stay out until dark, and maybe I was the bad guy for making her stay, but I couldn't just let her leave. Without reason, I began getting the urge to spend all my time on her. To show her all the remaining good I knew, however little it was. She deserved it.

Giving myself another moment, I stared at the shut door, my eyes traveling to the window I now knew was hers. The glow of her night light passed through and I sat a bit taller on my bike, willing her to look outside and see that I was still there, waiting.

But why would she?

Was I just delusional when reading the space between us?

The thumping behind my chest only worsened, going at a pace that seemed astronomically impossible. But the moment I saw her step into the frame, my pulse had halted entirely. She had changed into a similar pajama set as the last time I'd seen her at her window. Except this time, it was a pastel purple, her hair tied up in a scrunchie of the same color. I couldn't help but release the smile that grew unwillingly on its own.

Whether she matched them all for me, or if it was just her nightly look, I didn't care. She was mine to look at like this.

And for some reason, I wanted to keep her like she was my secret.

Not to hide her, but to protect her from all the bad that could come if she were to associate with me. I ran with the wrong crowds, I repeatedly got in trouble. We weren't right when put together in the same room. But at the same time, nothing could compare to it.

She shined her teeth as me, grinning while simultaneously grabbing onto her sheer curtains with both hands. Her fingers did a dance as she moved her mouth to say *bye,* disappearing behind the sheer fabric of her curtains and I found myself leaning towards it, trying to catch a final glimpse of her before accepting defeat.

The buzzing of my phone removed me from my fantasies and I sighed as I read the name that shined across the screen. There were multiple messages from Trevor and Colt on our shared group chat, all asking variations of *where have you been* and *we never see you anymore* and *hope you're doing okay.*

But how was I to tell them that all the time I had now had Sonia's name written all over it. Placing my phone back in my pocket, I revved up the bike, storming off into the night while mulling over the fact that what started as a dreadful tutoring session had turned into the only thing I ever looked forward to every day.

Sonia was becoming the most integral part of my life.

CHAPTER 28
Sonia

" They're coming!" Jyoti's projected voice was enough to silence the entire apartment full of noisy, slightly drunk friends. Scrambling, we all slammed the lights shut, finding places to hide under tables and couches, whispers passing through the air. Jyoti and I had kept our hands held, our heads clashing as we both decided that Addie's kitchen island would cover us.

"Oh my God," I said in between giggles, clocking exactly how tispy I had already gotten. I couldn't help it. That's what anyone would have done if they were being haunted by a tub full of ice cream and the memories of a handsome man bringing them coffee and breakfast.

Handsome? What the hell was wrong with me.

That man was *not* handsome. He was the spawn of Satan himself.

And I needed to stop thinking about him.

The lock clicked and anticipation rang through as we listened for the steps to pass through the doorway. Addie was already laughing at something Jaymin had said, her attention nowhere near her own apartment. Suddenly, the lights came on and all of us jumped out from our spots, a collective "Happy birthday" passing through all of us.

Instantly, Addie's eyes welled up, her hands flying to her mouth in shock as she figured out who to look at first. "I had no idea, oh my." She immediately embraced Jaymin, knowing he deserved all the credit for the night before making her rounds to the rest of us. "Thank you so much guys. This is amazing." Addie took in the pink decorations that were meticulously placed all around her home, streamers and balloons adding to the flare.

"Don't thank us, it was all Jaymin." Jyoti pulled the two of us for one of our signature group hugs. It was one of those embraces that made you forget about all the issues in your life and remember that there is real love, right here.

"That man has been organizing all of this himself. You've got yourself a good one." I pulled away from her, standing as straight as I could with all my focus.

"Yeah." She looked over her shoulder, watching her beau as he mingled with his friends. "I wouldn't have gotten him if you guys didn't push me towards him. So half the credit goes to you."

"Oh no, when something is meant to happen, it does. And you and Jaymin were meant to be together." Jyoti went on as her words struggled to reach my brain. My heart was pounding for an unknown reason and as soon as the door flew open, it fell onto the ground.

"No." I whispered, the attention of both my friends coming back to me.

The man who had been plaguing my every waking, and sleeping, moment was just strolling into the party like it was nobody's business.

And he was dressed in no other than that sinful shade of black and leather, looking all but heavenly.

Storming directly to Jaymin, who was grinning at the new guest, I stuck my finger into his chest. "What the hell is he doing here?" He simply smiled and stepped away. He knew and the smug look on his face did nothing to hide it. "Nuh uh. You owe me an explanation." I found myself suddenly wishing I hadn't had any alcohol because the sight of him was intoxicating me even more.

"Hi, shona."

Before I could say anything back, Addie had stepped in. "Kartik, right?"

"Yup. Happy birthday." He embraced my best friend like they had known each other for years, only managing to irritate me more.

There was no way I just let Jaymin ambush me like this, his smirk only confirming my doubts. Why, though, I struggled to answer.

"Why do I sense some weird tension here?" Jyoti pulled into the group, prompting my eyes off of Kartik.

Jaymin laughed, only managing to worry my friends more. "Are we missing something?" Addie chirped, her eyes quickly switching from focusing on me and then Kartik and then finally Jaymin. As if they had wordlessly had a whole conversation, Addie's eyes went wide while her voice jumped up a few octaves. "Oh, um, Jaymin, let's go get a drink, yeah." Her fingers were also tightly curled around Jyoti's arm, all of them sharing a look that excluded me and the man I needed so desperately to stay away from.

Before anything could slip through my tongue, they had dispersed with giggles, not even offering me a chance to rebuttal, leaving me face to face with the devil. Somehow he was closer now, our breaths sharing the same air. I couldn't tell who stepped up first, but our chests were almost brushing with every rise and fall.

"What the hell are you doing here?" I was sure my words were slurred but I couldn't seem to care.

"My *friend* invited me to his girlfriend's birthday party."

I took another angry step towards him, practically landing into his chest with no room to breathe. He didn't blink and although the alcohol was swirling through me, I was sure I didn't either. It was like we were having our own secret moment in a crowded room.

"We should talk." His voice was doing anything but calming me. I nodded instantly, shocking both myself and him.

What the hell was wrong with me?

Without looking behind me, I turned, walking straight to where I knew Addie's room was. It was the only place we'd get any sort of privacy, knowing whatever half assed conversation we were about to have could not happen in front of all these people, amidst all the noise.

He followed me wordlessly, silently, until the sounds of the partiers was hushed behind the closed door. It felt foreign, being here with him like this, but comfortable all the same. Like we somehow belonged here but simultaneously also nowhere near each other.

"What do you want to talk about?" I broke the silence first, the tension between us building as we both failed to put distance between us. My back was still to the door, remaining glued there since I had shut it at his arrival. He was still standing at my toes, forcing my head to fall back against the wood to see him properly. And yet, when all the warning bells should have been going off in my head, all I could think of was how he still made my heart pound.

"I want to talk about us." There was no mockery in his voice, almost sounding restless, like he couldn't manage to hold it in any longer. My eyes caught a glimpse of the way his hand twitched toward me, as if resisting reaching forward and holding on. I knew that's what it was because I had been feeling the exact same.

"There's nothing to talk about."

A noticeable irritation passed through him. "How long are we going to go on pretending like we've moved on?"

For some reason every word out his mouth was doing nothing but reeling me deeper into him. The problem was I couldn't tell if it was rage or frustration or whether it was just because he was constantly reminding me that he was still the same boy I grew to know and love. "That's the thing Kartik. I'm not pretending." My palm flew to his chest, breaking the silent agreement we had to not touch each other and I instantly knew I was opening Pandora's box. "I *have* moved on."

He scoffed, his hands coming around to cup my neck in a motion that made my breath stop. His thumbs rested on my jawline, one of them slightly making its way down my neck. I was sure he could feel the way I swallowed under his touch. "Is that why my necklace is hanging from your neck?" Kartik's gaze had been locked on the chain that deceivingly made itself visible through the square neckline of my dress.

"*Yours?*" The alcohol was making me appear bolder than I truly was, facing the emotions I'd run from for eight years. "I didn't even remember you gave me this." My hands flew up to my neck, reaching for the clasp but stopping once he latched on. His nostrils flared and I knew I struck a nerve.

"Don't even fucking think about it." Before words could spill out my open mouth, his fingers trailed lower, awaking heat under their cold touch. "Don't you dare lie to me when I was the one who tattooed this on you." He traced the exact stencil while keeping his brown eyes locked on mine like he knew it by memory. Like he had practiced it until he had perfected it in his mind. Perhaps he had. But this was dangerous territory.

And as bad as I wanted to leave it, something told me we needed this.

The fighting, the arguing. We needed it.

The silence wasn't enough anymore.

Not when our past was full of anything but.

"I know what the wave is for, shona. It was my safe haven. It was *our* safe haven. Humari jaga." *Our place.* I couldn't even deny his recognition, knowing that if I did, it would not only taint the security of it but also ruin its significance and all the moments we shared. The same moments I still kept boxed deep in the crevices of my closet. His hands were still wrapped gingerly around my collarbones, my breaths coming in pants, deceiving any distaste I wanted to have.

Instead, I couldn't help but watch how he panned down my body, his tongue slightly jutting out to lick his bottom lip.

It fucking blew that the one man I wanted to hate was the only one who could get me to quiet my thoughts, soothing me all the same.

After a silence, he sighed, shaking his head just once before attempting to take a step back, stopping as both our eyes shot between us.

I was holding onto his shirt and I hadn't even known it.

The black cotton fabric was tightly wrapped in my fist, pulling him into me as he attempted to give me the space we both thought I wanted. But his eyes darkened within seconds and as if the whole world collapsed, he let out a grunt, murmuring a silent *fuck this*, as he slammed his lips onto mine, dizzying me harder than any alcohol could have.

CHAPTER 29

Sonia

Everything happened so fast that I didn't even allow myself time to process how I ended up here, outside Kartik's rented house doorstep, impatiently waiting for him to throw open the door.

It didn't miss me how he was living here, rather than the home I knew was still in his possession. But I also knew it was no longer my position to ask and neither was it the time to.

We were making a very hot, very wrong mistake.

And for once, I didn't want to be right.

After he kissed me, I'd lost all sense. It was like it was my summoning, like he was personally sent from heaven to deter me from everything I knew was correct. And he most definitely wasn't. But as his lips encapsulated mine, our tongues dancing harmoniously, I couldn't deny that we were made to ruin each other in the most beautiful of ways.

We were doomed from the moment we saw each other again.

As he pushed off of me, we shared a look, the silence saying everything we couldn't muster the courage to say, and immediately, wordlessly agreed it was time to leave. Our rushed goodbyes were definitely deemed suspicious by our friends but I knew they'd figure it out. And as much as I wanted to worry about that, in that instant, with all the alcohol running through my veins, all I wanted was to live in the past for a moment longer.

And so as soon as we left Addie's place, our hands clasped together like they belonged and we stormed off right here, in front of his door. Which for whatever damned reason was *still* not open.

"Any day now."

I rolled my eyes as he chuckled, his laugh settling right in my core. "Eager now?"

"You wish." The sound of the lock unlatching was like music to my ears. "I just want to get this over with." Another laugh and the door was open, my heart pounding so loud it felt like my ears were bouncing at its beat.

He turned, locking those eyes that were almost as dark as night onto me, causing a rush in my body. "Before we go in," I grunted, about to complain again but he lifted a finger to my lips and I immediately fought the urge to wrap it tightly in my mouth. This was a *really* bad idea. "How drunk are you?" My brows furrowed, confusion running through me. "I don't want to do this if you're being influenced by alcohol."

God, did he really have to remind me that he was still the sweet boy I once loved? "I'm not drunk enough."

"I'm serious, shona."

"Kartik. Let's go inside before I change my mind." I was becoming restless. It was becoming harder to not latch my lips around the finger that still lay against me. And I knew he knew because the moment my tongue slightly brushed along it, he let out a primal grunt, letting me know he was just as impatient. "The alcohol isn't affecting me."

"Good. Because I want you sober enough to remember the first time I fuck you like you're mine." The unstoppable moan that left me was all the confirmation he needed.

In one swift motion, I was pressed up against the door inside his apartment, one hand clasping around my waist and the other wrapped around my neck, pushing me further into the wood so I had no choice but to offer him more of it as I looked up at him. Another sound left me and I was concerned how quickly I felt on edge.

No one had touched me like this before.

Like they were claiming possession over me. Like he knew I was still his.

"Dress off." He finally put me down, the same fingers that left me cold now reaching over his head to pull off his shirt. "Now."

For a moment, I couldn't pry my eyes off him, drinking in the harsh lines that made him irresistible. The sound that left him was enough to pull me out of my fantasies and realize that I was here, living them out in real time.

My hands slid under the sleeves of my dress, pulling it down until it had pooled around my feet. I hesitated for a moment, remembering how I was dressed in a mismatched pink bra and cotton panties, but all my fear wiped away when I saw the way Kartik was glaring at me. His eyes only darkened, now completely black, any trace of the soft auburn disappearing. Closing the space between us, his hands came around the back of my knees, lifting me until my ankles locked behind him, whisking me down a long hallway I assumed led to his bedroom.

I didn't even have time to register any of my surroundings, his mouth taking up all the space in my brain. His lips marked a path from my neck, jaw, shoulder and back up towards my lips. It was all so inebriating.

Kartik lowered me until I was lying on my back in the middle of his bed. The impact made my eyes open, a sound escaping me as I noticed he had nothing but boxer briefs on, the length of him already taunting me. His smirk only grew as he locked eyes with me, the need for him growing every second.

The bed dipped under him as he knelt over me, his fingers tracing lines along my waistband and dipping to the wet spot I knew was there. I moaned, unable to resist throwing my head back, exposing more of my neck and he took that as an opportunity to drop his head and pepper light kisses on it. The whole scene was like something out of the fantasies I refused to admit to.

"I so badly want to take my time with you right now." I eagerly let the sounds pass through me as he slid my underwear down my legs and pressed a finger into me, breaking the barrier easily. "But I don't think I can wait any longer."

"So don't." I managed to say through clenched teeth as he added another finger, moving them in and out at a painfully tedious pace. I was getting frustrated, in need of more, my hips moving with him in hopes that he'd do something, anything.

"Fuck, shona." He was watching his fingers disappear into me, shutting his eyes any time I made a noise, reveling in the way he was making me feel. "You're making me feel like I have no control."

"Kartik," his name dragged out from my tongue like it was where it was meant to exist. "Fuck me."

He groaned, leaving me feeling empty as he backed away and dragged his briefs off him, his cock springing out, taunting me. But even as I quivered with thoughts of whether I could take it or not, I was dripping even more, my mouth drooling when he moved closer. Kartik's brows scrunched, the obvious irritation at not being inside me matching mine.

As if remembering, he began looking around for his pants and when he couldn't find them, reached over to his bedside table, merging victoriously with a wicked smile. He ripped the foil between his teeth, grinning as he pulled the condom out and began rolling it down his length. I couldn't pry my eyes away. His thumb came up to stroke my parted lips, settling in my mouth while pressing against my tongue. "I so badly want to see my dick wrapped between those pretty lips of yours but I just need to be inside you right now."

Before I could even say anything, he buried himself deep within me in one thrust, settling in what felt like my stomach, pulling a pleasured scream out of me. There was no time to adjust as he went even further, stopping only when I could feel his body fully connected with mine. I was panting, unable to catch a steady breath, unable to see straight. His hands gripped my thighs pulling them up towards my head to give him an even bigger opening.

"Are you okay, shona?" I nodded, my voice lost somewhere between moans and screams. "Hold onto your legs for me so I don't hurt you." My hands were under his control, following his every command like they had pledged their loyalty to him. Still unmoving, he brought his hot mouth to my neck, using his hands to lower the lace of my bra so my breasts could fall out. Cupping one of them with a hand, he twisted my nipple, making me arch my back, pushing into him. Both our moans mingled in the air, mine stretching longer as he replaced his fingers with his mouth, carefully latching his lips around my buds, alternating between them until they both were hard peaks.

"Kartik." My eyes closed, the pleasure of his slight movements in me making me feel more on edge than I'd ever been.

"That's right, baby. Say my name again." With that, his fists fell on either side of my head, holding himself up as he slowly dragged out before thrusting deeply into me again.

"Kartik." I repeated, closing my eyes as the pleasure gathered in my core, dragging his name out and letting it slip through me like it was the most natural thing ever.

"You're mine." Each word garnered its own plunge. "You've always been mine." I was insanely close to bursting and it shocked me when most men struggled to even get me there. "Open your eyes, baby. Watch how pretty you look, swallowing me whole."

He was back in my view again, and I couldn't help but moan at the sight. He looked disheveled, like he was losing himself and I hoped he knew I was feeling the same. This moment was so much more than we'd intended.

This was more sensual than I'd ever experienced.

This wasn't just sex.

This was our damnation.

We knew it.

We willingly walked into our ruination hoping it'd save us from ourselves.

But I knew this moment would come back to haunt us.

And yet there was no stopping it.

His motions had gotten slower, dragging out so patiently I was becoming desperate. "Please, Kartik." I moaned, begging him like I was at his mercy. And in many ways, I was.

"Please what?" His voice was just as strained as mine, an indication that he too was right next to me.

"I'm so close." I was practically crying at his pace, sounding like I was ready to throw a tantrum if he didn't go faster. My hands wrapped around his bare back, running lines up and down his spine with my nails, goosebumps rising all over his skin at the connection.

He shivered as he lowered himself to my ear, whispering. "Be the good girl you are and tell me what you want."

After a couple of aggravated breaths, I knew he wanted to hear it. He wanted me to give into him and it was beginning to feel like there was no other choice. "I want to come."

He raised himself onto his fists again, a crooked, evil smirk now staring back at me and I couldn't help the way my pussy clenched him, fluttering like butterflies. If it was possible to get wetter, the look on his face coaxed it from me. "Whatever you want, shona."

I didn't know whether it was the nickname or the way he immediately picked up his pace, slamming into me like it were his only goal in life, but within seconds, the dam had broken, my orgasm forcing my legs to violently shake. He stiffened as soon as I started screaming through it, his dick pulsing in me one, two, three times, and then he was right there, coming with me.

We shared the most intimate parts of ourselves with each other, the high leaving us as exhaustion took over. He didn't pull himself out, instead, falling on top of me, being careful not to crush me under him. "That was." He blew out a breath of shock or wonder, which one I couldn't pinpoint.

"Yeah." I was definitely in shock.

We lay there for what felt like ten minutes, neither of us talking, just silently being present with each other for the first time in forever. But as the moments ticked by, my heart kept pattering louder and I knew we may have made the biggest mistake of our lives.

And yet I still didn't want it to end.

"I should put my clothes on." I attempted to salvage whatever I could, unwilling to sound like I wanted to stay when it was the only thing I wanted.

But as Kartik lifted his head, showing me his still black eyes, I couldn't help the feeling of joy that passed through me. "I'm not done with you yet."

CHAPTER 30
Kartik

Even as I sat here, in my childhood home, my mind remained shrouded in the taste of her and the way she disappeared as if I had dreamt her all night. Like she was just a mirage, nothing but a figment of my imagination. But I knew it was far from a fantasy. And if she *were* just a fantasy, she was the best kind. The kind that made good men stop dead in their tracks and change their entire being into bad. But to her benefit, I had already been there.

When I'd woken this morning, my heart had hoped for warmth and a five foot four teacher wrapped firmly in my arms but as I reached over, I was only met with a cold spot that hadn't seemed to have been occupied for hours. It was barren and immediately, worry overtook me.

I'd stormed through my temporary living space, looking for any hint that she had been there but even after looking through my phone, I knew she vanished into the night without making a sound. And that pained me.

Was it truly just a one time thing for her? Was that really all she wanted from me?

Shaking those thoughts out of my head, I finally let myself take in the scene in front of me. The walls that were once a bright pale yellow were now a rusty gold, the floorboards creaking with every step. It was as empty as the apologies that would bounce around the rooms.

All the furniture looked the same, safe for the dust matting the surfaces and as much as I wanted it to feel like nothing, I was scorned just the same. Because as horrible and horrid as my life was while living in this house, those same walls held memories that I cherished so deeply even today.

Memories with the only girl I truly ever loved.

The only girl who made me believe that taking a chance on love was worth the risk of it failing. Because even though we fell apart, we would have had the small precious moments to hold on to for the rest of our lives. Because even if it didn't survive the test of time, what we did have was legendary.

That was until life got in the way and ruined us.

Ruined the only good thing I had ever seen.

But I was determined to get it back.

Everything went back to her, even when I stared at the rooms ahead of me.

Climbing up the stairs, I let my feet lead me to the place that held the most of her.

Opening the door to my high school bedroom was like unboxing secrets I hadn't dared to peer into for years now. But now, it felt almost like I needed to. Like if I didn't, I'd be making the biggest mistake of my life.

The gray walls dulled with time, mimicking the lost memories that carried through them. My desk was still in good shape, cluttered with papers I couldn't even remember. A harbored chuckle left me as I rummaged through them, written evidence of a life I couldn't channel anymore. Song lyrics and poetry filled every page, and everything I wrote that meant something was all because of her. I couldn't even begin to imagine what it was like back then.

As I sat on the rustic chair, I smiled, reading some of the amateur work I had written back then with the band. I wonder where Trevor and Colt had ended up. Would they still remember me? Probably not. But on the off chance that they did, perhaps one day I'd find them and clear the air.

Although I had always been reserved to myself, they were the only two people who managed to make me feel welcomed, despite being of different backgrounds. They never needed validation from me, never needed an explanation for the way I was. In a way, they did for me what Sonia did, but somewhere along the way, I let that go too.

I laughed a little, seeing my room being untouched all these years. I was sure any attestation of me being here would've been gone just as I had been. But for some reason, it felt comforting knowing these walls never forgot me.

I continued sifting through the clutter, my eyes locking on something glossy sticking its corners out between the yellowing sheets. Slowly, I pulled it out, my mind being transfixed on exactly the day I saw in front of me.

My heart immediately stopped, all oxygen halting somewhere in my throat, making it hard for me to breathe.

It was a wallet size polaroid photo of sixteen year old Sonia, in her bright pink bedroom, a huge smile on her face. One that I gave her. One that was crafted just for me. She never smiled like that around other people and I used to take pride in it. But seeing it in photo form felt like there was a dagger in me with no way to remove it.

I no longer gave her those smiles, instead, only delivering insane suffering to her.

And it wrenched my soul knowing I had broken her somehow, making her lose that carefree part of her, the spark that made her glow, even when that was the last thing I had ever intended to do.

My eyes glassed over for the first time in years, remembering the ghost of her in my bed this morning as I stared at her in hers. In her hand was the exact acoustic guitar I had played in multiple shows, the same one she requested I bring to her that night when I went to see her. The same one I left with her, knowing it would be her reminder that I loved her. But maybe it was never enough. Maybe I was never enough.

I wondered if she still kept it or if it was gone, buried somewhere far with the rest of us.

"Fuck." I whispered to no one, a tear falling onto the photo. Even though it'd been eight years, a big part of my heart forever belonged to her.

With a deep breath, I pulled out my wallet, sticking the photo in the visible section of it and tucked it into my pocket again. I'd kept it then for the same reason but with the fear of anyone finding out how important she was to me, I refrained from keeping it on my person and assumed that eight years was too long for that photo to still be safe somewhere.

But seeing it here felt like a sign.

Pulling myself out of the cot of memories, I went through the rest of the house, examining all the things I'd need to do and tallying how much work I'd need to get done before this house was in selling shape.

But even with a task so depressing, I couldn't help but smile, knowing I was full of faith again. Because seeing the preserved pieces of us only made me sure of one thing.

It didn't matter if she pretended to be mad at me.

I would never give up on my goal of eventually winning her back.

I'd show her that I still loved her and there was nothing that could ever change that, not even her arrogance.

CHAPTER 31
Sonia

8 years ago

My hand flew to my chest as I slammed my locker door shut, the sudden view of Kartik leaning beside me startling me out of my routine. "Shit, Kartik. Don't do that again."

His devilish grin was like chocolate, causing my heart to skip a beat or two. To be honest, my heart's been betraying me often, warming up to the company I shouldn't be having. He wasn't good for me. He was a constant distraction from the level headed decisions I tended to make. Yet, despite knowing all that, I could never resist getting lost in him. "Kyun, shona?" *Why sweetheart?*

I glared at his playfulness despite feeling a blush creep up my body, my eyes wandering making sure no one could see us conversing. I didn't want to get in qualms with any of his many admirers, wishing to keep my head down and get on with my day. "What are you doing here, Kartik? Someone will see you."

"Dekhne do." *Let them see.* "Why does it matter?" I shook my head, taking a step away from him only to be stopped by the words leaving his mouth. "I like that horse of yours."

"Don't." My heart stopped for an entirely different reason this time. A deep ache overtook me as I thought back to the worst day of my life, freezing me exactly where I was.

"Hey." Kartik shook my shoulders, breaking me out of whatever spell I'd immediately been under. "You okay?" Attempting to not look like a mad woman, I cleared my throat and viscously nodded, realizing it probably only made me look worse. His brows furrowed, worry etched all over his face. After a moment, he dropped it, hopefully understanding that there was nothing that needed to be talked about. "Let's go somewhere."

"Huh?" He shrugged his shoulders like it was the most normal thing. "Kartik, what about tutoring?"

Although my mouth was saying no, something about spending time away and alone with him, like the rest of the world was shut out, was exciting to me.

"I'm already doing so much better on my classwork, and my teachers are convinced I'm on the road to graduating already." His bottom lip curled in a child-like pout that was hard to resist and immediately made me chuckle. "Please?"

I shook my head as he dragged out the last syllable like he was a kid begging their parents for outdoor time. "Fine." I shut my locker, following his lead towards the door. "But you're making this too often of an occurrence. We can't keep escaping like this."

"Yes, ma'am," he mimicked a military salute before placing my helmet over my hair.

*

"*This* is where you wanted to go?" I stared in disbelief at the restaurant in front of me.

It was a new Indian restaurant that had just opened a month ago called *Swad Dhaba*, the Hindi words for 'taste roadside cafe.' When they'd announced the opening, they had promised an authentic Indian experience, the food supposedly tasting just like it would if it were purchased and eaten at a food cart in the middle of the street in India. It'd been on my list of places to try ever since, and I would have never expected Kartik to be the one to bring me along.

"Yeah, why?" He began walking towards the door, holding it open and waiting until I stepped inside.

"I didn't expect you to be into desi food like that." Kartik put our conversation on hold while he spoke to the host who proceeded to seat us. The walls were bright yellow, covered in posters of iconic bollywood films and photos of iconic actors like Amitabh Bachan, Shah Rukh Khan and Madhuri Dixit. It was entirely like a picture out of a movie.

"Why wouldn't I be into our cultural food?" He took a seat across from me, letting me take the booth portion of the half table while he took the wooden chair like a gentleman.

"I don't know." I shrugged. "You're like an outcast with a reputation. Just figured you'd be running from your identity for the sake of looking cool."

He smirked, completely tarnishing any sense of sanity I had left. He was even more attractive in a setting like this. "Reputation, huh?" He chuckled, grabbing the menu from my side of the table. At my protest, he shushed me and ushered the waiter over, his hand flashing in front of my face to halt me from speaking. "I know what we're getting." A man walked over to our table, and Kartik whispered into his ear whatever it was he wanted to get for the both of us.

"What did you order?" I asked as the waiter strolled away.

"You'll see. But let's go back to what you were saying. I actually love my identity and everything about being brown. But I guess I've just never been around enough people like me to embrace it and now that you're in my life, I feel like I have a reason to love that part of me again." His smile tugged at every last string of my heart.

Something inside of me warmed, knowing I was helping him connect with a beautiful part of himself. I couldn't stop staring at him, the way he looked like he somehow fit in, although submerged in the darkest colors, like he was more comfortable than ever. It was always moments like these with him that befuddled me most. I had always been under the perception that he'd been his most authentic self at school in his little clique of mischiefs, but spending all this time with him, away from the manipulation of others and their words, I'd realized there was way more to Kartik Sharma than he'd let on.

And I liked him better this way.

It felt like I had a part of him that was just mine to keep.

Like it was an insider we shared.

I got dragged out of my thoughts as the workers approached our table, placing steel bowls of liquid in front of us along with a plate that was adorned with dried puris stuffed in potatoes. "Pani puri?" An unwarranted smile grew across my face.

"Gol gappe." Kartik announced, and I couldn't help but laugh at the decades long debate between the true name of the savory dish when there never needed to be one. Despite the different states in India calling it by other names, the love every South Asian had towards it was always the same. "I thought you'd like it."

I couldn't resist and as soon as the waiters had walked away, my hands quickly reached for a puri, dipping it into the green water, engulfing the entire thing in my mouth. The splash of spice and sweetness both clashed on my tastebuds, the most satisfied moan leaving my lips. At the sound, Kartik laughed and I swore an angel died and reincarnated into him.

Quickly, he followed my motions, taking his own bite in pleasure. For a moment, we stayed like that, quietly eating while just existing with one another. It was a different kind of solitude and I was beginning to enjoy it against all my devices.

"Why'd you start tutoring?" With my mouth full, I looked up at him, raising my brows and hoping he understood that I wanted him to elaborate. "Like was there any reason? Maybe you just needed something to do? Or are you just *that* passionate about math?"

I couldn't help but giggle at his assumptions. "I am most definitely not passionate about math. But I *am* passionate about teaching I guess. My mom was also once a teacher and that's kind of always influenced me towards it too." Kartik stayed mum, leaning slightly towards me while attentively keeping his eyes and ears on me. It was weird but I knew he was simply paying attention and that made me feel good. "I don't know," His smile grew as my fingers flew towards my neck to fidget with the exact necklace he'd given me. "I've just always loved helping people but not in the health care way, you know? Knowledge is the greatest power one can have but at the same time, I love kids as well. Someday, I'd like to be an elementary school teacher, preferably for kindergarteners."

His grin only widened, not faltering a bit, and I felt myself shutting away at his silence. "I can see it. You'd be an amazing teacher."

The reassurance caused my heart to skip a beat and I convinced myself it was only because I was thinking about my dream career and not because Kartik Sharma was sitting here, on what could be perceived as a date, telling me he believed in me.

"What about you? What is your goal after graduation?"

I took another puri into my mouth and watched as he disappeared somewhere in his mind. It was almost reminiscent of the same sad look from the first time I'd seen him at tutoring, but only for a second before it was lost again, like always.

"Not sure really. I haven't thought too much into it. I just know I want to move away somewhere."

Disappointment ran through my veins at his admission, knowing the time we had was limited. But then wasn't it always?

Even then, I wasn't someone who possessed the right to stop him even if I wanted but deep down I knew his motives were based on something he kept buried inside him.

"Why do you want to move?"

His shoulders lifted and quickly dropped. "Honestly, I'm so used to moving. My family has never really settled anywhere before, and this is the longest we've stayed in one spot and now I think they didn't want to mess with my education in high school." He scoffed as if disapproving his own statement. "Actually, scratch that, they probably didn't even decide to settle here for me. All I know is that once I'm done with school, I'm going to go to a college and pursue music and get as far away from all of this as I can." He shook his head, keeping his eyes downcast and refusing to look up.

"I'm sure they've had you in mind."

He let out a laugh that sounded anything but happy. "You have no idea, shona. They're too caught up in their own bullshit fights to care about their son. I'm nowhere when it comes to their thoughts."

Immediately, I clasped his hand that was curled in a fist on the table. Under my touch, he released the pressure from his knuckles but I knew the brick still sat hard on his heart. It saddened me to see the way other family dynamics ended up. I'd always grown up with a family that stayed intertwined with me and my friends and knowing what Kartik had been putting up with had brought me to tears. It now made sense to me why he continuously lashed out, even about something as simple as celebrating my birthday.

Perhaps I was wrong about him.

"I'm sorry," he started, "I don't know where all that came from. I actually don't really tell anyone about my home life." He put his thumb over my hand, brushing it lightly over my skin, the gesture so simple and soft.

"Don't apologize." I didn't make an effort to move, feeling like the point of contact had deepened our connection, like we were merging ourselves into one. "It's kind of why I want to teach kids too. So many kids have tough home lives and use their time away at school to escape it and it's hard for them when they're so young to even understand what's going on. I just want to give them a safe place to escape to, even if it's only for a couple hours a day."

Kartik was fully holding my hand now, and I was letting him. "I wish there was someone like you for me." The statement felt so unfinished.

Or maybe that was just my heart wishing for more.

Wishing he meant now.

Wishing he said now.

Because if he did, I wouldn't have hesitated to admit that he didn't need someone *like* me.

He could have me.

But at the same time, I felt relieved that he stopped where he did. Because if he continued, I wouldn't be able to stop the words from slipping out my mouth.

I watched him continuously, never letting my gaze leave him, taking in everything that made Kartik Kartik. This version of him, the real, vulnerable self, was so painfully beautiful, like Adonis, captivating with his beauty. He was so visibly broken that his scars made him appear like an aged painting that only increased in value with time. He was eternal.

"Is that all for today?" The waiter's voice startled me and I jerked my hand back into my lap, the loss of him feeling like I lost a piece of myself.

My breathing was irregular, my chest heaving, and suddenly, it felt as though I couldn't speak, my mouth drying with the seconds. Kartik answered for the both of us and I refused to look his way, afraid that my eyes would tell him everything my lips refused to let surface.

I was starting to fall for him.

And I could never let him know.

CHAPTER 32
Kartik

8 years ago

Every inch I made farther from her house all I could think of was the feel of her skin in mine, and how it was the only place I wanted it.

She belonged in my hold and after tonight, I was sure of it. I wanted to be around her at all times, wanted to stay by her side. But that was just an illusion in my mind. I knew it could never be.

She would never want me.

And even if she did, I didn't deserve her.

Sonia was too good to be corrupted by a rogue like me. I would only tarnish her life with all my mess, contaminating her calm with my chaos.

She was the light in the darkness, and I couldn't submit her to my shade.

But despite all that, despite knowing that it shouldn't be, my stupid mind couldn't stop being greedy.

Even if she didn't want me, it wouldn't stop me from continuously trying to be around her, whether that be as a friend or just a student. I could never walk away from her indefinitely.

Finding a parking spot, I pulled into the local record store for my weekly visit.

The bell chimed above me, alerting Roy, the older man at the register. Roy had watched me grow in the past four years, giving me his favorite album recommendations and listening whenever I wanted to play tunes on the guitar he kept behind the register. Some days, I'd just come and sit at the store for hours on end, but that was a tradition I couldn't keep up due to the insane amount of time I'd been dedicating to Sonia.

"Kartik, son," He made his way around the desk, meeting me halfway, throwing his arms around me in a tight hug. Roy was possibly the only person I showed physical affection to, the only man who had managed to find a place in my life as the closest thing I had to a father figure. "You haven't come around in a long time."

I stepped back, noticing that his hairs were slightly greyer than they'd been just weeks ago. "I've been busy in school." Turning away, I began shifting through the different aisles, talking to him over my shoulder. "They put me into tutoring."

"Back in my day, we sucked it up and taught ourselves." He strolled back to the register, our voices being the only ones in the shop right now.

"Nah, she's really helping me. Totally worth it." Browsing through the vinyls, my ears perked up when a familiar song began playing on the radio overhead.

"*She*, huh?" I refused to meet his knowing eyes, already feeling the warmth crawl up my cheeks at just the thought of her. "Is she pretty?"

Avoiding his question, I pointed up to the speakers. "Do you have the record for this album?"

"Ahh." He began treading towards me and I knew exactly what he was thinking, readying myself for it. "Hearing *The Only Exception* by Paramore and wanting the record for Brand New Eyes while being asked about this mystery girl. She's got to be something."

I rolled my eyes in defiance, though he was right. She was definitely something. And the song only reminded me of that.

I'd always believed that there was nothing worth loving in this world, my hindsight always telling me it was a waste of time. But every time I looked at her, there was just one thing I thought.

She was the embodiment of love.

She was the only exception.

"Here it is." Roy pulled the plastic wrapped vinyl out of a stack, handing it to me with a grin across his face. "Jeez, just thinking about her got you glowing like a matchstick."

"Okay now you're just talking out your ass." I took the album from his hand, walking towards the front of the store again.

"I'm just messing with you, kid." Roy stopped right in front of me, his hand clutching mine as I reached for my wallet. "Take it, it's on me." My brows pulled together, prepping for a debate. "You haven't looked this happy in a while, even more than you do when you play that guitar of yours. Whoever she is, I'm glad she's making you smile and if this album has anything to do with her, take it as a gift from me."

My eyes dampened at the gesture, unable to react in any other way. No one had ever been so kind to me when they didn't have to be. "Are you sure?"

"Mhm." He placed a hand on my head and it felt as though my father had just given me his blessing. "Just keep smiling okay? It looks good on you."

"Thank you, Roy." I wrapped my arm around him to pull him into another hug and exited the shop before I actually started getting emotional.

Placing the album on my bike seat, I pulled my vibrating cell phone out my pocket, reading the name *Trevor* across my screen.

Staring at it for a moment, I contemplated whether I wanted to pick up or not but as soon as my eyes locked onto my motorcycle, the answer was obvious. I already knew he'd be calling about the next show we booked for the upcoming weekend. Our conversations lately had only ever been about that or parties and frankly, now, I had other priorities.

Silencing the vibration, I placed the phone in my pocket again, the Paramore album reminding me of what's more important.

Sonia was the only thing that mattered.

CHAPTER 33
Sonia

What a mistake it was to end up wrapped in his arms like that. Because now, all day, all I could manage to think of was the way his limbs were tangled with mine just a few days ago. And it didn't help that I couldn't stop wanting it again.

Despite the constant urge to keep fantasizing about my personal Voldemort, I pushed all thoughts that revolved around him to the back of my mind.

Until now.

"Um, Sonia." Mortada knocked on the door, a frightened look on his face. My heart dropped instantly, knowing something big was going to happen.

"Mortada? Are you okay?" Turning to my class, I excused myself and walked towards the door. "What's wrong?"

"You have a visitor." He took a large gulp, as if he was being held hostage. "They weren't hearing me out when I said to just wait til class is over."

I took a step back to glance at the clock above the door. "There's ten minutes to the school day left. Who the heck came to see me?"

As if on cue, the familiar voice that hadn't left my head in the past week rang through me like a shockwave. "Hey, shona."

"I'm gonna go." Hurriedly, Mortada walked down the hall, leaving me face to face with Kartik.

For a moment, I let myself take in the beauty of him.

The same leather jacket paired with dark wash jeans and a white cotton collared shirt that had the top three buttons sinfully popped open. I swear a drop of saliva slipped out the corner of my lips.

I shook my head out of the nightmare, coming back down to the ground. Why the hell was I damn near drooling over this man?

And wait.

Why the hell was he in my classroom?

"What are you doing here?" As much as I tried keeping my voice low, seeing him here only served to make my blood boil, knowing he had been irritating me in my sleep. I didn't need him disturbing the peace I escaped to in my workplace more than he already had by plaguing my brain.

"I have something for you." It was only then that I noticed one of his hands had been hidden behind his back, holding something out of sight.

"You did not come all the way here to my school to give me something." When he refused to budge, my rising irritation surfaced. "Why are you really here?" My arms crossed against my chest and I immediately regretted it, dropping them, when I noticed his gaze dipping to the way it pushed my breasts together under the black blouse I had worn today.

Clearing his throat, he finally looked me in my eyes again and suddenly, I found myself wishing he was still focused on my boobs because eye contact with him felt like the world was melting while we were the only ones standing still.

"Teek hai." *Okay.* "You're right. It's not the *only* reason I'm here. But I do want to give you this." He finally revealed what he was concealing, all breath escaping from me in one loud gasp that I couldn't contain.

It was a bouquet. But it wasn't just a normal bouquet.

No.

This was a bouquet of snacks coupled with a few lavender stems, my favorite flowers, the smell of them spreading through my entire classroom. I observed the entirety of the gift, noticing the Kurkure chips, Twizzlers and Cheese Itz wrapped around a big bag of mini marshmallows. It was all the snacks I shared an obsession with that I told Kartik about eight years ago.

Eight whole years ago.

Yet another thing he still remembered.

"Kartik." I was at a loss of words, all sense of reality leaving me.

My eyes found his again, watching as he grinned proudly as if mocking me and saying '*I totally hit the nail with this one.*'

"You like it?" His cocky smirk was starting to piss me off.

"Why did you—"

My question got lost in the air as my students' voices made their way to my ear again. "Miss!" A young boy who sat in the front named Hector called to me.

"Sorry, yes?" It wasn't until now that I noticed that my entire class of nosey kindergarteners was watching the interaction I was having.

Hector giggled before finally letting his question slip into the air. "Is that your boyfriend?"

"No." I declared.

"Yes." Kartik stated at the exact same time.

My head instantly snapped to the infuriating man beside me, eyes bulging as I glared at him. The fucking audacity.

"No, he is *not* my boyfriend." The entire classroom erupted in disappointed groans.

Kartik took it as an opportunity to lean into my ear, his voice running down my spine like a drop of water, making me stand taller. "See, even your kids are rooting for me."

Not giving him any more attention, I stepped towards my desk again, attempting to ignore the fact that Kartik was still here, holding a concoction of my favorite items in his hand. "Alright kids, boyfriend or not, you guys are too young for this conversation. Your only concerns should be whether you finished your work or not." At that, the school bell rang on the intercom and all the students walked over one by one to give me their everyday hug before storming out of the room.

As I watched the last of them disappear out the door, a smile took hold of my face. This feeling was exactly why I loved teaching. Knowing I was someone the students considered important, someone they loved. Because I loved every single one of them back.

"I always knew you'd be an amazing teacher." My heart ached at the sentiment, remembering the first time he'd ever said anything remotely along those lines to me. No matter how much I didn't want it to, the things Kartik said always impacted me in a way no one else's words had. Maybe it was because he was the first person outside of the people required to accept me who sat here and made me feel like I was something.

Even if it turned out to be a lie.

"Thank you."

He walked around to the front of my desk, the wooden furniture the only thing preventing me from feeling the warmth I felt in his bedroom. And I was thankful for that.

If we had a chance to relive that night, I don't think I'd be able to survive it.

Just standing here, facing him, it was killing me all the same. Having a taste of him and knowing it was the first and last time was torturing me, the reminder of how perfectly we fit into each other's arms constantly scratching through the surface of my skin, causing me to bleed inside and out. I was being buried alive while not having the option to die, trapped in a constant cycle of torment.

"Go out with me, Sonia." He said it so simply, like it was the easiest question to answer.

He had no idea that after that night, I hadn't had a single night of proper sleep, constantly hopping out of bed to run to the corner of my closet that kept all traces of him. He hadn't known that he was the only thing I thought of, the only thing I was reaching for. And he most definitely hadn't known that I tried my hardest to forget him for eight years only for him to show up on a random day and make me remember everything again.

"Why?"

He placed his hands flat on the desk, leaning over it to eliminate whatever distance he could.

My goodness, he never failed to leave me panting.

"Because I know you felt it too. That's why you left in the morning." He didn't need to explain it further for me to understand exactly what he was referring to. While we were exploring each other's bodies, time after time, he kept chanting 'you're mine' and I could do nothing but agree. Because for just those moments, it felt like I was.

But it was temporary.

We were clouded by the euphoria from making a reckless decision.

"It was one night. We agreed."

"Fuck the agreement, shona. This is bigger than that." At those words, he made his way around the desk, walking to stand face to face with me, keeping a firm grip on my shoulders. His hands felt like they could burn through my clothes and merge into my bones. "This is us."

"There is no us, Kartik. You made sure of that eight years ago." I swallowed the lump in my throat, breaking out of his hold and attempting to put a sliver of distance between us despite the way my body flowed towards him like the moon pulling a tide. "Please go."

Defeatedly, he dropped his hands to his side again, nodding. "Okay." Just for a moment, the sadness was evident on his face before it was quickly replaced by a mischievous smile, reminding me of the seventeen year old boy who used to sneak into my bedroom to fall asleep in my arms. "But just know shona, I'm not giving up."

Before I could even reply, he was gone, vanished into thin air like he was never there.

The only proof of his existence being the bouquet full of all my favorite junk foods.

With a sigh, I plopped down into my chair, my head in my hands while the snacks laughed at me. My backstabbing stomach grumbled and I immediately reached for a pack of twizzlers, deciding against throwing out perfectly good food.

Kartik didn't need to know that I was enjoying his irritatingly perfect present.

What the hell had my life turned into?

CHAPTER 34
Sonia

8 years ago

"Hello." I no longer questioned it when Kartik called me at night while both of us were tucked into bed, looking for peace. It had quickly become an everyday thing and I wasn't complaining.

"Hey." His voice was dejected, different than normal, like he was in pain.

"Hey, you okay?" Sitting against my headboard and clutching my blanket, I furrowed my brows waiting for his reply only to be met with a distant sound on his end. "What's that noise? It sounds like someone's yelling."

"Nothing." I could hear him shuffling around, moving to a quieter part of his room in hopes to shield the receiver from the screams.

But he didn't know I heard them almost every night, sitting in my silent room praying that his home life had gotten better. Except today, with the voices came banging and it scared me for him.

"Do you want to go somewhere, actually?"

"Right now?" I feigned hesitation knowing there was actually none. I was down to go wherever he asked whenever. I knew that much for sure.

"Mhm. I'll come get you."

"Okay."

*

Watching Kartik hop off his bike was a sight I'd never tire of. There was something so captivating about it, like watching a dream play out in real life right in front of my eyes. And it was even more enticing how he'd gotten me so comfortable with the notion of riding on the bike despite all my efforts to deny it with my initial fear that I'd deemed unbeatable.

As he hung his helmet onto the handlebar, walking towards the empty park at midnight, I realized it wasn't really comfort that I was feeling. It was safety.

I was safe with Kartik.

And I was starting to wholeheartedly believe it.

Slowly, I followed him into the darkness, trusting that no matter what, he'd stand guard for me. He finally stopped in front of the swingset, gesturing for me to take one as he took the other.

A smile crept along his face as he slowly swung, keeping his eyes on the starry night sky. "Look, that's Orion." He said, pointing towards a cluster of bright spots above us. "It's one of the easiest to spot. Once you find his belt, the three stars lined up together in the middle, you can make out the rest of him." I looked towards him to see he was still directing his vision to his fixation. "And on the left of Orion, that's Canis Major. It's the thing that looks like a little dog jumping towards Orion." I met his eyes with a smile. "Canis Major has the brightest star in the sky, Sirius, right at his neck."

"I didn't know you were into stars and constellations like that." He shrugged and I looked back into the sky.

"It's just a small interest I guess." Kartik paused for a moment before continuing, his voice growing softer. "Started looking into it when I was younger. Any time my parents would fight, I'd try and direct my attention to things that could mute the outside world. Most of the time that was music but sometimes, I found myself getting lost in the stars, counting them and noticing shapes and then I just started researching them, talking to them like they were listening."

"That's beautiful." It began feeling like the stars were shining just for us.

"It is." I looked over at him, my heartbeat immediately stopping when I noticed he was no longer looking at the sky but directly at me. It was a common occurrence and it made me wonder how many times he'd glanced at me when I hadn't noticed.

Sighing, I removed my eyes from him, feeling a blush creep through me. "You know, you're different than I thought before."

"What do you mean?"

Still, I refused to look his way, feeling his gaze burning me in ways I didn't want to admit. "I don't know." I began swinging in place slightly, letting the cool breeze cut through me. "You have this reputation and I mean the first time we'd ever even interacted, you were kind of an asshole. And you continued to be one when we first started tutoring. And now three months later, after spending all this time with you, I realize it may have just been a mask." He stayed silent and I worried I offended him and in an attempt to salvage my mistake, I spoke again. "Your friends, Colt and Trevor, it's just the group you're around, you know."

"Yeah," he whispered. "They're great and we're really good friends but I guess I've never really found anyone who made me feel comfortable enough to drop the act." I finally looked at him and realized he wasn't just watching me, he was seeing me. Like *truly* seeing me. "Being around you feels like having the first sip of hot chocolate on a brisk snowy day."

What did someone even say to something like that?

How can someone say something so groundbreaking that shakes your entire life and expect you to just be casual about it?

"Are you cold?" I hadn't noticed I was shivering, the result of sneaking out my house in nothing but a pair of sweats and a black tank top.

I nodded, and immediately, Kartik hopped off his swing, making his way to stand in front of me. Still seated, I had to crane my neck up to look at him, his beautiful face never failing to make all oxygen recede from me. Meticulously, he slid his arms out of his staple leather jacket, pulling it around me to let it rest against my shoulders. The weight felt like a blanket and all I wanted was to drown in it.

I was definitely losing my senses in the scent of him now mixing with my own perfume.

My chest was heaving, his hands still on the collar of the jacket that now lined my exposed neck. "It looks good on you." His voice was so soft, so low and deep, like velvet. Every ridge in his syllables made its way to me, leaving me breathless like I'd just run a marathon.

"Thank you." I didn't know what else to say.

I'd never been this lost in someone's presence that I'd forgotten almost everything around us. I was no longer in a public park after dark.

I was no longer sitting with someone I once despised.

I was with Kartik, lost, somewhere only we belonged, somewhere like wonderland.

There were no more crickets chirping, no more wind whooshing through the air. The only sound that continuously rang through our ears were our panting breaths and beating hearts merging into one.

His fingers twitched on my collarbone for just a fraction of a second and I couldn't help but close my eyes, feeling him inching closer.

And just like that, all the things I knew right exploded in my mind, mixing with all the wrong, clouding me with nothing but the taste of Kartik's lips on mine. As if asking for permission he moved just slightly away from me but the moment my hands found his shirt, he was back, pulling me into him with a hand fisted deep in my hair.

My arms latched around his neck, desperate to remember this moment, like it could slip away at any moment. His lips danced around mine in harmony, his sweet kisses making my mind go blank.

There was no more outside world.

There was only Sonia and Kartik.

That *was* the world.

CHAPTER 35
Kartik

After a week of desperate texting, Sonia had finally agreed to come meet me.

And I was ecstatic.

She's inflicted every inch of my mind, setting up her anchor to make a permanent home in it. But she didn't understand that she didn't even have to do much. She was already living in my mind, in my memories, in my soul, unmoving, for the past eight years.

Looking at the text thread, I couldn't help but smile, knowing the only goal I had was to win her back at any cost.

When I had brought the snack bouquet to her office, I knew she softened just a bit, and if I just kept reminding her how much I remember about her, she may just be willing to hear me out. And that's why, when I sent her the address of the location I wanted to meet at, I smirked knowing she'd remember.

In the evenings, the park seemed to look barren, the chilly air taking over and sending everyone home. I glanced at my watch, reading 6:00pm, and kept looking towards the small parking lot adjacent to the swings, willing her car to come.

What if she decided not to show up?

I quickly brushed the thought out of my brain, keeping all strings of hope alive. If I had read her hesitation correctly when I stood so close to her, she would show.

And I wasn't wrong.

A small black car pulled into the empty spot beside mine, and all the world suddenly blurred. Just being in her space was allconsuming, taking every bad and turning it good. She was everything.

Her door opened and she stepped out, coming into vision, and I felt exactly as I did eight years ago, watching her mouth words through her window. It was so innocent and beautiful and it never made sense to me how we got it so wrong.

But it was finally time to right it all.

She strutted towards me, her black boots pressing into the dirt while she held up the loose material of her beige corduroy pants, preventing them from running along the unkempt grass. Disappointment coursed through me as I noticed her jacket, a small part of me showing up with the hope that she'd want to relive the same moment that changed our lives.

"Hi." She said as she stopped in front of me, looking up through her long lashes. It never failed to surprise me how stunning this woman was.

"Hi." I was a madman, twitching at the thought of pulling her into my embrace and holding her there so tight as to prevent her from ever leaving again.

She broke the time freeze, her feet moving like they had a mind of their own, settling exactly where we'd been once upon a lifetime ago. She sat on the exact swing she had been on and all of a sudden she was no longer twenty four year old Sonia Desai. She was sixteen again, dressed in her most comfortable clothes escaping into the night with the boy who only stirred up trouble.

As if being hit with a wave, I felt homesick just watching her, wanting to return to the home she crafted for me.

I took the seat beside her, letting my feet hit the ground, the creaking of the rusty metal the only sound against the beating of our hearts.

"Why did you want to meet me here?" She wasn't looking at me but my eyes were glued to her, captivated, just as they had been the first time. Under the setting sun and rising moon, her freckles glowed even more, adding constellations to her skin.

Since that night, I'd stopped looking for shapes in the sky and found even more beautiful ones on her face.

"For old time's sake?" She scoffed at my response, and all words left me as I stared, mesmerized by her. Everything I wanted to say had now turned into mush.

No words would ever be enough to make up for all the time lost.

"Why are you tormenting me, Kartik?" She barely spoke loud enough for anyone to hear but in the silence of the night, the only thing I could focus on was her. To be honest, though, it didn't matter the silence. Even in the loudest room I could hear her voice calling my name in an instant. When my lips remained sealed, she continued. "Why are you rehashing these memories? Why are you so intent on seeing me all the time now? Even when I say no."

"So why did you come?" I was facing her now, resisting the urge to reach over and grab onto her hand.

"What do you mean?"

"I mean you're here, shona." I waved a hand to the empty park ahead of us. "I asked you to come and you came."

"It's because you're so goddamn persistent." She was yelling now, unable to control her voice, her emotions making their way to the surface. "It's infuriating to consistently tell you I don't want to see you."

"Fuck, Sonia." Without another thought, I took one step and landed directly face to face with her, my hands gripping the chains of the swing she was settled on. The swift movement coaxed a breath that I was sure she didn't intend to release out her mouth. "So block me." Her eyes widened in shock. "You can't, can you?" I shook my head once in disbelief and for a moment I felt exasperated at the fact that she kept running from her feelings. She kept running from me. "It's why you still had my number saved even after eight years. You couldn't delete it. Just like I couldn't resist using your new one."

"No." She was shaking her head, refuting the words I was telling her. "You said it was the forms. It was the fact that I showed up."

"Yeah I used them to make sure you hadn't changed it again. But fuck Sonia, you showing up wasn't everything. Your old number had never been gone from my phone. But ever since I got the new one, I've stared at it every waking second. Shit I could probably recite it back to you with how many times I looked at it wishing I had the right to use it again." Her eyes were glassy, her forehead creasing in confusion. "You keep acting like I'm nothing to you but here you are sitting with," I reached for her neck, finding the small pendant, and pulled it out, "this still on you everyday." She let out a shaky breath, her eyes locking on the way my fingers gripped the guitar pick.

"Kartik."

"No. You don't get it, do you?" I stepped away from her, dropping my arms to my side. "I *miss* you, shona. And I know." My hands were back on her, lightly holding onto her neck while my thumbs painted circles along her jaw. With the feather light touches, her eyes shut, her fingers wrapping around my wrists. "I know you miss me. But you just keep this barrier between us and I don't even know why."

I was desperate now seeing her sitting still in my arms.

"Say something, shona. Kuch bhi." *Anything.*

A resigned sigh left me and I almost stepped away, only to realize her hands gripped me tighter, keeping me rooted in place. I let my thumb travel down her chin, lightly tapping her bottom lip until she shuddered, her breath hitting my finger. Her lids were still glued together, but her chest was now moving at record speed and I took it as a sign to inch closer to her.

I knew she could feel me approaching and if she wanted to stop me, she could and I would leave immediately. But as her fingers slightly twitched towards her, pulling me just the smallest bit, I knew.

My lips crashed onto hers, taking them in like they were mine to devour. *She* was mine to devour.

My teeth grazed her bottom teeth just slightly, dragging it towards me and she let out a sound that made my hand fist her hair, pulling her even closer. If it was possible to absorb each other to become one, that's exactly what we were doing.

She was my destination and I'd do anything to make sure I made it back to her.

My tongue pushed past her lips, intruding her space only to be met with hers tying itself with mine. She let out a moan as I caressed her face with another hand, her arms locking around my waist. Sonia's fists gripped the back of my jacket as I leaned over her, her body being held up on that swing with my grip.

I could feel her tense up but the moment I bit onto her lip again, she relaxed in my hold, latching onto me like her savior.

As if coming to her senses, she harshly moved back, almost slipping onto the ground if it weren't for the way her hands shot up to my biceps. "Wait." Sonia was panting, her face just inches away from mine, the loss of her lips leaving me cold. "Wait, Kartik." Lightly, she pushed me up, fixing herself before standing tall in front of me. She refused to meet my eyes, like if she did, she'd fall under a spell again.

"What happened, shona?" I tried to reach for her but her hand stopped me.

She was profusely shaking her head, wrapping her thoughts around us. I didn't understand what she was thinking, and she wasn't letting me into her brain. "I shouldn't have come. This was a mistake."

That was all she said before she slipped past me, disappearing into the night like the ghost of my dreams.

CHAPTER 36
Sonia

"Shit." I couldn't stop repeating the word on the entire drive.

Now, I was sitting in the driveway of my childhood home, with my head slumped on my steering wheel.

What the hell did I do?

I knew I shouldn't have gone there. But I assumed I would have some semblance of control around him. I should've known that the moment there was an opportunity to blur the lines between us, I'd hop on it like a hormonal teenager.

And the worst part was, I didn't even want it to stop.

I wanted to continue absorbing the feeling of his lips on mine. I wanted his breaths to become mine, to merge so intently with me that we couldn't tell each other apart.

"What is wrong with me?" I groaned as my forehead lightly tapped the car horn, startling me.

At the sound, the front door opened, my mom standing confused, her eyes locked directly at me.

"Here we go," I whispered, stepping out the car door and walking towards the woman who always offered me a shoulder when needed. "Hi, ma."

"Sonu." She wrapped her delicate arms around me, immediately making me feel better. "Kya hua?" *What happened?*

"Nothing." I stepped inside, smiling at my father who sat at the couch, all his papers scattered on the coffee table. "Papa, it's about time you take a break. It's not healthy. You need rest."

He stood up, making his way to us and pressed a kiss to my forehead. The small token of affection never failed to make me smile. "I'll rest when you're married and gone. Tab mein chain ki saans loonga." *That's when I'll take a breath of relief.*

My mom lightly slapped his arm, both of them breaking into chuckles while I rolled my eyes. "We all know I'm not leaving you any time soon."

"Yeah, that's our misfortune." My father had always grinned while roasting me, a back and forth we've had since I was extremely young. In reality though, no matter how many times he'd say he wanted me gone, I knew he couldn't stomach the thought of me actually leaving. We were too close for it to never bother him.

"Harsh," my mom directed towards him, "when it's her vidaai, you'll be the one crying most."

My father feigned a dramatic sigh, recalling the exact moment he'd be giving me away at my wedding. "You just heard her. She's never having a vidaai."

My laughter escaped me, my vision alternating between the two, my heart already feeling better about the night that had started with my biggest mistake yet.

But that satisfaction only lasted two minutes.

"So what brought you here so suddenly, Sonu?" My mom snapped me back to the real problem.

"Ma, I wanted to talk to you." She looked at me worriedly for a moment before nodding.

"Oh yeah, let's all forget papa exists." My dad exaggeratedly announced before returning to his seat in the living room again.

"What a drama queen." I laughed towards him before going after my mom into her room.

My mom was already sitting at the edge of the bed, tapping the side beside her, prompting me to occupy it. Whenever I was around her, I never felt the need to say words, knowing that she'd understand me regardless. "Is this about him?" I let out a breath before falling back onto the bed, staring at the plain white ceiling. "Tell me." She followed suit, laying just as I had.

"I saw him." She let the silence linger, giving me the time to gather my thoughts. It was one of the things I loved best about my mother. She never let me feel pressured to say anything, always waiting until I was ready no matter how long it took. "Not just once. A couple times, ma." I sighed, my hands flying straight towards my face, catching the groan that came with it. "And I just came straight here from seeing him. And on the entire drive here, I kept thinking how I wanted to be back there with him."

A sigh sounded from my mom, one that felt like equal parts relief and grief. "Okay." I watched as she calculated everything in her head. "Sonu, what do you want to do?"

What did I want to do?

It was such a simple question but the answer was anything but.

I wanted to give Kartik a piece of my mind and tell him all the reasons I hated him.

But I also wanted to run right into his arms and never leave even if he begged me to because I didn't hate him.

I couldn't hate him even if I tried.

And I hated myself for it.

"I'm scared, ma." I turned to rest my head on her shoulder, her hand shooting up to my hair the same way she'd always done when I was in duress. "He keeps saying these things that make me want to trust him. He keeps making me feel things I thought I'd never feel for him again. But I'm so scared. Because I know if I believe him again, and he leaves me dry again, I won't be able to pick myself up again." I hadn't realized I'd been crying until I felt my mom's fragile touch brush away stray tears. "It's like he's had this control over me and when I finally got it back, he's taking it again. And I'm handing it to him too. I'm willingly seeing him. I'm willingly entertaining everything. And I'm getting sad when I'm not around him knowing he's so close. But I can't do it. I can't put myself in that position again."

"Shh." My mother's soft voice quieted me, her fingers still brushing through my hair. There was truly nothing better than crying in your mother's arms. "Sonu, have you thought about the fact that maybe you're holding onto something negative in regards to him just so you don't have to face your real feelings?" I took a moment to think about what she said. Was I really just causing this turmoil for myself? "What do you really want?"

"Perhaps I am. But that doesn't change anything." I wiped the last of the tears, forcing myself to stop crying. "I want him to apologize and mean it. But ma, I don't even think he knows what he did wrong and why it broke me so bad."

She froze for a moment, her voice coming out still and chilly. "Sonia, have you thought, maybe you don't know the whole story?"

"What's there to know?"

For a moment she didn't say anything, her quietness making me feel queasy. "I don't know. But sometimes we jump to conclusions because that's what feels comfortable. It's easier to not take the risk of opening your heart up especially when it's been injured before. But it shouldn't stop you from getting you what you deserve. And in this case, I think you and him might just need to have a conversation."

"Ma," I propped myself up on an elbow. "Just a couple weeks ago you were telling me to be careful and now you're telling me to go talk to him."

"Haan." *Yeah.* "But you've already played with fire. And now you're too scared to get burned. But maybe you won't. Maybe if you talk to each other, you'll find whatever closure you need." I nodded, swallowing her words like a pill. "Even then, I'll say what I said the first time. Be careful, Sonu. Don't do anything you know will one hundred percent hurt you, okay? I still want you to choose yourself first so take your time."

Dropping my arms, I fell onto my back again. "Maybe you're right."

Could she really be, though?

Did I truly not have the whole story?

And did it even matter?

CHAPTER 37
Kartik

8 years ago

The drive back home after a show was always the toughest. It was never known what I should be expecting, whether I'd have a quiet night or be in a need of an escape.

Especially now, when Sonia had started showing up to all my shows.

Leaving her to come to my shit show of a family was never easy.

I pulled into the driveway and sighed, noticing a car that I'd never seen before. Grabbing my guitar case, I opened my door, making my way to the Black Audi Q7, brows pulling together.

"What the hell," I whispered, trying to cup my hands to see the interior for any clue as to who I'd be encountering inside. But the windows had been so tinted, nothing was visible to the naked eye.

Strapping my guitar onto my shoulder, I made my way to the door, unlocking it with caution so as to not disturb whoever was inside. It felt weird, coming home to a quiet house, where the screams weren't heard from miles away.

It was so off putting that having a non-hectic home was starting to feel concerning.

Stepping through the doorway, my brain was on high alert as I kept my eyes open for anything out of the ordinary. Red flags were written all over the front door, causing my footsteps to run stealthily through the steps.

There were soft voices in the living room, two recognizable as my parents and one deeper, of a man I'd never heard from before.

I kept my distance, not wanting to be found out, glaring from afar, trying to make out the words being said. My parents were seated on opposite ends of the couch, and the other man was on the accent chair angled towards them. He was dressed in a full suit and I found myself wondering why anyone in their right minds would show up to another house dressed like that at midnight. The coffee table, which normally sat unoccupied, had scattered papers that they'd been all shifting through, my parents' attention varying from the sheets to the man across from them.

"We'd also need to consult your son." The stranger had a voice of authority that sounded anything but soft.

"No need." My mother replied. "He's just a kid."

What the hell was going on?

In an attempt to get closer to try to decipher the words on the papers, my guitar case accidentally jammed into the wall, and I cursed myself, realizing I had miscalculated the distance between us.

In a fury, both my mother and father turned, shocked and startled faces looking back at me.

"Kartik." My dad stood up, hurriedly making his way towards me. "You're home already?"

"What's going on?" I tried to maneuver around him, trying to get a glimpse of the scene before me over his towering frame.

"Didn't you have a show tonight?" He attempted to stop me, my mom rising and stepping towards us.

"Ended early. And again," I looked at her face this time, "what the hell is going on here?" When no one responded, I prodded further. "I heard you guys talk about me. What am I too young for?"

"Kartik." I shook my head in a questioning way at my mother's harsh tone. "Go upstairs."

"Not until you tell me what's going on. And who is that?" I pointed to the man who continued to keep his distance from us, watching the scene unfold uncomfortably. "And what were you guys talking about?"

"Kartik!" My mother's screams could rattle the entire house. "We'll talk to you later. For now, get in your room. It's midnight."

"It's a Friday night." My rebuttal was weak and I knew it wouldn't get me any extra hours to stick around.

"I don't care."

My gaze shifted between all three faces, waiting, wishing for anything.

I knew something was tremendously wrong.

But I also knew that I had to pick my battles.

"Fine." Reluctantly, I made my way up the stairs, keeping my ears alert in case I could hear anything else but it proved to be a lost cause.

As I shut my bedroom door, I vowed, somehow, I'd figure out what the hell was happening in this house, even if it meant spying.

CHAPTER 38
Sonia

8 years ago

Glancing at the clock, I debated packing my books up and leaving. Kartik hadn't been late for a tutoring session since the first week.

Was something wrong with him?

No, it couldn't be.

He would tell me if there was.

Especially when we'd only been getting closer.

Exhaling, I piled up my books, standing at the table for a minute longer before deciding to leave. Even in my disappointment, I couldn't help but think back to all the nights before.

The way he'd hold me every night.

The way he'd squeeze my hand, fitting so perfectly into the crevices of his knuckles.

The way his lips would feel while pressed against mine, like they were opposite ends of a magnet finally meeting.

Him. The way he felt like he was always mine.

It couldn't have all been a lie, right?

Lost in my thoughts of Kartik, I failed to realize the crowd that began to form around me while I shuffled through my locker.

The sound of a cough had startled me, and I turned to find Casey, Layla and their other friend, Taylor, all standing being me, their arms crossed over their chests with a smirk.

I never found myself inclined to talk to them, the clique of popular girls always thinking they were better than everyone just because they were conventionally pretty. They assumed everyone would fall at their feet, worshiping them and everything they did. It was the sole reason I always hesitated in making friends in this school.

Everyone had this deep desire to be liked.

I just wanted to exist.

"Hi. Sonia, right?" Casey questioned, taking a step closer.

"Mhm." I nodded, trying not to encourage much from her. Suddenly, the urge to bolt was building up my chest and I struggled to stay rooted, my fingers and feet buzzing with the need to peel away.

"I don't see it." Taylor raised her brows, and I looked back at her, confused at what she was speaking of. "What is it about her?" She tilted her head, examining me further, her gaze making me want to crawl out of my skin and bury myself where no one could see me.

"Yeah," it was Layla who spoke next, loudly, her voice attracting onlookers. Thankfully, since it was after school hours, the amount of people still here was limited but it was humiliating nonetheless. "What *is* it about you?" Her hand came up to brush a strand of my hair but I flinched away before she could touch me.

"What do you guys want?" I prodded them, anticipating and knowing whatever answer was coming was not one I wanted. My eyes roamed around the hallway, meeting a concerned Travis in the crowd. He looked apologetic, like he wanted to step in but was at his wits ends.

"We just want to know why you." Casey was back in my face, the two inches she had on me feeling like a foot. "I've been trying to get Kartik's attention for two years now and he's never even looked my way. Can you believe that?" She scoffed and I thought better than to respond, standing quietly as panic bubbled through me. Suddenly, I was craving the safety of Kartik's arms. "I'm captain of the cheerleading squad. And you're, well, you." A chuckle left her, as diabolically as her. "So why?"

Just as the words left her mouth, her eyes zeroed in on something behind me, my heart immediately falling to the floor. It was so sudden, the way her hand reached over my shoulder, grabbing the only thing I considered extremely dear to me.

In an instant the ceramic horse I made sure to protect for the past two and a half years was dangling between her two fingers.

My entire world shifted as she waved it in front of me, grinning like she knew she could hurt me and figured out the best way to do so.

"What the hell do you want?" I hopelessly reached for it, a gasp sounding from my lips as she threw it back towards Layla. "Give that back." Casey's hand shot up like a barricade, stopping me from further going towards her friend. Glaring at her, my rage took over. "You know what the difference is between us? I'm not pathetically looking for validation from any and every one. I'm pretty fucking happy with myself. When you," I made sure to exchange looks with all three of them, "you guys can't even take a breath without thinking everyone loves you. And if they don't, you confront them like you're some superior goddess but earth to fucking Casey. You're not even worthy of being worshiped." Her eyes were bulging out her head as I grabbed her wrist, throwing it to her side. "You're just pathetic."

"How dare you!" The walls shook with the ripples of her voice.

The world stilled, time moving slower than ever as I watched her reach behind her, grab the only thing I vowed to protect all my life, dangling it once, twice, and never making it to a third, my eyes shutting tight and my hands covering my ears to shield myself from watching it shatter on the floor right beneath my feet.

As badly as I wanted to appear strong, I couldn't help the tear that escaped from my eye, pressing my lids tighter together to prevent any more.

A chuckle and the sound of familiar heavy footsteps prompted me to take a peek, realizing everyone was frightenedly looking towards the door.

Kartik had just walked through the door and he was visibly angry.

Immediately stepping in front of me, he cupped my face, examining it before turning his back towards me, facing the girls. "You have a fucking problem, talk to me about it and I'll give you a million reasons why it'll never be any of you."

"But Kartik—" Casey stopped as Kartik took a threatening step towards her.

"Leave."

Dejected, she peered over to the side, shooting me a nasty look before grabbing her girls and walking out of the building. Slowly, everyone dispersed, the only people left in the hallway were me, Kartik and Trevor.

Kartik turned, grabbing my chin in his hand, attempting to lock eyes with mine but I couldn't look away from the shards on the floor. His gaze followed and I could feel him shrink under it, stiffening as he continued to keep his grip on me. "I came as soon as Trevor texted."

Now, I was glaring at him, and an indescribable rage bubbled inside of me. I don't know what I was mad at. All I knew was that as irrational as it was, I blamed him for it. "Where the hell were you?" He cringed and I could feel myself clawing through him. "Where were you Kartik?"

"Shona."

Before he could give any justification, I put a hand in the space between us, broke out of his hold, gave him one last glance, and stormed out of the school.

CHAPTER 39

Sonia

Our monthly trips to the mall were something we always looked forward to.

Currently, Addie and Jyoti had dragged me into a small boutique that had just opened up in hopes to find cute clothes to add onto their wardrobe. My hands shuffled against the aisles, grabbing hangers and scouring around, while my mind continued circling and winding, lost and unable to lock onto anything but those dreamy eyes.

My mom's words kept playing in my head the entire week, the fact that she could have been right all along. But it'd been eight whole years.

Would knowing the full story even make a difference?

And was it even worth it?

Lost in thought, I almost hadn't noticed the person walking directly towards me in the empty aisle.

Almost.

"Hey!" She approached me with a smile. "Sonia, right?" Her arms wrapped around me in an awkward hug, my body hardening under her touch. "It's good to see you again."

"Hi, Kaitlyn." I managed, frantically looking around for any help out of this conversation. How was I supposed to face the girl Kartik had once fallen for on a casual Friday evening?

"How have you been?" She was still so chipper, and it confused me why she hadn't hated me over the falling out they had.

"I'm okay. How are you doing?" Kaitlyn brushed a loose strand of hair behind her ear. God, she was so pretty, it made sense why he liked her. "I mean, after the whole, you know." My voice trailed off and I found myself wishing I hadn't said anything at all.

"The break up, you mean?" I nodded coupled with a slight shrug. "I'm okay, really. I knew it was coming."

My brows pulled together, my thoughts scrambling for a place to stop. "What do you mean by that?"

"I knew from the moment you walked in that day." It shocked me how she still wore the sweetest smile, although now, it was masked by something bittersweet. "I always knew what I had with him was temporary, honestly. He wouldn't shut up about this girl from years ago, truthfully, and it worked out because I was running from something similar. We both were just two people who connected because of our mutual sadness. It didn't take long until we realized we had a lot more in common and actually worked really well together."

He'd been talking about me to her?

"You know, at first, it used to make me sad. Hearing someone who was my boyfriend talk so highly about some woman from his past but I understood it. He was surrounding himself with things that reminded him of her and it hurt for a bit until I realized it was never my right to say anything. He told me she'd have a part of him forever and I still went after it because I just wanted to just run with him. I was tired of having to escape by myself, it was becoming lonely. And Kartik isn't bad company."

If my hand hadn't gripped onto the shelf beside me, I was sure my knees would collapse to the ground.

"But I knew it the moment he looked at you in the shop. It was you he'd been talking about." She let out a breath, her eyes traveling from my head to my toes and back to my face. "And I can't even be mad at it. You're beautiful. And he was never mine to have. He's always been yours. I was just holding onto a spot that was never meant to be filled by anyone else."

I shook my head, her words not making any sense. How could that be? "No. There's no way."

If what she was saying was true, then was it also true that my perception of whatever went wrong was also incorrect?

Had I been wrong this whole time?

My fingers immediately shot up to the necklace still adorning my neck as if it were scorned by the revelation as well.

"Sonia," she took a step closer, softly touching my shoulder. "I'm not upset at it, nor at you. I get it. The heart is a messy, messy thing to play with. And honestly, Kartik and I, we're better off as friends than anything else."

"Kaitlyn, I'm so sorry." There was nothing else I could say. Nothing to make it better—the way she felt *and* the way my whole perspective was now questionable. Nothing made sense anymore.

"Honey, there's nothing for you to apologize about. I'm still employed and have a great friend in him. So there's no love lost." She shot me an innocent wink, her mouth only spewing sweetness.

"Sonia?" Addie and Jyoti were standing behind me, and I almost cursed, wondering how much of that they had heard.

Before I could say anything, Kaitlyn pulled my attention again. "I should get going though. It was really great seeing you again. And Sonia," she leaned in closer, as if letting me in on a secret that was meant for me only, "don't break his heart again. As his friend, I won't forgive you if you do."

She chuckled lightly before walking out the aisle, leaving me there with my meddling friends and mixed up thoughts.

"What was she talking about?" Jyoti was now pursuing me.

Sweat beads lined my hairline, my breaths getting quicker, realizing I finally had to face my past in front of my friends.

"Kartik as in *Jaymin's* Kartik?" Addie stared at me expectantly.

Fuck.

"Yeah," the admission slipped my tongue, my shoulders feeling featherlight for the first time in years. "Jaymin's Kartik."

"Oh my God," Addie came forward, her hands flying up to my shoulders as if she knew I'd needed to be steadied. "What? How?"

"Tell us everything." Jyoti grabbed my wrist, letting me know she was with me too.

There was no avoiding it anymore.

So for the next hour, I finally mustered up the courage to tell my best friends everything I'd been keeping from them for eight years.

CHAPTER 40
Kartik

She was detrimental to my life the way I so unhesitantly shut down the shop and postponed the rest of my appointments for the evening, feigning a sickness, at just one text.

Stepping into my car, I glanced at my phone screen again, making sure my eyes hadn't deceived me.

Sonia: *Can you come over? I need to see you.*

At first, my heart dropped, immediately going to the worst case scenarios, wondering how she'd hurt herself.

But then I'd remembered Kaitlyn had come into the shop later than usual today, going on about how she had run into Sonia in the morning. I had made her recount every detail that it was now recitable by me as if I'd been the one who had seen her instead.

I'm sure Sonia's sudden urge to see me was solely inspired by the events that transpired this morning.

And I was fully prepared to succumb to whatever she'd needed.

The drive to her apartment was dreadful, my left leg bouncing at an unexplainable rhythm, each mile closer causing my breaths to become even more erratic. As I parked in front of her building, I allowed myself a moment to calculate all the possibilities of showing up here.

Sonia could possibly let me in and we could rehash old memories and finally give us a fair shot.

But she could also be calling me here to tell me to leave her alone, rubbing salt in a wound that refused to close, despite however much time had passed between us.

From what Kaitlyn had told me, the conversation seemed to favor me but knowing Sonia, she could have misinterpreted the whole thing as Kaitlyn wanting me still. She was like that, always thinking of other people and what they wanted over herself.

Whatever it was, however, I knew I would respect her wishes and abide by whatever she said.

Stepping out the car, each footstep seemed heavier than the last, finally bringing me up the elevator and to her door. My hand flew to my chest, unknowing of what would find me on the other side. With a deep breath, and a hurried mental pep talk, I rang her doorbell, waiting.

Within seconds, I could hear someone moving inside, footsteps approaching closer. My breath halted as I heard the click of the lock and then the door was open.

And I still couldn't breathe.

"Hi," my voice was so small I was unsure if it even left me, until she moved away, allowing me space to step beside her.

But she didn't move away as I got closer, the door shutting behind me as she panted just an inch from me. The light yellow tank she wore stooped so low it practically hid nothing, and my throat immediately went dry. It stopped right above her belly button, exposing her midriff until down to the waistband of shorts of the same color.

She resembled sunshine.

But she also reminded me of the darkness in the night.

She was fucking bewitching. A goddess if I ever knew one.

"Just one time." She gave me no time to think, moving at the speed of light, stealing my breath like the million times she has before.

Except this time, it was literal.

Her fingers curled into my gray tee, pulling me down as she pressed her lips into mine, stealing whatever sense of sanity I had left.

I was begging the heavens above to give me any sign to let me lose control because, here, with her lips in mine, I couldn't even think straight. She pressed her tongue against mine and I took that as an acceptance to grip onto her hips and pull her into me, coaxing a moan out of her mouth and into mine.

Or maybe it was mine.

I couldn't tell.

Right here, in this moment, every part of us was connected, our anatomies merging until neither of us were recognizable without the other.

"Shona." I managed to slip between us while she pulled apart to take a breath.

She finally opened her eyes and I swear I could've died right there. They were glassy with need, practically pleading with me.

Her chest was pressed onto mine, rising and falling with her heavy pants as she let her hands travel through my hair. "Sonia."

"Hmm?"

"What happened?" She pressed her brows together, her eyes refusing to look anywhere but at the way her fingers wrapped around me. Something must have been wrong for her to so boldly call me here and act this way. "Are you drunk?" I couldn't smell any alcohol on her but my mind began racing at the possibilities.

After an eternity of silence, she shook her head, and nothing could prepare me for what slipped through her lips. "I haven't stopped thinking about you." She leaned onto her tiptoes, pressing her lips into the corner of mine, my fingers lightly brushing the exposed part of her lower back. I felt a shiver run through her, goosebumps rising at every movement. "Ever since that night. I need it again."

She was pressed so close to me there was no mistaking that she could feel the way my cock had hardened between us. "Sonia, what are you saying?" Something was on her mind, but I couldn't find myself pushing her for further information. Her hands moving lower down my body were my biggest distraction.

Through hooded eyes and wispy lashes, she begged. "Fuck me, Kartik." She squeezed my dick through my pants, a groan leaving my mouth. "Please."

Fuck it. It was the only encouragement I needed to finally lose my composure, pulling her flat against my body. My hand gripped onto her thighs until they wrapped around my waist, my teeth grinding against her lips in sloppy kisses.

It didn't matter that her mind seemed far away because despite it all, it was on me. I could read it in the way her eyes blackened each time she glanced my way, luring me in like a siren.

She was my undoing.

Within seconds, we'd reached her bedroom, our lips and limbs still unable to free themselves from each other. Her hands raked against my hair, pulling the strands against my neck, forcing a groan out of me.

In response, my lips latched onto her neck the sweetest song of pleasure leaving her lips. Placing her softly onto the bed, I hungrily took her in, all her curves looking delectable under the dim light. "Clothes off. Now."

Under my command, she scrambled, swiftly removing every piece of fabric that hugged her. I'd unintentionally been holding my breath, just observing her as she lay there baring her golden skin to me. Her hair fanned across her chest, falling against the curves of her breasts and down to her stomach.

"Fuck." The word left me by accident, an immediate reaction to seeing her. But my mind was always stunned by her, it didn't matter whether she'd been clothed or not.

"Are you just going to stand there or do you plan on joining me?" Even with a distressed mind, she hadn't lost her wittiness.

I smirked, reaching for the back of my shirt and pulling it over my head. "I was just remembering what you look like before I go and ruin you to the point of unrecognition."

Without giving her a moment to craft up her response, my hands latched onto her ankles pulling her to the edge of the bed, angling her legs so they'd rest on my shoulders.

As I removed my pants, I watched her eyes trail along my body, stopping at the waistband of my boxer briefs. She'd been so entranced by it that a surprised gasp left her as I swiped a finger across her bare clit. "Your pussy is practically salivating for me." Pulling my dick out the briefs, I stepped out the fabric before running it against her wet folds.

The moan that left her would be imprinted in my brain forever. "Hurry up, Kartik."

"Don't rush me sweetheart." But she was right. I'd been so desperate alongside her, wanting to have a taste of her just once more. Unable to hold back longer, I trailed a hand up her body, resting it behind her neck as I pulled her up. Reaching for a condom from my wallet, I ripped open the plastic with my teeth, rolling it down my shaft. "Watch how easily you swallow me whole."

She groaned, struggling to keep her eyes open, but my girl never backed down from a challenge. Treacherously, I entered her, pulling out slightly with every inch that went in, until I was fully rested in her, our blondies flush against one another.

"Fuck," both our voices mixed into one, like a harmony so perfect it would be a crime to never let it play again.

"Hold onto me, shona." Her nails dug into my wrist as I held her up with my hand. "Ready?"

She nodded her head like it was the only thing she knew, her teeth gliding across her bottom lip.

Slowly, I pulled out, almost entirely, preparing myself before slamming into her in one thrust. Her head fell back, claws digging further into my skin. But it didn't matter, because this was the only way to satisfy how deeply I craved her.

Repeating the motion again, I began thrusting into her animalistically, like I'd been starved and she were the only one who could satiate it.

Just a few moments later, she began panting, reaching everywhere until she wrapped her arms around me, bending her body so I could go deeper.

"Kartik," she moaned against my neck, shivers traveling down my spine and building deep in my core. "I- fuck." Her soft lips marked a path against my collarbone before she pulled away again, unable to stay still while I continued ramming into her.

"You're all mine, shona." My brain ceased to work, her body wasn't close enough. Sweat pooled between us, mixing with the scents of sex in the air.

"Kartik, I'm gonna come," her words were choppy, slow and calculated.

"We'll come together, okay?" I shut my eyes tight, wanting to remember the feeling of her skin on mine forever. She nodded under my hand, prompting me to hurry up. I couldn't handle it anymore, my dick thumping as it strained in her. "Now." I grumbled, and she instantly moaned, her orgasm causing her to spasm in my arms while mine shot out in the warmth of her.

Sonia fell back against the mattress, eyes fluttering shut, ecstasy overtaking her. "Open your eyes, beautiful." My fists fell against the sides of her head, my lips skirting over hers. "I promised to ruin you. I'm not done yet."

CHAPTER 41
Sonia

8 years ago

The first time I heard the tap, I assumed it was just a branch or pebble that'd flown in the wind. But when it sounded a second time, my heart dropped over the prospects.

All of the fear subsided when, through glistening eyes, I could make out the familiar figure that cupped his hands to glance through the window. Wiping the back of my palm across my cheeks, I hopped off the bed, slightly raising the glass. "What are you doing here, Kartik?" The cold wind hit my face as I peered over him, seeing as he jumped across from the big tree into my balcony.

"Let me in." He used a hand to prop the window open and I crossed my arms over my chest, conflicted feelings running their course through me. I was still upset at him, but for what I couldn't figure out.

Maybe it was the fact that he hadn't shown up to school today.

Maybe it was the fact that one of my biggest prized possessions was destroyed because of him.

Maybe it was both.

He climbed across the ledge easily, just as he'd done almost every night for the past few months, the routine becoming a dance he learned. In a sense, it was perfected by the both of us. But seeing as though he'd been a missing all day, it felt almost wrong for him to act it out tonight.

"You haven't replied to any of my texts." He stood directly in front of me now, his hands twitching as if wanting to reach out. I took a step back, his face contorting in pain. "You're crying." It was an observation, one I had no desire to confirm to him.

"What do you want, Kartik?" Turning away, I took a seat on the edge of my bed, Kartik following immediately. Even in my sadness, all I wanted to do was reach out and hold him. But was it even my right anymore? "You have been MIA all day and then come to my window complaining about *me* not texting you back? What do you want?"

He sighed, taking my hands in his. Just his touch alone was enough to soothe my building nerves and turn the horrid memories of the day into dust. "I brought you something."

"No, thank you." The proximity was getting to my head and I desperately needed to get away. Looking for an escape, I rose to my feet, attempting to put a lousy excuse for space between us. "You can go now."

"I think you're gonna like what I have." I opened my mouth to speak but he slightly tugged me until I was beside him again, his finger shooting up towards my open lips. "Shona, stop talking for a second."

I didn't need this. He was already on my last nerve, and I wanted nothing to do with him anymore for the rest of the night.

Pulling away from him, I attempted to walk towards the door only to be stopped with his hand clutching onto my wrist. In one swift pull, I was against him, my arm pinned behind me. My neck craned to get a glimpse of him towering over me and suddenly it was like the whole room was void of oxygen. Being this close to him would always leave me panting.

There was a sadness in his appearance—not the same kind I'd seen before, this one was new. Like there was something he was hiding. And it made me forget all my problems and only focus on him. "Are you okay?" It was just a slight whisper but the corner of his lip quirked up.

"I'm not here to talk about me, shona." He leaned down pressing the lightest kiss onto the top of my head, managing to knock me off balance at the suddenness of it. He reached into the backpack I hadn't realized was strapped onto him, producing something that I would have never guessed.

My eyes bulged out my head, my body freezing at the sight, unaware of what to do.

My hands shot up to my mouth, the tears I had so carefully managed to keep at bay finally escaping. He was holding a clay horse. It took me a minute longer to glance at it until it finally dawned on me that it wasn't an ordinary horse. It was *my* clay horse. "I picked it up when you rushed off." He chuckled nervously, not realizing how he made me lose all my composure. "But I figured it needed a little fixing." Still unable to move, I examined the clay figurine which was now adorned in chains and a saddle. "Is it too much?"

As if it'd combust at my touch, I lightly ran my fingers across the jewelry before finally looking up at Kartik again. "Thank you."

His thumb wiped the water drop that began staining my cheek, smiling in return. "Where should I put it?" I immediately grabbed a hold of it, wrapping my arms around him as well. My tears were staining his shirt, but he didn't seem to care. Kartik began brushing through my hair, soothing me the best he could. But he had no idea what he had just done for me. Composing myself, I moved away from him, placed the clay object on my dresser and turned to watch him with a smile. "You've never told me why you protect that so much."

I let out a breath, moving silently towards the bed again, urging him to follow.

Like usual, we both took residence in our unspoken spots, laying beside each other staring at the faint lines of the ceiling above.

"It was a gift from my cousin." He didn't say anything, allowing me time to gather my story before I presented it to him. I was unaware of how he would take it, if he would realize why I acted the way I did and if it would make him understand me. "He passed away two years ago." Immediately, he clutched my hand, pulling me into him so there'd be no space between us. Just like every other day, all anger aside, we were ending the day off in each others' arms.

"I'm so sorry."

I shook my head against his chest, finally feeling the burden of grief pass through me. "He was basically my brother. He got me that little horse from India." I chuckled, remembering the moment. "Him and his family had gone when he was twelve, and as badly as he didn't want to go, he was excited to finally explore somewhere. He was like that, always wanting to see more, to travel and find the beauty in every place. He wanted to make a home everywhere he went. Little did he know that he didn't have enough time to do it all."

The tears weren't stopping but Kartik wasn't complaining. With a shaky voice, I continued. "So his family dragged him to Rajasthan for a family friend's wedding and he complied. And he pretended like he hated it but I knew, like I always did, that he loved it. His eyes would sparkle any time he spoke about it even if his words were saying something else." For a moment, I could almost picture him, the scene playing out in real time.

"But anyways, after the wedding was over, they finally got the chance to see the beauty of the land there and they ran into a pottery shop where a woman was making them by hand. There, he saw that exact horse sitting on the shelf and for whatever reason, wanted it so badly that he spent part of his saved up allowances on it just so he could get it for me.

"When he brought it to me, I was so happy, it was my new toy and as a ten year old, it made me so happy that he thought of me when he went because I always saw him as my inspiration, my role model. I didn't realize until his parents blurted it out that he spent his own birthday money on me. I knew we were close, I knew he was the only person in my blood family that I would run to despite anything, but it was then that I realized I was that person for him too. And it made me feel so loved. *He* made me feel so loved." I clutched onto Kartik's shirt, hoping he'd hold me until I was steady to stand on my own again.

"What happened?" He pressed his lips into my hair, his fingers tracing circles on my slightly exposed back.

I still couldn't manage to look at him, the pain resurfacing like a scab that's been scratched and violated, the healing process being halted only to begin again. "He loved the thrill of new places but along with that, he even loved the thrill of life." I choked on a silent sob, feeling myself tense under Kartik's soft hands. "When he was about to turn sixteen, he wanted so badly to ride a motorcycle, even though everyone said no. His parents were worried for his safety but he managed to convince them he'd be safe." I shook my head, remembering all the times I'd seen him ride fearlessly through the night. "So they agreed that they'd buy him a bike if he went through it the right way.

"They got him the bike and since my uncle used to ride one back home, he took it upon himself to teach him and help my cousin get his license. And for a while, everything was fine. But then he started getting bold with it, doing tricks and racing down empty roads but he still promised he'd be safe. But it wasn't really him everyone was worried about, it was the situations he'd land himself in if he wasn't careful. And I guess everyone's premonitions played out in ways we didn't think they would."

I took a breath, composing myself and the shaky breaths before continuing, Kartik still silently rubbing my arms, though he'd also gotten stiff. "That night, he had been with a couple of his friends coming home from a party. And he was always careful to never ride unless he was completely sober and okay to ride. So it's just ironic that that same night where he decided he wouldn't drink a bit, he was driving down a barren road and got struck by a drunk driver making an illegal turn." I was fisting his shirt, holding on as I let the pain run through me. "He was only eighteen." A shiver caused me to flinch as I thought about the fact that I was going to outlive him soon.

After a long silence, Kartik finally spoke. "This explains why you were so hesitant to sit on my bike. I could tell you were scared but I thought it was just because you weren't used to it. I'm so sorry, shona. If I had known—"

I shook my head against his chest, stopping him. "You couldn't have known. And it was my choice to get on." He pressed his lips against my forehead, letting a comfortable quietness take residence, feeling kind of like peace. I felt lighter knowing I finally talked to someone about it.

Knowing that that person was Kartik.

Knowing that in this very moment, I could love him.

I clung onto him tighter, wishing to cement this moment forever onto my skin so that I could feel him even when he wasn't near.

"Can you stay the night?" My voice came out in a whisper, almost begging.

In a swift movement, he turned towards me, pulling me even further into him so we would be inhaling each other's air. "Whatever you want."

CHAPTER 42

Sonia

Football Sunday was now an occasion that we spent together, me, Jyoti, and Addie all gathering with our parents at one person's home to watch our favorite player, Jaymin, on screen. Today, it was at my home, the one I grew up in, watching my entire family indulging in the activity.

Reaching for another slice of pizza, I fell back onto the couch, smiling at the solace I was feeling here, despite my mind hovering over the way Kartik had tainted my apartment.

Okay, maybe taint wasn't the right word.

But my place was now infiltrated by him, covered in the remnants of him I allowed in. And it was cursing me, taunting me like it was all that could harbor in my mind.

"Sonia?" Jyoti's hand came upon my shoulder, shaking me until I turned to her. "You okay?"

"Yeah, sorry. What's up?" I could tell both girls had found it suspicious but instead of pressing, they continued their conversation. It was something I loved about them. They never dragged anything out of me, knowing I'd let them know when I was ready.

But would I ever be?

"Nothing, I was just talking about how irritating it is that my parents are hosting an international student next semester." She had spoken loud enough to gain the giggles of all the moms that were gossiping within themselves on the other side of the room.

"Oh, chup." *Be quiet.* Jyoti's mom waved a hand towards us, grinning. "You'll probably never even see him. You're always in the city anyways. *We* barely even see you."

"But ma, that's my house. What if I do see him?" I couldn't help but laugh. Jyoti had opted out of dorming for the year, saving money by commuting through the subway since her parents had bought a house in Secaucus a couple years ago, costing her just a thirty minute train ride to school.

"Toh dekh lenge." *Then we'll see.*

We all bursted into laughter at the thought of carefree Jyoti having to share her space with a stranger. She groaned, dramatically announced that she needed to pee and wavered away from the rest of us.

At her departure, Addie scooted closer, her eyes examining me in a way that felt like she could see through me. She had a talent for that, for understanding and empathizing with others before they'd even uttered a word. "Are you okay?"

I nodded, but it felt like I was a traitor. A liar. Scoffing, I started, "Actually, I don't know." Running my hands down my face, I threw my head back against the top of the couch, staring up at the ceiling.

"Does this have to do with Kartik?" After I had opened up to the girls, they had convinced me to talk to him, believing that he was misunderstood. But it only proceeded to confuse me even more, resulting in him being naked on top of me for the rest of the night.

Gosh, I was stupid.

"What happened after the mall yesterday?" She pressed a reassuring hand on my wrist and I sucked in a breath remembering the way he held them pinned above my head.

"I called him over." Blurting it out was the only logical answer I could come up with. "And we did *things*." Her eyes bulged out of her head. "Again." I was sure she was going to collapse. Addie had never been so animated in her reactions and an incoming Jyoti was even more surprised. However, I refused to mention how this time, I'd kicked him out as soon as day broke, the reality of my actions settling in with a clear mind.

"What the hell did I miss?"

Addie pulled her down onto the couch before reiterating my words into her ear causing Jyoti to screech, gathering the attention of everyone around us.

"Sari duniya ko bata do." *Tell the whole world, why don't you.* I groaned, clutching her hands in warning, regretting mentioning it but also knowing that it would've eaten me up inside if I hadn't. "Can I ask you something, Addie?" She raised her brows, allowing me to proceed. "When it came to Jaymin, how did you know you could trust him?"

As if on cue, the television screen cut to a shot of Jaymin running off the field towards the bench. The longing look Addie immediately had on her face made my chest tighten, knowing that, to an outsider, I must look like that every day.

Distractedly, she sighed, grabbing both my hands into hers. "To this day, I don't really know how I knew. It kind of just happened. It was a gut feeling."

"Yeah but there must have been something, right?"

She glanced into the sky for a moment, mulling it over. "Actually, if I think about it, I knew from the moment I met him. And I think I started believing it when he set up that picnic for me. There were so many times where I tried my hardest to convince myself that he was just playing a part, that he was going to betray me over and over. But time and time again, he continued to prove me wrong and he didn't get irritated by the constant need I had for reassurance.

"I think knowing whether someone is trustworthy or not just comes from your heart. No one can tell you how to let someone else in. It's the biggest thing I've learned from being with Jaymin. Sometimes it's okay to jump into the unknown because whatever is waiting on the other side might be exactly what you needed but just didn't know. Honestly, Sonia, wouldn't you rather explore the possibilities of being wrong than live a life full of *what ifs?*"

"Has he done anything to prove he's untrustworthy?" Jyoti asked.

I truly let her question sit for a moment, thinking back to all the years we spent. "Well, he disappeared once."

"And you guys were kids then. Has he done anything *right now?*" I was reminded of all the moments he's shown up for me, starting from when I was drunk dialing him to him unpromptedly bringing snacks to my classroom. Shaking my head, I looked over to my grinning friends. "Well then there you have your answer."

"But he's only here for a couple months, I believe. What if I have to deal with the same thing all over again?"

"And what if you don't?" My mother's voice cut through us and I realized she'd heard it all. She placed a hand on my head, caressing my hair, reminding me of everything she said when I'd told her my doubts the other day. "It's been eight years, Sonu. It might finally be time to have a conversation. And this way, you already aren't expecting anything so what do you have to lose?"

Everything, all over again, I thought but refused to voice.

My heart was so close to combusting atop itself at the possibility of everything going wrong again.

But maybe they were right.

I needed to finally talk to him, even if it was just for the sake of closure.

I'd held off for long enough.

CHAPTER 43
Kartik

My phone continued buzzing with no end in sight. And each time I glanced at it, hoping it was the girl of my dreams, I'd only been met with disappointment.

I contemplated throwing it across the room at the fiftieth text from my father.

I had no intention of speaking to him but a quick scan at the words plastered on my screen verified that he knew I was back in the city, and he was trying to see me. I had no idea how he found out, no premonition about who could have even told him. But it seemed like he wouldn't leave me alone until he got what he wanted.

The last text rolled in two minutes ago, my phone glowing as I recited it aloud.

Please meet me, son. There is a lot of stuff we need to talk about.

I sneered at the use of the word *son*, as if he ever considered me one. When it really mattered, I was nothing but an inconvenience, being thrown to the side like I had no thoughts, no feelings, almost as though I wasn't human. Like I was just a child that was expected to heed to their every command.

Throughout childhood, I truly did like my father, our bond strengthening with all the times he took me along with him on any of his day to day tasks. Back then, I'd been under the assumption that regardless of the submission he was subjected to, he continued to show up for his son. After all, he was the one who suggested I take on music, encouraging my love for music and songwriting. But he was also the reason I stopped it all.

Now, it seems that I've forgotten what it felt like to ever love my father, his mistakes costing me everything I loved, including Sonia.

My phone sounded again in my hand, my attention going immediately to it.

Dad: *I know you don't want to see me and there's nothing I can say to make it better but I would like the opportunity to be able to apologize to you face to face. I'll stop bothering you now. I'm sure you must be busy. Please message me if you ever want to talk. I'll be looking out for anything from you.*

The fact that I still couldn't bring myself to change his contact information pained me, knowing a part of me will still be stuck there, holding onto the small part of him that showed me true compassion.

But as much as he taught me to savor the important moments in life, he handed me the worst ones in a spoon that he forcibly shoved down my throat.

And as much as I didn't want to, I knew, eventually, I'd have to meet him to let him know I wanted to sell the house he had transferred to my name, which I still had no idea why he did. Or even when.

The chime at the door startled me out of my thoughts, reminding me that I was not in the comfort of my bedroom but in my place of work. Shaking my head, I stuffed the phone back in my pocket, making a mental note to figure out how to reply to him later.

CHAPTER 44
Kartik

8 years ago

"Wake up Kartik." An angelic voice was whispering directly into my ear, making me feel like I'd been transported to an alternate reality where I'd been reeled in by a phantom. But that immediately got proven wrong by the way soft hands had roughly shaken me awake. "Kartik, you need to go!"

I groaned, wrapping my arms around Sonia and pulling her back down onto me. A chocolatey giggle left her and all the memories of the previous night flooded back in. The way she was quivering in a pain she had kept within herself finally deciding that she would let me in. It all rushed through me like it had just happened seconds ago and my grip on her tightened, a gasp leaving her lips, the puff of breath hitting the vein that ran down my neck.

She pushed away from me and I moaned, wanting to feel that sensation again, experiencing emotions I thought I never could. This girl was special to me, she was the stillness in my storm, holding me steady while I constantly fought the urge to fade away.

I had no idea how but she had somehow become my reason to keep going.

And I didn't intend to let her go any time soon.

"Kartik!" Her voice was just loud enough to prompt my eyes open, her room coming back into sight.

It was then I realized I never really saw it in daylight, only in the darkness of the night, comparing the shadows to the ones that had always followed me.

But seeing her pink and purple room convinced me that not every morning began with a burden of the night, coated in hues of blacks and grays. Mornings could bring color too.

"Kya hua, shona?" *What happened, sweetheart?* Rubbing my eye with the heel of my palm, I forced my vision to fade back to normal.

"You have to go." She continuously kept looking over her shoulder at the door despite being comfortably wrapped under my arms.

"Why?" My bottom lip jutted out in rebellion and although she pretended to be annoyed, I didn't miss the way the corner of his mouth shot slightly higher.

"My parents can't catch you here." I groaned again, closing my lids just to tease her some more. "Kartik!" She dragged out my name on her tongue and suddenly, I wanted to taste it on mine.

Fuck.

She was becoming my addiction and just the thought of leaving her, even if it was just for a day, was killing me. Especially when I knew where I would have to go once I did.

I was happier here, in her room, with just her. It was the world we created, one that was just ours to keep. But with that came the crash of reality every time we had to step out of our fantasies.

"Do I *have* to?"

She mimicked a cry, her eyes locking at the digital clock that read 6:00am. "Yes!" She pushed out of my hold, landing on her feet beside the bed, and began messing with the covers, throwing them off me. I attempted to grab them back but her limbs were moving faster. "My parents normally come to check in on me at 6:30 to make sure I'm up for school and they cannot see you here! I'm not supposed to have boys in my house, let alone in my room. And it doesn't help that you're, well, you." She waved a hand towards me and I caught her wrist, lifting myself up until I was face to face with her.

"I'm me?"

The gulp she took was as audible as it was visible on her throat. "You ride a bike and wear leather all the time. If anyone was the definition of trouble to my parents, it'd be you." She furrowed her brows while pleading with her eyes. It was the most attractive look any woman had given to me and I wanted to snap it into a photo so I could stare at it longer. "You need to get going. I'll see you in school."

Bringing my gaze to the window, I released her. The thought of going home after a night like this was burning me from the inside out but I knew I couldn't linger for any longer. If my parents had found out that I wasn't home all night, I'd be in big trouble because despite their negligence, they had a zero tolerance policy when it came to spending the entire night outside of the house without telling them.

"I'm sorry for rushing you out." Sonia whispered. "I wish you could stay longer."

"It's okay, shona. I don't want you to get in trouble." Lifting off the bed, I wrapped my arms around her waist, pulling her into me. A couple weeks ago, I would have hesitated. But after the past few hours, I knew this was my birthright. She was mine in one way or another. And I would no longer run from that. Pressing a kiss onto her forehead, I cupped her cheeks, forcing her to look up at me. "Can I come back tonight?"

She disappeared into her head for a moment before solemnly nodding. "My dad has a client in Philadelphia that I think he's going to visit and my mom is going with him. They'll most likely be staying the night there and coming back tomorrow evening. I'll be alone."

"Okay."

Hesitatingly, she perched up on her toes, bringing her lips closer to mine, waiting, and I couldn't help but smile. "If you want me to kiss you that bad you can just ask."

I chuckled at the way she lightly smacked my arm, her surprised pout coming to attack at full force. But before she could pull away, my hand came up behind her neck, holding her in place as I captured her bottom lip between mine.

I was never going to get tired of this feeling.

Reluctantly, I broke away from her, her lids still fluttering as I made my way to the window.

"I'll see you later, okay?"

She ran towards me as I took a step across the ledge. "Wait. Can you bring your guitar?"

I grinned at her request, knowing I wouldn't want to share my music with anyone else. "Whatever you want, shona."

With that, I pressed one more kiss against her lips before jumping down her roof, leaving my heaven to go meet my personal hell.

CHAPTER 45
Sonia

8 years ago

Kartik's kiss still lingered on my lips halfway through English class, my eyes continuously darting to the empty seat beside me.

He missed class again.

My mind shuffled any possible reason it could come up with, the fear of yesterday's absence still making my pulse race.

Making sure Mr. Hemly couldn't see, I placed my phone on my lap, shooting a text to Kartik asking where he was and when he was coming. He said he would this morning and I was beginning to worry something had gone wrong.

The class bell rang, time flowing effortlessly, and immediately, avoiding the glares of all the girls who targeted me yesterday, I speed-walked towards the tutoring office. The deepening pit in my stomach grew stronger as I saw both Trevor and Colt standing near the door, their faces twisted in concern.

Both of them seemed to quiet as I approached, their silence churning my stomach. "Do you guys know where Kartik is?"

Colt remained quiet, sharing a look with Trevor before he spoke. "No." I glanced at the phone in my hand, still with no reply. "He might be home, I'm not too sure. I haven't heard from him today and we were wondering the same thing." After examining his face, I dropped it, nodding before brushing past them and into the office.

The office was empty, the only staff member being the head of the tutoring department, Ms. Reily. With a smile, she waved me towards her, pointing at the empty seat. "Sonia. What can I do for you?"

"Hi, Ms. Reily." I placed my bag on the ground as I occupied the chair. "I just wanted to know if Kartik had stopped by. He hasn't shown up for a couple of tutoring sessions and I also noticed he wasn't in class either. As his tutor, I just wanted to make sure he passes his classes, you know?"

An uncomfortable stillness harbored the air and her face instantly dropped. "Oh, Sonia. I'm so sorry we must have forgotten to tell you. Had you not received the email?"

"What email?" I confusingly asked, scrummaging through my phone to figure out what she was speaking of. At the same time, she began clicking her keyboard, scrolling her computer for whatever it was she was talking about. "I didn't get anything."

"Oh here it is!" She pulled up a letter that seemed to have been undelivered. "We may have gotten your email address wrong. That is completely our mistake." Turning the computer towards her again, she placed her folded hands on the desk. "Kartik had dropped out of tutoring a couple days ago. He said he felt that he was good to pass and his grades were a fabulous reflection of that, all thanks to you."

She was grinning with joy, unaware of how I was breaking all the same.

Why would he not tell me?

Ms. Reily kept talking but her words were no longer making sense to me, all merging into one question: What was Kartik hiding from me?

"I'm sorry Ms. Reily. I have to go." Promptly cutting her off, I excused myself, rushing out the door and leaving the office even more dazed than I had been before entering.

Mindlessly, I made my way to my locker, gathering my books while my head roamed around all the possibilities.

What wasn't he telling me?

I almost slammed the door shut with anger if it hadn't been for the buzz that sounded from my phone.

Pulling it out, I let out a sigh of relief, reading *Kartik* in bold with a text message below.

Kartik: *Family emergency, I'm sorry. Will see you tonight shona.*

A queasy feeling passed through me, his excuse not sitting right with me. It didn't explain why he canceled the rest of his tutoring sessions when we still had two months left in the school year. It didn't explain why he was so crass and cryptic, along with his friends.

I knew he was concealing something big.

And I'd make sure to find out when I see him later.

CHAPTER 46
Kartik

As everyone filed in, I shuffled on my feet, waiting for the only one that mattered. Within minutes, I could hear her laughter circulate through the entire parking lot, her smile brighter than the spring sun above us. She was alluring.

She was walking beside the same coworker that she was always with, the one who tried to resist letting me in the last time I was here. I knew he had his own girlfriend but my nostrils flared watching as he wrapped his arms around *my* girl, pulling her in for a hug.

It took all my wits to stop myself from walking over and peeling his skin off his hand.

But I couldn't do that to Sonia.

So I waited.

Still, she was standing beside him, entangled in whatever conversation they were having, and it wasn't until she turned that her entire smile dropped, her eyes finally peering towards me. I couldn't stop my grin at her repulsed expressions, knowing they were all fabricated and fake. She was never truly upset at seeing me.

"With the way you were scowling, I was afraid you'd end up crushing those coffee cups." I looked down at my hands, having completely forgotten about the treats I had brought. "What are you doing here?"

"I brought you a morning coffee." She reached for the cup I extended between us, her fingers brushing mine while latching on, igniting every spark in my body. "Hazelnut with oat milk."

"How did you know my order?" Questionably, Sonia brought the straw to her lips, taking a satisfied sip.

My shoulders went up in a nonchalant shrug, although I was feeling far from it. "Lucky guess." Tilting her head, her brows shot up. "Fine. I saw the hazelnut creamer and oat milk in your fridge and figured it's what you normally would get."

She let out a *hm* before sipping again. "Why are you here?"

I didn't want to seem like a jealous boyfriend but my mind kept going back to the smile she wore before walking towards me, as if I were the one who stole it. "That teacher you work with. What's his deal?"

"What?" Her brows furrowed and I gave her a moment to ponder. "*Mortada?*" I nodded before taking my own sip of coffee. The bitter taste washed down my throat. "Don't even start, Kartik." I shivered as she uttered my name, craving to hear it again. "He's my friend. His girlfriend is a sweetheart. And if I remember correctly, you've met them both." Memories of that drunk call came rushing back, the way she asked for the bike, the way she noticed the scrunchie I still kept. It was all so nostalgic. She shook her head as if she still couldn't pinpoint a reason. "Actually, what's it to you?" Her finger shot up to my chest, my eyes locking directly at the point of contact, hoping she could feel the heat from my body transfer into hers. "Why does it matter to you?"

I let out a small laugh, meeting her gaze. "You don't know why it matters to me?" Her pupils dilated, eyes darkening for just a moment before going back to normal. But it was all I needed. I knew she was feeling the undeniable string towing us together, shortening with time. "It burns me everytime I see you smiling at someone who isn't me, shona. When I don't make you smile it makes me want to destroy everything that could get in the way of it. Those smiles are mine. Everything about you is mine. It's about time you admit it, too."

For a moment, it felt like she was ready to agree but as logic kicked in, she retreated. Taking another large sip, she finally spoke. "Are you going to tell me why you're here, Kartik?"

Nodding towards the building behind her, I answered. "After you're done with your day, I want to see you."

"Nope." She was profusely shaking her head. "Not happening." I could practically see her thoughts turning around to the nights we spent together but as badly as I wanted another one, I also understood that there were more important things that needed to be discussed.

But that didn't stop me from wanting to pull her into my arms and run my hands all over skin, claiming her lips like they belonged between mine.

"I promise, just talking. I don't know if you ever found out but I'm selling the house." I knew I didn't need to tell her any more, that she'd figure out which house I meant. "I'd like it if you came with me." She seemed to disappear for a moment, her silence only to be broken by the harsh breaths. "Shona?"

With steady hands, I shook her shoulders, pulling her back to the ground. "Your house?" I nodded. "Why?" Her brows pulled together, furrowing in pain. "Actually, *how?*"

"I don't know, really. But the house doesn't hold anything valuable for me anymore." A pained scoff slipped out of my mouth, prying Sonia's attention directly onto it. "Will you come?"

Stepping out of the shock, she finally met my eyes again, a different kind of sympathy washing through them. "I'm not sure, Kartik." Throwing her thumb over her shoulder, she shrunk. "I have a lot of work to do. I should get going."

Without another sound, she stepped away, still facing me. It wasn't until she turned away that my heart clenched and desperation took hold of me. "I'll be waiting for you!"

And just like that, she left without a second thought.

CHAPTER 47

Sonia

The entire school day passed in the memory of Kartik and his words.

I'm selling the house.

The house doesn't hold anything for me.

Come.

How could he expect me to go to that house without feeling like I was walking through our field of dreams that was now engulfed in fire? How was I supposed to go there and pretend it didn't mean something for us, for me, to be there, together, eight years later?

How could he be so selfish to sell it?

And how did he even have the power to?

Lost in the questions, I hadn't realized when Mortada had walked into the room. "Sonia, you okay?"

"Mhm."

Gathering my papers, I piled them into the corner, sorting through all the submitted homework my students had dropped into the bin I kept for them. Placing them neatly into a folder, I slid it into my bag before rising off my chair.

"What's the history?" I raised my brows as I walked alongside him, his question knocking me off balance. "With that guy. I can tell there's some push and pull and I think you and I are pretty good friends to be talking about things like that." He opened the door for me, waiting until I stepped out, following behind. "If you don't want to tell me, though, I'll respect it. But I notice whenever he's around, it's like you lose all sense of sanity."

"It's nothing important."

He examined my face, not believing a word out my mouth but, as promised, he refused to push further. "Okay."

But it was all eating me up inside, keeping it like a curse that was rotting in my bones. I needed to release the qualms to someone who didn't know Kartik on any level. And the only person that qualified under that requirement was Mortada. I sighed, fathering exactly how I would weave my entire past life to him. "He's one of the biggest reasons I even teach, honestly. He believed in me in a way no one had."

If he was shocked at my confession, he didn't say anything to indicate it. "How so?"

"I knew him eight years ago, in high school, and he was quite literally part of the popular kids' group. And I was just a tutor that unfortunately got assigned to him." We were standing beside my car, Mortada listening intently. "When I told him that I wanted to pursue teaching, he was one of the people who encouraged my dreams, telling me that I could really make a difference as a teacher." A longing sigh left me, the feeling of being validated by him still comforting me so many years later. "Long story short, we got a little too close, perhaps closer than we should have, and feelings got involved and then we just never spoke again. He just packed up and left my life like I never mattered and now he's somehow returned and keeps attempting to get me to see him."

"Wow." Exasperated, my friend took in all the words I blurted out. "So what's the issue that's got you so wound up? Just tell him you want nothing to do with him."

"I can't," I admitted, for the first time to myself. "You know, he was my first love and there are so many times where I've sat in the *what if* curse. And my friends think I'm crazy for it because they believe if I just go and hear him out all the little hopeful butterflies in my stomach would disappear. But I don't know." Hiding my face in my hands, I groaned. "There's this undeniable attraction between us but he's hurt me too much to just give him a shot."

"What did he want today?"

"He asked me to go see him after school. At his old house." My gaze traveled to the sky as if all my answers were written in the clouds. "The one he's selling."

"I hate to admit it, Sonia, but your friends might be right."

"How so?"

"Look, you don't have much to lose right now. I assume you're just caught up in rekindled feelings because you saw him. And who knows, you might hear him out and finally be able to let it all go. Or maybe," he paused, waiting until I looked at him. "Maybe, you're the one who's got it wrong. I mean, he's kind of scary around me but I've seen him around you and as an outsider it looks to me like he cares about you. I mean what asshole would pick you up when you're drunk, bring you bouquets of snacks or even coffee in the morning?"

"But—"

"No buts. Stop doubting everything. You do it every single time. This time, try giving yourself a little push. Give yourself a try. Get the answers you need and who knows, it might just be beneficial for you."

Pondering his words, I groaned, knowing he wasn't wrong. No one was.

Especially after knowing everything Kaitlyn had said and the night after it.

Why was I suddenly feeling like I was missing an important part of the story?

"Look," Mortada continued, "if anything, think of it like you're giving him a chance to explain. Everyone deserves the right to their words. There's always three sides to a story and right now, you only know one. Yours. The other two, his and the truth, are both unknown to you and it's probably best if you find them out to give yourself the satisfaction of knowing."

I leaned over, wrapping an arm around him. "You're a good friend."

"I know." Cockily, he smirked and I immediately felt lighter, the burden of secrets lifting off my shoulder.

"Thank you." I unlocked my car door, smiling at Mortada.

"Of course. Good luck." He tapped the top of my hood, nodding once, and walked away.

As I turned the ignition on, determination rose within me.

I knew what I needed to do.

CHAPTER 48
Sonia

8 years ago

Opening the front door, for the first time, I allowed Kartik Sharma to walk into my house like a proper gentleman. My nerves were skyrocketing watching him observe everything that was carefully used to decorate the empty house, wondering what exactly was going through his head. He walked through the corridor, his gaze halting at the shoe table that held frames with childhood pictures, the sudden embarrassment making me want to crawl into my skin.

"Is this you?" He was pointing to a photo of me with my best friends from childhood, posed alongside all our parents. It was a trip we took to Canada, all of us standing on the boat getting drenched under the Niagara Falls. This was before any of us had any idea how tough high school would be without each other while residing in different counties of the same state.

"How did you single me out?" Cocking my head, I tried to envision what he was seeing.

"You have the same smile. It's the brightest of anyone there. Even now, when you're smiling, you're even more beautiful than when you're not." My cheeks warmed, my gaze looking anywhere but at him. "I could recognize you even if you were lost in a crowd of a million people. It'd take me less than thirty seconds to get to you."

I didn't know whether I was flustered or shy, but either way, all I knew was that it was becoming all too suffocating with him, even in an entirely empty home. He was invading all my senses, clouding all my judgment until I no longer knew wrong from right. "Let's go upstairs." I didn't wait for him to follow, rushing up towards my room.

But he didn't take long, his steps quickly falling in step with mine.

As he stepped into my room, it suddenly felt tighter, as though the walls had shrunk. My brain kept reminding me that we were alone, my heart beat making its way up my throat.

I desperately wanted to know what he was ruminating but all my courage had vanished into thin air, any scrap of it gone like it never existed at all.

Taking a seat at the edge of the bed, my fingers shot up towards the strands of hair that were falling out of my messy ponytail, fidgeting with them until they tangled. He cleared his throat, moving towards me like he wanted to stamp me in his name.

Like I was his.

This time, if he said it, I wouldn't be able to deny it.

"I brought my guitar."

Did he feel it too? The tension?

Was he getting nervous with me?

He knelt on the floor, uncasing the instrument, looking up at me with soft eyes.

My jaw slightly dropped, the scene like something out of a movie.

I never expected that I'd be the one who made Kartik Sharma drop to his knees.

The mattress dipped as he took residence beside me, strapping the guitar across his shoulders. "You seem lost in your head." He pulled me out of my brain again and I finally took the time to look at him.

Really look at him.

His hair was tousled, like he ran hurried hands through it immediately after waking up. His gray tee hugged him so perfectly, the creases of his body causing me to salivate. His usually dark brown eyes were even darker, coated in a shade of black that matched his hair.

If I stared at him any longer, I would begin panting, wishing for things no good girl should be thinking about.

And yet I couldn't stop reminiscing about the feel of his mouth on mine, wanting it again.

I forced myself to stop thinking about the way his arms flexed as he brushed his fingers along the strings, a sweet note filling the quiet night.

"Where have you been?" I chose the safest conversation we could have right now, afraid that if I gave him any indication of what I was truly thinking of, we'd both trudge into territory that would have the power to destroy everything between us. "You haven't been showing up to school."

He sighed as if he'd expected it, articulating his words. "It's a long story."

"I've got time." I rested my palm on his, which was now pressed onto the space between us. It was then I realized I wanted to be his safe place, understanding that he was running from something, and I desperately just wanted him to sprint towards me when he fled. "You can trust me." It seemed so small but I found myself holding my breath, hoping he'd believe it.

"I know." His lids closed over those beautiful auburn eyes, shielding him from the world around him. "It's just a lot of fighting at home, nothing I'm not used to."

"Fighting?"

"My parents." A defeated breath left him, the same broken Kartik sitting in front of me that I saw a shortened glimpse of the very first day he'd shown to tutoring. "I don't think they ever really liked each other. And I think having me was their attempt at fixing their relationship, thinking a child would bring them closer, but it never seemed to get better." He shrugged it off but it was churning my stomach, finally understanding why he was always hesitant in accepting concern from others.

He was simply never loved.

Not even by the people who were obligated to love him.

But he was by me.

And I was too fucking scared to tell him.

"It's not that serious." I almost blurted the words out, but as he spoke again, it allowed me to cower within myself, knowing that if I said it now, he would think I was only pitying him. "Let's not talk about it anymore. What do you want me to play?"

Accepting his retrieval, my attention was back on the guitar that sat against him, perfecting the portrait he was. "Whatever you want."

"Hm." He thought for a moment, mindlessly strumming before deciding upon a tune. He nodded once, then twice, turning to me. "Alright."

As the opening chords of *Yellow* by Coldplay filled the air, an unavoidable smile grew on my face, his lips curving upwards in response.

In the softest voice, he simply stated, "This song reminds me of you."

I swore my heart stopped for a beat before resuming at twice its normal speed. "Why?"

He shrugged, continuing to play while dissipating into the wall ahead. He was avoiding my gaze, and I didn't mind, because if he dared to look at me, I was sure I wouldn't be able to stop myself from leaning over and pressing my lips to his.

But his confession continued to play through my head as the song progressed and I leaned back until my back hit the sheets.

This song reminds me of you.

The more I thought of it, the hotter I felt my cheeks grow.

My vision caught sight of the horse Kartik brought back to me, restored and embellished in a way that would color all my memories in him. He was unknowingly reserving a spot in my life that I was sure I'd never give away.

"You know," he whispered over the sound of the acoustic, the song coming to an end. He waited until the ending keys to continue. "All my life, I'd been living in this kind of shadow." Sliding the guitar off his shoulders, he fell onto his back beside me, still unwilling to look at me. We just lay there, the both of us, next to each other, facing the ceiling like it was writing a script from the heavens above. "I was clouded in gloominess, like there was nothing better for me. Like this was the best it could get, my life just staying stagnant there. And then you happened."

I opened my mouth to speak but as he turned his head, all words were now null in my head. There was nothing I could say when his face was this close to mine, our noses brushing with every inhale.

"I stopped looking at the constellations because looking at you was like looking at a thousand stars that light up the night sky. I stopped counting the stars above me for relief and started counting the freckles on your face instead. You took off the cloak of darkness I was trapped in and showed me daylight. You're as bright as the sun, shona, and you don't even know it." He let out a breath and my eyes shut. I was sure he could feel the bed thump alongside my heartbeat. "You're my yellow."

A visible gulp passed his throat, his Adam's apple bobbing in response. He took his time running his vision down my face, his tongue jutting out for a moment as he stopped at my lips. Instinctively, my eyes shut, waiting for something, anything.

His hand came up to my face, caressing and running down my cheek before brushing a stray strand of hair behind my ear.

Sucking in a breath, his gaze bore into me and I felt him closing the minimal distance.

Our breaths were now synchronized, our bodies working with each other.

Without another thought, his lips latched onto mine, no warning delivered, like they finally found their home within me.

He groaned into my mouth, his tongue dancing melodiously with him. Kartik's hand found my hair, pulling me further into him, so close until I was straddling him with my legs bent beside his chest.

Pulling away, a lopsided smile appeared on his sinful face and I couldn't help but lean back onto him. Wincing, I felt the pain rise through my body and end right where his lips found mine again.

With a final wrenching thought, a stray tear left my shut eyes, threatening to drown us with it.

He kissed me like it was a final goodbye.

CHAPTER 49
Kartík

8 years ago

Even in my dreams, the image of her played on repeat, luring me deeper into her. My mind kept envisioning scenes of the night before, the taste of her kiss haunting my lips, the feel of them like a ghost brushing onto me.

After the kiss, Sonia urged me to play her another song under the condition that I taught her the same one. But to my surprise, in the midst of my fingers moving along the strings, she'd reached over and grabbed her pink polaroid camera from her bedside table and flashed it to me, capturing the memory.

I let her have it though, seeing her face brighten as the picture developed. And I knew then that I wanted that memory for myself as well, handing her the guitar while capturing an identical picture that I'd never let leave my hold.

It was too precious to lose.

She was too precious to lose.

I'd been so lost in her that I almost didn't hear the screaming at first.

But I did.

And it startled the both of us awake at the same time.

A frightened look took over Sonia as she frantically pushed off of me, attempting to hide, whether herself or me, I couldn't tell.

When we'd carelessly fallen asleep, we knew we were alone, Sonia's parents trusting her to be fine. But we never accounted for the possibility of them coming back earlier than they had originally planned.

"Sonia, yeh sab kya ho raha hai?" *What the hell is going on?* A woman I assumed had been Sonia's mother roared. "And who the hell is that boy?"

"Sonia," her father started, disappointment lacing his tone.

"Papa, ma, I can explain." Sonia left the bed, leaving a cold patch of air beside me that only served to heighten my guilt.

This was my fault.

"What explanation, Sonia?" Her mother's face was growing redder by the second. "We leave you here alone and *this* is what we come back to? Is this how we raised you?"

"Mumma, no." Sonia profusely began shaking her head, her eyes brimming with tears.

"We expected better. We came home early thinking we'd bring you some breakfast and spend the rest of the day together but it looks like you had other plans." Her mother waved her hand towards me, still refusing to look my way.

"Mumma." Sonia sounded defeated and it was killing me all the same.

This was all my fault.

"Aunty—" I started, only to be cut off by her sharp tone.

"I don't care what you have to say. What business do you have with my daughter in her bed?" She was raging, Sonia's pleading eyes begging me to stay silent. "We don't know you and you're spending the night in a girl's bed."

But how could I stay silent when she was standing here breaking in front of me by the second?

"I'm sorry, aunty." I stood beside Sonia now, alternating my gaze between both her parents. "I'm Kartik. I go to school with your daughter."

"Oh, so your school allows disrespectful boys like you? Sharam nahi hai kya?" *Have you no shame?*

"It's not what it looks like. I was just here because I get tutored—"

"I don't care." The walls shook with her words, her hands wrapping around Sonia's wrist, pulling her towards her, presenting a barrier. "Get the hell out of my house."

"No!" Sonia broke away, wrapping her arms across my waist, burying her face into my chest.

This was all my fucking fault.

"Sonia!" This time, her dad screamed, the girl in my hold now fragile and shaking.

"No papa!"

"Sonia, let go of him!" Her mom attempted to pry her off me, all her efforts failing.

Without releasing me, she turned her face towards her parents, the words that left her next shaking the ground beneath me. "No! I love him!"

My eyes immediately found hers and I knew how wrong this was.

How wrong *I* was.

Suddenly, all the oxygen in the air had vanished, her confession stopping time.

I needed to leave.

Reluctantly, I peeled Sonia off of me, pressing my lips against her forehead before returning my attention back to the two angry parents at the door.

"I'm sorry." Keeping my head down, I choked on the sob that threatened to leave me as Sonia continued peering up at me. "I'll leave."

No one dared to speak another word, Sonia too shellshocked to utter anything, her parents too angry for me.

Without a sound, I crossed through her bedroom door, doing everything in my power to not look back.

As I stepped out the front door, I managed to black out the fighting that resumed at my departure, my mind only clouded with one thing.

She loves me.

I should leave her alone.

She loves me.

I'm not good for her.

She loves me.

I can't give her everything she wants.

She loves me.

This won't end well.

She loves me.

She loves me.

She loves me.

And despite it all, I was a fucking selfish fool.

I wouldn't be able to stay away from her.

Because as much as I couldn't admit it, I loved her too.

CHAPTER 50
Kartik

It never seemed to get easier walking into this house. The memories of what could have been taunting me, bouncing off the walls as if they were laughing at the outcome.

I'd already fixed up most of the house the first time around but my limbs always halted when I saw the corner of my childhood bedroom, untouched.

It's almost as if my feet navigated on their own, a pull drawing me right back where I peeling my heart out last time. Kneeling on the floor, I clasped my aching head, wondering how it went so wrong.

Reaching for my wallet, I propped it open, staring at the same picture I'd found here.

"Where did you go, shona?" I whispered to no one in particular, the ghosts of our relationship's past mocking me in response.

The life we lived together seemed so far away, its existence part of a different reality where I wasn't me and she wasn't her. A reality where we didn't have so much animosity between each other.

I smiled at the photo, knowing it was the only thing that could get me through this process.

I had only come into town for this one reason, not realizing that my biggest purpose in life was still here and if she'd ask, I'd drop everything and stay back in this godforsaken town for her. But if she didn't, I would convince myself to be content in the remnants of her that I'd found and the new memories we made that I never thought we'd have a chance to.

Anything she'd give me, I'd take.

No matter how covetous I wanted to be.

The doorbell sounded and I rose to my feet, hopeful, making my way towards the entrance while tucking my wallet back in my pocket. I couldn't resist grinning at the sight of her. She could make the strongest men fall weak in their knees.

"You came." Opening the door wider, she allowed herself to step inside, the scent of her floral perfume coating my nostrils. She glanced at every corner without uttering anything, and I realized she'd never truly been inside of my high school house before. "Do you want me to show you around?"

She shook her head, still taking in the bleak walls and lifeless furniture. "I want to see your room."

It almost came out of her as a question, the sentiment warming me the same, knowing there was a part of me she still wanted to discover. And maybe seeing what she would, she'd understand why my heart still beat her name.

Sonia followed close behind as I led her up the stairs, falling in step as I swung open the door. Her eyes immediately glistened, her lips upturned. I tried envisioning it as she would, as someone who had only seen it with virgin eyes. The bed was still half covered in my black sheets, the rumpled pages on the desk and floor giving the illusion that this place was lived in. Like it was loved.

But in actuality, every moment that I had spent here, I spent dying, wasting away a life I could have been living.

There was nothing special about my bedroom but having her next to me felt like it was something out of heaven's gates itself.

"I've never been here before." She almost sounded like the Sonia that I once knew—the one who would always run to me and never *from* me. My heart quenched the thought only further reminding me that she didn't want to be mine anymore.

"I wish I could have brought you here back then." I whispered to her as she walked further inside, immediately stopping at the desk, her hands skating over the scribbled pages. "All the music I used to write."

"Feels like a lifetime ago." She sounded as though there was more on her lips she was refusing to say, straining herself with locked up words. For a moment, she seemed to lightly smile, mumbling some of the words that were messily scratched over the pages. Looking over her shoulder, her eyes pleaded for more, and instantly we were seventeen again, the bittersweet taste of an innocent and fabricated youth clouding the air.

"I don't even remember what it felt like to write, honestly." I took a seat on my still messy bed, watching as she continued flipping through the pages, reading whatever caught her sight next. "Ever since I started finding a passion for drawing, I decided I wanted to tattoo people, starting with myself."

She spared me a glance, my fingers twitching at the urge to grasp at her waist and pull her down onto me. Now that I had known how she felt on top of me, I never wanted her to be anywhere else.

"You're covered in tattoos. Why?" It was a simple question but her curiosity assured my hopeful soul that, whether she believed it or not, she still wanted to know me.

I had kept hurtful truths from her enough in our lifetime that I knew I would no longer put her through that pain again with a half honest answer. "It was for the pain." Sonia turned to me, leaning a hip onto the wooden desk for support. "I guess I was always just looking for a way to pour my pain into art to mask it as something beautiful. It's what I did with music. After everything went wrong between us, I knew you no longer wanted to speak to me and it was probably the hardest pill to swallow. To know that you wanted nothing to do with me anymore. And music reminded me too much of you. So I found my new outlet.

"The pain felt good for a while. I could pretend that the only reason I was aching was because I'd just had needles stabbed into my body. And for just a moment, I could forget that I was missing a part of my soul. So I covered myself in ink to try and navigate through the pain. But life was playing its biggest joke on me. Just when I thought I was able to live with the fact that maybe the pain was just something I was destined to carry with me, it threw me back into this life with you."

Sonia straightened her spine, her brows furrowing as she took a step back. "What do you mean?" Disoriented, I stood up, trying to recall what I had said that could have made her react in such a way. "What do you mean *I* didn't want to talk to you, Kartik?"

"What?" My arms wanted to reach for her but something in the energy shifted boldly as she pulled back from me again.

"You said you knew *I* didn't want anything to do with you?" I opened my mouth to speak but her hand shot up in the space between us. "You know what, I don't even want to know." Glancing at the ceiling, she let out a laugh that was anything but humorous. "I'm sorry. I shouldn't have come."

Her feet shifted towards the door but my hand caught her wrist, ensuring she didn't make it far enough. "Stop. You do this every time."

"Let go of me." Her chest was heaving, her eyes fuming.

"What are you so angry about?" A tick in her jaw told me she was clenching it to prevent swords from falling forward. "Why do you keep running from me?"

"Let go of me, Kartik." Her voice was louder but calmer, as if it were her pathetic attempt to tame herself. But if only she knew that I wanted her to let go.

Because I'd take anything she gave me.

I'd take her anger if it meant I'd no longer have her silence.

I'd take her hate even if all I wanted was her love.

But she refused to give me even that.

"Shona," I started, my mouth clamping shut at her interruption.

"Kartik, what were you trying to do calling me here? What was the purpose?" Her words cut like sharp knives. "Was it just some sick ploy to see how you could fuck with my head again?" She was breathing into me, her chest pressed into mine, and even in anger, her eyes seemed to darken.

"Shona, what are you talking about?"

"This was a mistake." She twisted her hand, roughly pulling out of my grip.

The only sound that followed was her footsteps as she stormed down the stairs and out the door, leaving me alone in this house all over again.

CHAPTER 51
Sonia

8 years ago

There was not a moment in the entirety of the week that hadn't been spent with tears streaking down my cheeks. In between classes, I'd find myself running to the bathroom, holding my breath and waiting for him to come scoop me up and take me away.

Even this morning, as I had gotten into the car for the drive to school, a punishment my parents began enforcing, I attempted to soften my mom up.

"I love him, ma." I had screamed, hoping it made her open her eyes to her daughter's pain.

"You're seventeen years old! You know nothing about love." The veins in her neck protruded any time I'd brought up Kartik.

"I know enough." It was my response every time, followed by silence for the rest of the day.

I was willing to risk it all when it came to him.

Nothing mattered if it wasn't for him.

And that's why, when he decided to stop showing up to school again, for the entire week since that night, rage resurfaced within me.

After the last bell, I stormed into the hallway, locating the two people I knew would have any sort of information. "Trevor!" He turned, his face immediately turning stoney, deception written all over him.

"Hi, Sonia." He feigned a smile but I knew it was all for show.

"Let's cut to the chase." Colt appeared behind him, looking equally as distraught. "Where's Kartik?" Crossing my arms across my chest I glared at both the boys who seemed to cower. "Seriously?"

"It's not our business, Sonia." Colt spoke up, causing me to raise my brows at him. I didn't know whether I wanted to believe him or not but something made me feel defeated, like they couldn't help me even if they tried. "Look, honestly, we really don't know what's been going on."

"When I called him earlier, he turned his phone off. You can't possibly think I'm just going to take your word for it. He's closest to you both."

"Not since you came into his life." Trevor replied in a hushed tone. "He blows us off to go see you and we're not complaining, really. But if anyone would know what's going on, we'd assume it's you. All we know is that he was having issues at home, nothing more and nothing less."

I let out a breath and suddenly, worry crept up my bones like a spider. He had said his parents were fighting a lot and had been progressively getting more distressed. Had something gone wrong at home?

As if the universe had heard my pleas, my phone chimed, an incoming text curing all my doubts for a second.

Kartik <3: *Meet me outside. I'm waiting for you.*

"Is that him?" Colt leaned towards me as I nodded.

"He's here."

"Look, Sonia." He sighed. "As close as we are to him, he never really opened up to us fully. I don't know if he just didn't want to or what but he seems to be taking a liking to you. He chooses you and as much as we seem like assholes, he's our friend and we wouldn't want anything but for him to be happy. And you're what makes him happy. We can see it." Something about his words were reassuring, although the story Kartik's absence told was the opposite. "Go see him and make sure he's good, yeah?"

Without another word, I picked up my pace, storming out the door and frantically looking around for the boy I'd been desperate to find. After a minute of standing there, a hand slipped between my fingers, pulling me off to the side and against a wall. I had to crane my neck to see him but even then, I could never get my entire fill.

Each time I looked at him, there was a new beauty to him, like he just continued to get more enchanting, more irresistible.

"Shona." I closed my eyes as his whispered nickname fell against my lips, his kiss like a spell casting me into him.

As he pulled away, I allowed myself to breathe, the anger and hurt and anguish of the barren week falling heavy against my shoulders. "Where have you been?" He was calculating his answer, his eyes seemingly distant in a way they'd never been before. "Please don't lie to me." If I could drop to my knees and beg for an answer, I would.

"I've never lied to you, shona." The truth was laced throughout his sentence but there was still a hidden secret between each letter.

"Then tell me everything." My hands gripped his biceps, running up until they reached his neck, clasping behind him.

"Baby, there's nothing to tell."

My arms dropped to my sides, irritation stringing through my sentences. "Stop lying to me, Kartik. You haven't spoken to me in a week. You stopped showing up to school. What the hell is going on?"

"I promise, shona. It's just a lot of family issues." He rubbed a hand across his face frustratingly.

If that's all it was, why hadn't he just told me sooner?

"Kartik. Whatever it is, I want to be there for you. I want to show you that I care for you. I want to show you how much I love you." His eyes widened at it, his hands cupping my face instantly.

His lips said all the words his mouth refused to utter, pulling me into him for another kiss.

But I couldn't help feeling like there was something rancid waiting at the corner.

Waiting until we crashed and burned and fell apart.

I couldn't help feeling like his wordless confession was nothing but a vow of silence.

CHAPTER 52
Kartik

8 years ago

Hearing her consistently say those words only managed to cause the dagger I'd put into my heart to twist and twist until I was profusely bleeding internally.

There was no easy way to tell her everything that had been going on and I assumed seeing her today would lighten the blow, but then there she was, in all her glory, pained because of me and I couldn't find it in myself to give her more. I couldn't hurt her more than I already was.

I had to tell her soon that I was leaving.

Sitting on the parked bike for a moment, I glanced at the front door that was slightly ajar. The images in my mind flipped through every moment with Sonia like a slideshow, stopping on how she looked when I dropped her off just moments ago on what possibly was the last motorcycle ride I'd take with her arms wrapped firmly around my torso.

My eyes dampened and, for the first time, I wasn't afraid of letting the waterworks fall through.

I was hurting and I couldn't even tell the person who could take away my pain because her knowing would only serve to make us both upset.

I let myself linger for another moment before hopping off the bike and heading for the house. Upon entering, I could already sense the shift in environment. My parents were no longer fighting but the same mysterious guy I had once seen when I'd snuck in the house was there again. Except now, I had the knowledge that he was their lawyer, drawing up plans for their divorce.

They agreed upon a settlement, wanting to avoid the trips to the courthouse, and it wasn't that long ago that I found out they'd been planning this for a while. Originally, they wanted to wait until I had graduated but I guess they easily got sick of each other, wanting to separate, putting me in the middle of their personal crossfire.

When they told me that we had to move away, I assumed we all were leaving together like we always did. But then, they dropped the other bomb.

Not only were we moving away, we were also selling the house which was under my father's name. Which not only meant that he'd still be here, but that I was being forcibly taken with my mother to live with her family.

And despite all my rebels against going with that careless woman, my father didn't budge, like he wanted to let me go, like I was just a lint on his jacket that he could dust off.

You're a minor. You don't have a choice.

My parents' voices kept revolting in my head and every time I heard them, they grew louder, fury building within me.

"Kartik, make sure you pack everything. We're leaving tomorrow night." My mother had never sounded sweeter but it was nothing but a facade.

It's okay, I consoled myself. *I'll finish school online and go to college. I'll get away and all will be right again. I'll make it right again.*

Storming up the stairs, I slammed the door, not caring about the hinges when my life was falling apart.

I needed to tell Sonia. I couldn't keep it from her any longer.

Fishing through the clutter on my desk, I found a loose sheet of paper and a black pen, the ink filling up the page.

My hand hadn't stopped moving for an hour, writing out everything I couldn't say in words that would hopefully make her understand.

Folding it like a pamphlet, I sealed it in an envelope, holding it to my chest as if it could absorb the sound of my breaking heart.

Lost in thought, I hadn't noticed when the door had opened, my father standing as if waiting for me to speak first. "Son." I cringed at his use of the word, knowing I no longer meant that for him. "Can we talk?"

I shook my head, unwilling to even look at him in his deceitful face. "I have nothing to say to you and I don't care for anything you have to say."

"I understand." He sounded broken himself but I wouldn't be fooled anymore.

I'd always been under the impression that despite all the arguments, at least my father had loved me in his own sick and twisted way. But it seems it was always just a big role he had been playing, so well that I began believing it.

Defeated, I rose from my chair, closing the distance between us. He stared as I brought the letter up between us, hesitantly grabbing it from my hand. "If you ever cared about me, give this to Sonia. I've put her address on the front. I don't expect you to tell her anything. Just hand it to her." He examined my face for a fraction of a second and I wondered if he could see just how grief-stricken I had been. "Don't make me regret trusting you for one last time."

"I won't let you down."

CHAPTER 53
Sonia

8 years ago

One week, six days, ten hours.

That's how long his silence came this time around.

On top of that, I had visited the principal's office after school and discovered that he'd dropped out of school.

A month before graduation.

A graduation he worked his ass off for.

And that's how I ended up here, walking 20 minutes to his street after lying to my parents and telling them I had senior year after school activities to attend so that they wouldn't show up to fetch me from class.

But I couldn't help it—I had to see him.

As I turned the corner to where his house appeared, I didn't see it at first. But once it came into my line of sight, my chest nearly cut itself open, my heart falling onto the neatly cut grass.

A *'for sale'* sign.

There was just one car in the driveway and I figured the only thing I could do now was walk up and knock on the door, hoping for some answers. Hoping that all my answers were there, just shielded by a wall.

I stared at the brown wood for a moment, wondering if I was even ready to know what lay on the other side. But anything was better than nothing.

My fist thudded onto the door twice, waiting for what felt like an eternity.

Until finally, the lock clicked and a man appeared in front of me.

Kartik's dad.

There was no mistaking it. The resemblance was uncanny, the same lips pulled into a straight line, the same fluffy hair, those same cheekbones. I now knew where Kartik got his looks from, his father looking exactly like an aged version of him.

If his father was still here, that could mean Kartik was too? Right?

A sudden wave of confidence pulsed through me, the hope I managed to push down resurfacing.

"Hi." I had almost questioned it, unsure if I even possessed the right to interrogate. "I'm Sonia." Extending a hand, I put on my best smile. Hesitantly, he grasped it, his expression giving no insight on his thoughts. "I'm looking for Kartik."

"Oh. Sonia." His face immediately dropped, averting his eyes like if he let me see through them, I'd find something he intended to keep secret. "He's not here."

My throat was growing drier by the second, the panic almost showing itself. "Okay. Um. Do you know when he'll be back?"

He sighed and I prepared myself for the blow he was going to deliver. "He actually won't be back. I'm sorry. He's gone."

If I hadn't been outside, I would have collapsed to the ground, falling until I no longer were in this realm. Did this mean he left forever? "What do you mean he's gone?"

A pained sound left him, almost as though he, himself, were choking on a sob. "He and his mother left almost two weeks ago. I'm only still here because I intend to sell this house. Did he not tell you?"

No.

This can't be happening.

"Okay. Thank you," I managed before running off his porch, not hearing the rest of his words that called out behind me. I made it one street down before I fell to my knees, my face buried in my hands as the tears uncontrollably pooled into them.

I clutched my chest, the pain getting almost physical, feeling like someone had run a knife down my skin and squeezed all the life from my beating organs.

My entire life had crumbled apart right in front of my eyes.

And Kartik had been the orchestrator of it all.

I allowed myself another five minutes to dwell alone before grabbing my phone and calling the only person whose arms I wanted to fall asleep in now.

"Mom, can you come pick me up?"

CHAPTER 54

Sonia

Turning into the parking garage of my apartment, I'd expected to come home and relax. But right beside my usual spot was a bike I knew all too well and a man that nonchalantly leaned against it, helmet still secured and a leather jacket that pulled at his every curve as he crossed his arms across his torso.

Letting out a deep breath, I stepped out of my parked car, grabbing my bag and marching directly towards him. "What do you want?" Like a madman, the scent of him, bleeding with oak and whiskey, cascaded through me and I let myself bask in it for just a moment hoping he couldn't tell while he pulled his helmet off. "Why are you in my lot?"

"You haven't replied to a single text since that day you walked out and never even let me explain." He was carefully crafting his words, being concise as if he feared saying the wrong thing.

But he had to know there was no 'wrong thing' to say. The whole idea of him being here *was* the 'wrong thing.'

"It's called being ignored. Can't take a hint?"

He smirked just slightly, as if holding back to not let his full amusement show. "Not by you."

"Well, too bad." I wanted to reach over and wipe the laughter from his face. "What?"

He shook his head, my foot tapping, prompting him to explain. "You've always been so fiery with me. I missed this version of you."

"Is this why he came here? To dwell in the past? Was it not enough to invite me to your home the other day that you need to rub it in for some narcissistic idea you have about the past?"

For the entirety of the week, I'd been angry.

Angry at myself for going.

Angry for how I was so foolish eight years ago.

Angry for believing him again.

Angry that I let him mess with my head again only for him to blame me for the way it all went down.

He was the one who left without another word.

And the thought wounded me like it was fresh every time. It built up my resentment towards him and everything he brought alongside him for all these years.

"I just want to talk, Sonia." His feet drew closer, stepping into a territory that skirted around being too close to be clear minded.

I wanted to pretend that the way he used my name for the first time hadn't affected me at all. But it did. And he saw it in the way I winced immediately.

His eyes shone regret like I'd never seen before.

"Shona—"

My hand shot up, now eager to get through the conversation as quickly as possible. "Kartik, I hate to break it to you but I have no interest in rehashing our history. There's just too much pain and I don't want—"

"You think I haven't hurt, Sonia?" His frustration was evident causing his voice to rise as if it were just begging to be heard. "You think I haven't spent the last eight years wondering where the hell you and I went wrong? God, Sonia. Get out of this *I did nothing wrong* mentality!"

"How dare you? You left me Kartik." Each word came out with a punctuation mark, enhancing its effect.

"See, that's the thing." His hands reached for mine, clasping them together, the familiarity of the action causing me to shiver. Tears were on the brink of falling but I wouldn't allow him the pleasure of basking in hurting me again. "You keep saying I left you. And it confuses the hell out of me. You keep pushing back but then you call me to your house and kiss me on your own and make me feel like we're somewhat getting somewhere. But then you ignore me again. Tell me what the hell I did wrong. Tell me how to fix it, shona. And I will."

No longer could I pretend to be tough, my whole body aching as huge drops of water began falling between us. They coated my cheeks, Kartik's eyes trailing each tear as if he were directing them.

"You really don't get it, do you?" Unsureness marred his face, stabbing me further. Slipping my hands out of his, I let the breeze hit me, a chill passing between us. It was all too poetic, knowing we couldn't be warm with each other anymore. I couldn't allow it. I wouldn't allow it. "Eight years ago. Do you remember that night you slept in my room? The night my mom caught us?" My heart twisted as I pictured us in bed, once upon a time, happy.

"How could I forget? Of course I do."

"*That* is why I can't be around you." If he wanted the truth, I'd yell it until it'd get through his hard skull and he'd understand. His jaw opened as he contemplated words but it was now my turn to tell my side. "Every time I see you, Kartik, it's like the bandaid on that pain is ripped off like it's fresh. And it hurts me because that's the day you left me."

He stepped forward, his hands reaching towards me again but dropping before they could latch onto mine. "I saw you after that. I remember it."

A laugh escaped me, unable to contain it, almost presenting an evil undertone. "Do you not remember a single moment of that morning, though?" His brows pulled in, his mind clearly shifting through the files marked eight years ago. "It's actually insane. The one moment that changed everything and you don't even fucking remember."

"Please." He bordered misery, the only difference between him and a stubborn child being that he was still on his feet.

What a ghostly fucking scene.

"I can't be around you Kartik. I can't. Every time I'm near you, every time we touch, every time you kiss me it's like it's taking a piece of me. It's taking a piece of my heart."

"Why is that so wrong?"

Was he serious?

"Because." I was gasping for air, unable to control the words spilling through my lips. "Because if I allow myself that, I'll fall in love with you. *Again.*" The pain I'd felt at never hearing him utter those words was now bleeding through me. "And you won't fall in love with me. *Again.*"

If his bike weren't his support, he'd have fallen over. His face fell as if his world had shattered, churning in a hurt of his own. "You're fucking joking, right?"

My gaze focused on the gravel, counting every piece of rock willing it to take my mind somewhere far. "You never said it back," I whispered.

Immediately, his hands came up to my shoulders, shaking for my attention. "Look at me." I shook my head, attempting to pry my body from his grip. "Goddamnit, Sonia, look at me."

The whole lot shook with his voice as he released me, my eyes immediately finding his. He took a step back, slowly peeling off his jacket by the sleeves. Time halted as he moved, as if it were made just for him, crafted to shift with his every movement. Draping the leather along the handlebars, he stood in front of me again, painfully stunning in a white tee.

"Look at me and tell me I don't love you." I struggled to see him through my wet eyes, wiping at them ferociously. "Fuck, Sonia. I'm covered in remnants of you."

For the first time, I got a good look at the man before me, who once appeared to only be covered in ink and sins, my attention running anywhere but near him.

But I noticed it now as the pictures became clear in my head.

"All of my tattoos, Sonia. Every single one of them goes back to you." I met his gaze again, a stray tear marking its path down his cheek. Looking at his arms again, my breath halted, calculating them all.

Emily's skeleton hand and butterfly from Corpse Bride.
A lion.
The numbers 116, right along his wrist.
A wave wrapping around his bicep similar to the one on my neck.
Lavenders climbing up his forearms.
A sketch of Stitch from Lilo and Stitch.

A microphone with the words 'You're just too good to be true' signifying the scene where Heath Ledger sings on the bleachers in 10 Things I Hate About You.

All of those caused me to stop in my tracks but the piece that lay on his left bicep almost made me stumble, my hands flying to my mouth.

It was an outline of me from the same day I claimed he didn't remember.

It was the night I told him I loved him.

It was me with his guitar, the exact picture he must have kept a polaroid of.

I searched his face for any hint that it was a cruel joke but these were permanent marks that he'd sketched onto his body.

"For eight years, Sonia. Eight years I wondered what *I* did wrong and whether I was just truly never enough. I didn't deserve you then and I don't deserve you now but God, if I wasn't a selfish ass man I would have never bothered you. But I can't go another year after knowing what I do now. How you taste, how you feel, it's all become a part of me. You're a part of me." He was closer now, the distance between us disappearing with the sobs. "I loved you then and I love you now."

This didn't make any sense. Breaking free from his hold, I caught my breath. "So why didn't you ever call?" He stared at me as if I'd pulled a rug from under his feet, causing him to tumble. "In all these years, you never called me Kartik. Why?"

"What do you mean?" He ran his hands through his already messy hair, my sight locking on the tattoos now. "I left the ball in your court, Sonia. *You* never called *me*. And even then, I tried but you changed your number by then." My brows pulled together, my jaw dropping at the sheer audacity of him to continue placing blame on me. "Of course you don't remember." Before I could ask, he proceeded to challenge everything I knew right in my mind. "Of course you forgot the letter."

All sounds ceased to exist, everything blurring as the shock hit me. "What letter?"

For a moment, panic shot across his face, as if he were calculating all the outcomes in his brain. "The letter I wrote you. The day I left Sonia."

"*What letter?*" I was pleading with him, begging for something I didn't even know. But whatever it was had the power to destroy us.

"You didn't get my letter." It was a simple statement but the weight of it drowned us both. Kartik began shaking his head as he chanted the words over and over, each time his sadistic grin spreading wider. "Of course you didn't."

"Kartik." I tried reaching for him but even as my hands fell against his skin, he went cold to the touch.

"I have to go." And without another word, he hopped onto his bike, as I continued getting full of a million rising questions that still wouldn't have answers.

As I watched him ride away, I stayed right there, right where he left me.

CHAPTER 55
Kartik

She didn't get the fucking letter. It was almost laughable how I hadn't thought that possible. It was even more laughable that I assumed it would get to her safely in the first place.

As much as an asshole she must have seen me be, just leaving her in the parking lot without an explanation, I had something far more important to get to.

The root.

The wind cut through my helmet and I contemplated yanking it off so I could feel it on my bare skin. But as I neared my destination, the fury was enough to fill me up with steam.

Parking the bike on the driveway I'd known for years, I yanked the phone from my pocket, typing the text as fast as I could so that I wouldn't throw it across the street.

Meet me at the house.

I didn't have to wait long.

The sound of the car pulling in roared through the living room, my feet immediately taking me to the front door.

I watched through the window, as he did the same as I had, taking in the sight before him like if he didn't, it'd disappear the second he blinked. My heart longed for any feeling of nostalgia, of love, but all it was met with was despair and anguish, coupled heavily with wrath.

After a breath, the door swung open and there he was, the man who had single handedly ruined the only good thing in my life. "Hi, dad." I laced the word with vexation, hoping he felt how I had for the past eight years.

"Son." He stood there, unaware of what to do, as I took him in. My father was always handsome and age never worked against him. He still appeared to be young, save for the now slightly peeking grays that stuck deep in his hair. "How are you?" Stepping into the living room again, I heard him shut the door and follow, sitting across from me on the couches. "Thank you for meeting me. I've been waiting to be able to speak to you."

"I'm selling the house." I had no interest in small talk with him, my resentment piling up until it was nearly overflowing.

If the news shocked him, it wasn't evident on his face, his roaming eyes taking in how fresh and new every piece of furniture looked. "I can't say I blame you. This house never gave you anything but pain so I understand."

The silence stretched for a moment longer and I tried to read his face, seeing if there was any indication of whether or not he knew how effortlessly he ruined my life in more ways than one. "Tell me how you still had it. And why is it under my name now?" Leaning back, I propped my leg up, crossing it above the other.

He seemed to contemplate his answer for a second, settling on one as he placed his elbows on his knees, folding his hands together. "All those years ago, I knew it was wrong the way we, your mom and I, separated, putting our seventeen year old son in the middle of it all when he was just an innocent bystander. But your mother, she was adamant that she wanted to push the divorce early. And for a long time, I never understood why and so it was always just her bluffing, just the fights you must have overheard every night. But then one day, when she was asleep, her phone continued to ring and I looked over," he paused, taking a breath as though it had been the first time he'd been telling his story. "It was the night I found out she'd been cheating on me.

"I didn't bring it up to her until after you had gone to school. And that night I saw a side of her I never knew existed. She was a different person when she was scorned, she began throwing things across the room and I realized as I watched it all play out that I didn't love her anymore. I'd been tolerating her for the sake of you, hoping that maybe if you saw that your parents were still together, you'd feel like there was a sense of family. But that was such a flawed opinion, one that only harmed you. Because sometimes, when two people aren't meant to be together yet decide to stay alongside each other, they tear apart everyone in their path, including the life they share. Sometimes, the best thing for a kid is when their parents realize their paths don't lead to the same destination.

"And so I made up my mind. That night, we called the lawyer in. That was the same night you had that show, I'm not sure if you even remember it." I nodded because I did. There was not a moment of those wretched memories that I let myself forget. "Your mom, however, had her own plans on the side. I tried keeping you here but somehow she had maneuvered the whole divorce to side with her and told me she'd go through court to get legal custody of you under whatever bullshit argument she would have made. And I didn't want to put you through that when you were almost done with high school."

The scoff that left me was unintentional, but it prevented him from speaking further. "You don't get how screwed up you made my life. She made my life hell."

"I'm sorry." There was a genuine look of remorse on his face but it'd been too long for me to ever consider it.

"While you were off living life doing whatever you want, you left me with someone who didn't care if I lived or died. Every night I'd come home to a mess of a house and a drunk woman who was supposed to be my mother on the fucking couch. I was counting down the days until I could move into a college dorm and get the hell away from her." I hadn't realized how much I'd let the weight of the past burden me until the words spewed out my mouth without hesitation. "What a fucked up way to protect your son. And to think I used to think, even despite everything, *you* cared."

"I do, beta." He sat up straighter, his fingers inching towards me before retreating again.

"Save your breath. I just want to know why the house is in my name."

He nodded, slightly dejected, but continued nonetheless. "So after the settlement, there were a lot of demands from your mother and she kept threatening to completely pull you legally into her custody and stage a scene where it'd look as if I had caused harm to her. Like she had gone through falsified domestic abuse. She had the contacts for it, which was her biggest advantage. The costs of the divorce and the move were all adding up and originally, she had the man she cheated with on her side, willing to take on her costs, but halfway through, when he found out she wanted to take you with her, he left her too, leaving all her bills in the air as well.

"He wasn't ready to be a father to a teenage boy, he had adult kids of his own. And so your mother said that as your father I should be expected to pay for your share of life and with that, I was struggling to make ends meet and she suggested that I sell the house. At the time, it seemed like the only option. It was the home I'd made to shelter you in but it turned out to be the one I ruined your childhood in. There didn't seem to be any point in keeping it. And so I agreed.

"But then you moved and I sat in that house and realized it was a mistake. I decided I was going to work hard and pay off all the debts that came upon me because of your mother and keep the house. Not for me, but for you. I wanted you to have it to turn it into what it originally intended to be. *A home.* I wanted you to write a new story here, one where you're happy. Your story. And in that, I conjured up the documents with my lawyer to transfer the house to your name once you had graduated from college."

If I hadn't already had ulterior reasons to be angry, his explanation may have made sense to me. But even despite all of his fabricated care for my life, he still managed to ruin it all the same.

"You have something else on your mind." My father was always someone who could read through the lines on my face. One look and he'd know exactly what I was thinking and it was one of the reasons I always assumed he was the parent who didn't regret bringing me into this world. "Tell me what it is."

I stared at him, hoping I could see his answers as clearly as he could see mine. But to my dismay, he was a mosaic of unknown words. "The letter."

His brows pulled together, calculating through memories I assumed he'd rightfully shelved away for years. "Kaunsa letter?" *Which letter?* The whispered tone of his voice chilled my bones.

"The day we were leaving, I handed you a letter." My father's eyes bulged, a light bulb appearing atop his head. *He remembered.* "I told you to give it to a girl named Sonia." I waited, giving him an opening to confess his mistake but when he made no move to do so, I had nothing stopping me from my accusation. "You never handed it to her."

"What do you mean?" The fact that every syllable of his was laced with confusion did nothing for my rising anger. "I did."

"Don't lie to me. She never got the letter." He opened his mouth to debate but I strongly cut him off. "I met her, *dad.* And she told me she never got the fucking letter. And because of that, the love of my life hasn't spoken to me in eight years." I had risen from my seat, baring my teeth to not say more than I should. However, the pent up emotions had no intentions of keeping themselves suppressed. Pressing two fingers between my forehead, my nostrils flared, attempting to calm the nerves. "I'd been missing her for eight years and she's been hating me thinking I never even loved her."

I hadn't realized when he'd gotten up from the couch and made his way over until his hands pressed against my shoulders. "Son, I promise you. That letter was delivered the night you handed it to me." He sounded sincere and I hadn't known my father to be a liar but was it truly a good idea to trust him when he gave me up so easily? "It was one of the only things you had asked of me after music. I wouldn't have just let it in one ear and out the other." I searched his eyes for any trace of indifference but failed to find it. "I know you may not believe me but trust me this time, please. I've never lied to you, Kartik, and I wouldn't when it means this much to you."

"So then where is it?" This time, it was less accusatory and more fearsome, understanding that perhaps fate had interfered and declared that she never did belong to me. I was just a selfish man who wanted someone who was far beyond perfect and I didn't deserve her. This was the universe's cruel way of dragging me back to reality. And I had no choice but to accept it.

My father shrugged, his hands coming up to his temples, rubbing them in an attempt to release the information. "That night I went to drop off the letter and no one was home. I remember because I tried looking through the windows if I could see any sense of life and even waited there for some time. But whatever was in that letter, I knew it was important and I wanted to hand it to her as soon as possible so I left it in the mailbox." He sighed, his frustration at the situation only building. "I should have waited for her. She came to look for you a few days after it too and when I went to ask her if she got it, she stormed off and didn't hear me." He stood in front of me again, compassion written all across his features. "I'm so sorry."

"It's not your fault," I admitted.

The urge to run right back into Sonia was captivating me inside and out. But I knew it now.

There was no outside force holding me from her.

It was all a big play from the heavens, proving time and time again that I never deserved to have her.

"If I could go back in time," my father's voice rattled me, my limp body falling against the couch again, "I would hand the letter to her." The furniture dipped as he took a spot beside me, hesitating to come any closer with the fear of rejection. "I would make it right."

Shaking my head, I finally met his apologetic gaze, feeling sadness towards my father for the first time in years. We were all just results of the shitty circumstances life had put us through with no way of changing the past. "It's alright, dad."

Despite everything, after today, there were two things I was sure of.

One—My father never gave up his messed up notion of love towards me, thinking this house would have changed if I gave it new meaning. But he failed to understand that there was nothing here for me, his sacrifice amounting to a sheer nothing.

Nonetheless, I'd realized that perhaps I had been too hard on him, undermining all the things he was doing and dealing with when I hadn't been looking.

Perhaps he would one day be deserving of a second chance, one where apologies were not received on deaf ears.

And two—The only girl I had ever truly loved was never mine to begin with.

CHAPTER 56

Sonia

The bedroom floor was covered in his memories, my hands working thoughtlessly to find whatever paper he'd been talking of. I'd taken apart the entire shoebox that held all the remnants of a life I never thought I'd want back and went through each one numerous times. All for the letter he mentioned.

The words had left him so nonchalantly, expecting that I had known exactly what he meant but the moment they were cast into the world, mine shattered.

Grunting, my hands closed around a teddy bear, throwing it across the room.

My body went limp as my back hit the wall, my eyes scanning the way the floor was in shambles.

All the pictures, toys, anything that had to do with a reality where Kartik Sharma was mine was spread all over the room.

Except *the letter.*

Ever since he'd mentioned it, it had been the only thing running through my mind, searching for any possibility that I may have missed it. Hoping this was my mistake that could be reversed.

But, unfortunately, life was never that easy.

My fingers landed on the polaroid photo, the one that was a mirror image of the tattoo he'd had on his arm. Except in this version, he was the one holding the guitar.

God, my soul ached to be freed from the torment. It began feeling as though whatever I'd been feeling for all this time was falsified, tampered with like it was some cruel joke.

Like we'd never been just two kids who found solace within one another.

Whatever the case, I knew there was no turning back now. It was cemented into the world, that perhaps we'd been wishing for a fairytale that should have never existed in the first place.

It didn't matter how many memories we'd gotten scarred onto our skin, we were never meant to be one.

A lone tear fell onto my hand and I followed its path until it slipped off onto the hardwood, spreading into a tiny puddle of its own.

It'd been years since I had been surrounded by these memories, all the emotions threatening to flow through. For the first time in eight years, I allowed myself to be upset again.

Upset about the silence.

Upset about losing Kartik.

Upset about loving him.

Without a second thought, my hands reached for the instrument that I had settled still inside the closet. The one that I was unsure if he even remembered.

How couldn't he?

He had it permanently marked on his soft skin, coloring it with reminders of a relationship we were both delusional to think existed.

Sliding the strap across my shoulders, I shuddered. Suddenly, I was sixteen years old, sitting in a pastel pink room with the dreamy broody boy sitting across from me, a lopsided grin on his perfectly sculpted face.

My fingers began strumming with a mind of their own, playing the tunes of all the songs he'd taught me. I could feel his hands on mine, his body against mine, moving in rhythm to play the most perfect melodies; all the songs ripping bandages off old wounds.

It took two whole songs for the realization to set in.

I wasn't in my childhood bedroom with the boy I snuck in anymore.

I was now on the floor of my all white apartment, covered in a lifetime supply of hurt in physical manifestations without the boy I loved.

I was alone.

CHAPTER 57

Sonia

" Hi ma," I said as she slid open the door. I couldn't wallow by myself any longer, making the conscious decision to head over to the only person who would understand.

"Sonu!" Immediately pulling me into her, she wrapped her arms around my shoulders, holding me tight as if she hadn't just seen me a couple days ago. "Kya hua?" *What happened?*

Walking into the corridor, a chuckle escaped my lips. "What? Your daughter can't ever just want to see you?"

"Na." My mother's laughter was magical, almost medicinal to any injured. Without fail, a smile peered upon my face, making me forget all the pain I was subjected to for just a brief moment. But in that small moment, she was watching me intently, waiting. "Tell me what's wrong."

Slouching onto the kitchen stool, my elbows sat against the marble island, my head resting against my palms.

A worried look passed against my mother's face, her emotions attempting to remain hidden until I had spoken. But she was always an animated woman, wearing her emotions so heavily on her sleeves, her expressions giving away everything her words refused to.

"Ma, chill. I'm not dying." My smile fell flat against her growing saddened face.

"Aisa mazak bhi nahi karna." *Don't joke about that.* She took the seat beside me, her soft hands grabbing onto my arm, immediately comforting me. "Now tell me, what's bothering you?"

"Kartik."

Panic flooded through me as she briefly stiffened against me, my brows pulling in as she straightened in her chair. "I told you to be careful with him, Sonu."

Something wasn't right.

"Ma, what's wrong?" I was fully facing her, watching as her face contorted into an emotion I couldn't place. Slightly shaking her head, her lips moved into an uncomfortable smile, my heart thumping in warning.

"I just warned you when you first told me he had come back." My mother brought her hand to my head, resting against my cheek reminding me I was still her little girl. It was the safest place to be, in her embrace, knowing she was there to protect me. "I just knew he'd hurt you again. I didn't want that."

How was I to tell her that this time it wasn't necessarily him that hurt me? It was the situation.

"Mom." Releasing a breath, I focused onto the words I knew I'd have to push through. "Technically, it's not really something he did." Lines formed against her forehead, questions lacing on the tip of her tongue. But she continued watching me, wanting to hear manifested in my voice. "I've been seeing him recently."

"Sonu—" The disappointment coursed through her voice but I couldn't help focus on the way her features continuously gave off a feeling I couldn't figure out.

"No, ma, wait." A heavy breath left me, with it, the weight of all the sadness leaving as well. "It's just something he said."

"Tell me everything."

Taking my time, I filled her in on the past few months, spilling every moment he'd shown up unannounced and every mistaken night we'd spent with one another pretending there was no malice between us. Although, I couldn't find myself being able to rehash those buried feelings that I refused to resurface, but I knew I didn't have to. It was telling from the way I spoke about him.

My words halted as soon as the reminders of our last conversation settled in, the struggle of finding exactly how to cope with it overtaking me. "There was something he said this morning that I still don't understand."

"What was it?" My mother clutched my arms in anticipation.

"Do you remember that day when he called me continuously? You suggested that I might not know the whole story." The world slowed, her nods seeming to take longer than usual. "You might have been right." There was a trace of fear on her face, and I failed to understand whether it was towards me or the circumstances. But whatever it was, it didn't fail to make the air between us turn to a cold chill. "He mentioned a letter, ma. He kept saying that I didn't get his letter." My cupped palms held my head as I sighed into them, her hand releasing me suddenly. "I don't even know what letter he's talking about or if there even was a letter." It was eerily quiet as the revelation was now in the air.

Peeking through my fingers, my mother's shocked face did enough to cause my heart to crash against the floor.

"Ma?"

As if she'd seen a ghost, her eyes shuffled around the room, struggling to find something to focus on. "I knew this day would come."

She rose from her chair, my voice falling against her back as she disappeared into her bedroom.

What the hell was happening?

She'd been gone a minute, the sound of shuffling taking over in the place of her. She walked out, her hands clutched against her chest, an apologetic look deep within her eyes. "Ma, what's going on?"

"I know you're probably going to be angry with me." My breath had stopped in my throat as she placed an envelope onto the marble beside us, my name scribbled onto it the same sloppy handwriting I spent years staring at. "But you have to understand, Sonu, you were sixteen years old. You had your whole life in front of you. And you were throwing all that away for a boy."

"Mom, what is this?" The moment the question left me, I already knew its answer. My hands shot up to my mouth, eyes welling with tears. "Oh my God."

Hesitantly, she sat back down, guilt written all over her. "I never thought he would be back, you know. And he wasn't. But it was my mistake, fully." Trembling, my fingers traced the outline of the envelope. "I didn't open it. I didn't read it. But I knew one day I would have to show you."

The flood of emotions pouring through me didn't allow for it to settle anywhere.

Was I mad? Hurt? Betrayed?

Or was I relieved?

"Why do you have this, ma?"

A saddened sound left her, her shoulders falling along with my years' long resentment. "That day, you were still in school and I had just gotten home." Stuttering her words, she continued, "And the mailbox seemed to have an envelope sitting inside. I don't know how it got there, who dropped it off, but it had your name on it as well as his in the corner." Her soft hands pressed atop mine, a mix of feelings muddling to the surface. "And I was your mother. I know that doesn't justify it. But you were sixteen and I was your mother. You had a long life ahead of you and there's a lot of times where young love like this leaves you ruined rather than fulfilled. I didn't want that life for you. You'd already lost your brother, I couldn't put you through the pain of losing a boy who was only looking for fun."

"Ma, he wasn't just a boy." It felt like we were reliving the day she'd walked in on us, my heart being torn from within me for the hundredth time.

"Ab mujhe pata hai." *I know now.* Her gaze was now locked onto the letter under my fingers, filled with all the answers to the questions that piled up for eight years. "And I wanted to give it to you eventually but by the time I thought I could, it was too late. It didn't seem like there was much reason to. When he left, I thought you would soon get over him, and I was so wrong. I thought you were just infatuated by the boy but God, I was the cause of my daughter's despair. My motherly heart could not handle it if you hated me for keeping it. So I selfishly never showed it to you. And then you got over him and I thought why dig through old memories and rehash something that was better left shut.

"This is all my fault. I should have said something when you said he was back." She was profusely shaking her head, as if the guilt was clawing through her. "I should have been honest with you. But I was so worried he would hurt you again. Never did I realize how wrong I was. How *I* was the one hurting you instead."

If I was sixteen, I would have been mad at her.

I would have settled upon the silent treatment and went about my days.

But I was twenty four, no longer a child.

I could try to put myself in her shoes and understand, even while it was hurting me all the same.

This was my mother, the one woman who never wished ill towards me, the woman who would pick me up whenever I was down.

No matter how hurt I'd felt, I couldn't find myself to be completely furious towards her. Half of it was my fault in the end.

Even when I hadn't received the letter, I gave up on Kartik. I stopped reaching out. I stopped trying. And he did too.

She was just being my mother but the love we claimed to have should have been bigger than it all. So was it really fair to put all the blame on her when all she wanted was to protect her daughter?

"Ma." Her apologetic eyes locked on me and I could feel my soul tearing as I watched her overcome with regret. Her mouth opened to speak, closing as my hand shot up. "I get why you did what you did. I won't lie and say I'm not hurt. I am. But I can also try to understand." The thumping of my heart filled the silence, the paper warming my palms from underneath. "I just wish I knew there was a letter. If I had known." My words trailed into the air as I allowed myself to stare at the secret of my past, debating whether it was even worth it anymore.

"Khol do." *Open it.* My mother could always read my thoughts with just a glance at my face. "It's been too long. You deserve to know what was in there, no matter how late it's become." Without another word, she walked out of the kitchen, her steps rushed as if she'd taken the grief with her.

Releasing the breath I'd been holding, my fingers lifted the corners of the fold, peeling it back until it had opened. There it was.

The sloppy penmanship never failed to twist the corners of my mouth, the familiarity piercing like a million needles.

Blinking my vision to focus, I began reading.

My Shona,

I'm sorry.

One, I'm leaving you with just a letter.

And two, I'm leaving.

I'm a coward. I don't think I could have done this if I was looking at you because I know the moment your beautiful face would contort into sadness and your eyes would shed tears, my whole heart would shatter. My parents are getting divorced. And I have to go with my mom. I tried so hard to convince them to let me stay but it was of no use. They're making me leave. And I'm so angry.

When I first moved here almost four years ago, I never thought I'd ever have an attachment to this bland city. I never thought I'd want to stay. There was never anything here for me.

Until I met you.

Shona, the day I met you was the best day of my life. You've changed my world, you've made me a man. You taught me to stop running and appreciate every moment. You made me believe there was more to life than just becoming something.

You've made me believe in love.

Two days ago, you said you loved me. Not to me, but to your mom. And it felt so good but I knew I'd be so selfish if I were to say it back. I knew I needed to leave. The day was coming faster than I could even process. But now, I'm wishing I hadn't. I wish I held your hand while your mom accused us of being just another high school fling. I wish I held you while you were crying. Fuck, I wish I was with you in those pink blankets right now.

I wish I had been the selfish man I wanted to be when it came to you.

I don't know how long it's going to have been by the time this letter gets to you. I'm going to give it to my dad, hoping he'll do this one thing for me. For some reason, I want to trust he will. He's always been the one who at least tried to be a parent. I know you might hate me for leaving without saying anything, I know you'll hate that I'm writing a letter. You may even try and find me, you're just so resilient and stubborn like that. But I'm moving to Chicago with my mom.

I know she's going to want to tie me down, to hold me til I break, but I won't let that happen.

I'm going to come back for you. I promise.

She's gonna expect me to fall at her feet, and if I had been alone, I would have. But shona, you've become my only purpose in life, my true destination. You've taught me what it means to love. You've taught me what it means to let someone in. You've been the best tutor, not only in math but also in life, and in everything surrounding it.

Please, when you get this, if you can forgive me for leaving, write to me, text me, call me. I'll leave you with my address on the envelope. Just because there's distance between us doesn't mean I want to lose you. I can't lose you Sonia Desai. But if you don't write to me, if you can't forgive me, I'll understand. In that case, I'll just thank you for showing me the best five months of my life. You've become my muse, every song I've written is about you. You are my biggest dream come true.

I hope one day, you can forgive me and our time will align. I hope I get to kiss you again. I hope I get to hold you like you're mine again.

I love you, my pretty girl.

Yours forever,

Kartik

Sucking in a breath, a drop of water fell into the pool of tears that had gathered onto the table. As I held the piece of paper against my chest, only two thoughts repeatedly played through my head, everything I believed being challenged.

Kartik never really left me.

And Kartik always loved me.

CHAPTER 58
Kartik

It was almost as if my mind worked on auto pilot, automatically remembering every chord and strum on a guitar I hadn't touched in years. Although my favorite guitar was somewhere lost amongst her memories, I bought my own as soon as I turned eighteen. Back when I had first left, I tried continuing the craft, but the passion slowly left when everything I wrote, everything I played, reminded me of her. Everything I did was strung in the memory of her. The girl who never forgave me for leaving.

Or so I thought.

For so long, I'd been assuming she hadn't believed my words, but I've only now realized that they never reached her in the first place. They were foreign to her, unreal and nonexistent, fleeting like a quick memory of what could have been.

It was the biggest *fuck you* delivered straight from the world.

My fingers swelled as I began strumming *Look After You* by The Fray, my heart shrinking as the words left my lips with its melody.

It wasn't until the entirety of the song was over that my ears caught onto the violent buzzing coming from my phone. Turning it over, the message almost yanked the world from under my feet.

*

"Your cafe latte, sir." I smiled at the waiter as he placed the white ceramic mug in front of me before walking away. However, my eyes continued to peer through the window, willing her to come.

"Watching the sidewalk isn't going to make her come here faster," I whispered to myself, staring at the brown liquid swirling in the cup. The scent of the coffee overtook me as I let myself indulge in it, trying to distract my mind from the nervousness.

"Kartik?"

Glancing up, a woman I knew far too well awkwardly smiled, standing directly in front of me like a ghost. "Aunty." As I stood from the seat, Sonia's mother closed the distance, wrapping her arms around my body like it was second nature. For a moment, I stood in her embrace like a statue, unaware of what to do, before finally deciding to return her embrace. Although the only memory of her I had was in relation to the day my life fell apart, I could tell she hadn't aged a day.

She was still radiating, a mirror image of her daughter, skin as clear as water.

She seemed to battle with a dilemma, her turmoil so evidently written across the delicate features of her face. "Do you want me to get you anything?" Startled, Sonia's mom removed herself from her thoughts, her smile widening a bit before shaking her head. "Please, let me get you something."

Taking a seat, she agreed. "Okay, just a chai is fine." Quickly rushing towards the counter, I placed the new order before settling across from the woman I hadn't seen in years.

There was something oddly comforting about her presence, the warmth encompassing me with every passing second. Even after getting comfortable, however, her hands continued to fidget, her foot bouncing beneath the table, slightly shaking the ground beneath us. "Aunty, is something wrong?"

"Kartik, there's a reason I needed to talk to you."

Something was definitely wrong, a hollowness appearing deep within my chest. "Is Sonia okay? Did something happen to her?"

"No, no!" She immediately looked up, her eyes widening as she witnessed the panic escaping me. "Nothing like that."

"Then what?" The beating against my chest heightened at her dragged silence.

Before she could answer, the same waiter from before had placed a cup on her side of the table, flashing her a grin before walking away. She wrapped her fingers around the heated mug, never lifting it from the wooden table. Her downcast eyes constantly found new things to focus on, shifting from the cup to the napkin holder to the little drop of coffee that dripped alongside the handle. "You've grown so much, Kartik. It's really good to see you."

I couldn't shake the ill feeling that was building within my stomach, a nauseousness making its way through me.

She took a large breath, still refusing to let her sight focus anywhere but the drinks on the table. "I wanted to apologize."

"There's no need, aunty." The reality of the situation was finally clear. We would have never lasted. "Whatever happened was for the best," I admitted, solemnly.

"Let me finish, Kartik." She seemed distraught, my lips clasping shut as she recouped. "Eight years ago, I made a mistake. It's one that has taunted me every day, reminding me of what I had done and how wrongly I've acted."

My elbows rested against the table, my attention fully engrossed in her words. "What mistake?" It was as though a bubble had dropped over us, shielding us from any outside noise or distraction.

"Before I get into all that, I need to know something, Kartik. Sach kaho ge?" *Will you be honest with me?* Sonia's mom looked almost identical to her daughter, mirroring exactly the same expression she wore when she was frightened.

"Of course, aunty. What is it?"

"Why my daughter? It's been eight years of not talking. I saw her fall apart in my arms for years before she had learned to be okay without you. But I can see now that she was faking it all. It was all for show, her steps ahead, because she's still stuck there. So I need to know now, Kartik, why my daughter?"

With the memory of the first tutoring session in my head, my smile exponentially grew. "You know, aunty, the first day I met her, I actually bumped into her in the hallway. In high school, everyone always huddled around me, wanted to talk to me, never just wanted to be *my* friend. They only wanted to befriend the popularity I brought. And they made it quite obvious in the way they acted around me." A shudder traveled from my head to toes as the slightly pained version of Kartik Sharma before Sonia Desai showed itself. "Sonia wasn't like that.

"She didn't care that I was the most known kid, she didn't care that other girls wanted me, she didn't care that they all wanted to be in my life. For all my life, I felt like I was just a thing everyone wanted to acquire, like I was some kind of trophy that everyone was trying to win. She made me feel human. She listened to me when I spoke, she understood me when I was sad and she never stepped back from calling me out on my shit.

"Sonia changed my life, aunty. Ever since I was a child, I felt like I was a pawn in my parents' lives, just a tool they used for leverage against each other but Sonia never made me feel like I was any less than her. And God knows, she's the most divine woman in this world, no one could amount to her."

By the time I'd finished speaking, her dark auburn eyes had been lined in water. "She really is special." Her agreement did nothing to calm me, instead, raising the trepidation within my soul. "I just feel so guilty."

My hands reached over towards hers, covering them to minimize the tapping. She instantly relaxed under my hold, her eyes peering up towards me. From this angle, she looked tired, whatever secret she had kept visibly holding her down. "For what, aunty? I understand what you did that night. I get it. Any parent would have been angry to see a boy in their daughter's room. It's not your fault. Instead, I didn't try hard enough to prove to you and to Sonia's father that I wasn't just messing around, that I loved Sonia with all my heart." Sighing, I found myself unable to meet her vision anymore, the disappointment of the reality settling in. "That I'll always love her. Even when she doesn't love me."

A drop of water fell against my knuckles and it wasn't until then that I'd realized she was crying.

This wasn't how I imagined my first conversation with the mother of the woman I loved would be. I never wanted to be here, grieving, but instead, celebrating.

"Kartik, I'm so sorry." Her voice came out frantic, rushing to build sentences as her mind struggled to focus on one thought. "Sonia loved you too much and I was an inconsiderate parent. I thought I was doing the right thing keeping you two apart but it seems maine dono ki zindagi ke sath khela hai." *I've played with both of your lives.* My body knew the words she would speak before they were ever manifested into the world, my palms immediately turning cold from her touch. "The letter you wrote to her was in my mailbox and I was so angry with her and with you and I thought she was straying from her purpose. I thought you were her biggest distraction. I was so wrong, Kartik, beta, and in the end I was the one who caused you so much pain."

If I had been holding the coffee mug, it would have slammed to the ground, shattering with every preconceived notion I'd arrived with.

My father never did wrong by me.

"I thought she would be over it all in a couple months, maybe a year, but now eight years later she still keeps everything that reminds her of you in the corner of her closet. She plays the guitar you left in her room even when I've tried to take it from her. She has never forgotten you and she never will and I kept her from her love for eight years. What kind of horrible mother am I?"

The entire dictionary ceased to exist as I struggled to find the words to say. But my lips were sewn shut, my eyes bulging out of their sockets. My muscles froze, the world around me froze. Everything was frozen.

Nothing made sense anymore.

"Please, just talk to her, Kartik. I gave her the letter already and I'm sure she's read it. Please, allow me to fix this. I'm not asking you to forgive me, I know that's a lot to ask of. But please vada karo, tum use baat karoge." *Promise me, you'll talk to her.* "Just don't give up, please."

How was this possible?

With a hollow chest, my legs prompted me up, the table shaking slightly at the sudden movement. "I have to go aunty."

Refusing to even look at her again, I rushed out the coffee shop with my heart laying somewhere crushed on the ground.

CHAPTER 59

Sonia

The letter was engraved in my brain, each curve of the alphabet visually memorized. I'd read it about a thousand times in the past two weeks, crying harder each time I heard his voice along with it.

For the first week, I attempted to call him, finally making a move first, only to be met with the voice box telling me he was unavailable. Texts went unanswered, calls ignored, and with it, my built up hope had vanished too.

I couldn't find myself to hate my mother for her actions, understanding her position in it all. Perhaps I would never fully comprehend why she did it until I had a child of my own, but she'd never been a woman of malevolence, never wanting bad for me.

She'd been there when I had wanted to disparage into the air and waste away, holding me down and giving me the support I struggled to accept.

My mother had also told me she spoke to Kartik, but due to his silence, I'd convinced myself that he didn't seem to care much.

Maybe our last fight was too much. Maybe I'd given him the impression that I'd given up.

Maybe he simply didn't want this anymore.

This apartment had never felt more empty.

The sun reflected upon the light wooden floors, casting shadows that engulfed me fully. The Stitch plush sat on the edge of my couch, mocking me as my eyes welled up.

Allowing one more glance at my phone, I flipped it over, seeing messages from my friends crowd the home screen.

The group chat with the girls had been blowing up, their concerns over not hearing from me manifesting through the phone. With a reluctant sigh, I avoided opening it, the regret of stepping away from everyone piercing me.

But I should have known that there was no escaping those girls.

They'd been with me through thick and thin, our bond unbreakable.

Within minutes of the last buzz, a banging sounded against the front door, followed by two voices who knew me better than myself.

"Sonia Desai if you don't open this door right now," Jyoti proceeded thumping her fist so loud it could have awoken the neighbors.

"We'll break it down." Addie's soft voice finished the sentence, prompting a chuckle from me.

Those girls would break their bones before even coming close to breaking open a door.

"Sonia, I know you're in there!" I rushed to the door as Jyoti's voice got louder, the sound causing a rumble under my feet.

"Okay okay! Ek second." *One second.* Clicking the lock open, the girls pushed inside, anger latching onto their faces. "Jeez, no need to wake up the entire floor."

"Sonia Desai, why the hell are you ignoring our texts?" Jyoti had her fists pressed against her waist, exactly reminiscent of an image of a scolding parent.

"My whole government?" Scrambling to wipe the apartment clean, I began shuffling towards the couch. "I was busy."

"Yeah, we can see that." Addie was the exact counter of Jyoti with her hushed voice. She'd been here before, locking herself in her apartment while crying profusely over a boy. And just like today, Jyoti and I had barged in to pull her out.

That's why I knew this was an intervention.

"Guys, I really don't have the energy for this today." Holding the letter tight against my body, I managed to turn, their curious faces observing.

"Sonia, tell us what's going on?" Addie placed her palm softly onto my forearm, her eyes softening at the pain I was sure was visibly written all over my skin. "What is that?" Sliding the paper through my fingers, she turned it over, her eyes skimming through the words. Jyoti came over her shoulder and I could practically hear each syllable in my head as they read.

"You guys helped me when I was like this." She looked up from the paper that had all the confessions of a teenage boy written all over it. Her smile grew wider, more fonder, while folding the paper neatly as she walked over and placed it on the kitchen counter. "Now tell us what happened. Where did this letter come from? I thought you guys would have worked out your issues after the party, seeing how close you were when you left, but it seems that things have just turned messy."

Plopping onto the kitchen stool, I stared at my two women who continued to look at me expectantly. These were the girls who had vowed to never leave my side, the two girls who proved time and time again that although we didn't share the same blood, they were my sisters.

"My mom had it." Jyoti was now fully invested, her eyes almost popping out of her head. "Eight years ago, he left me a letter that I never got. Ma told me just two weeks ago that it was left in the mailbox and she kept it from me because she thought we were just kids who would be nothing but a distraction to each other."

"Aunty really pulled the Bollywood mother move, huh?" Jyoti perched up on her chair, her jaw dropping with the revelation. "Wait, but then why did she wait so long to show you?"

My shoulders dropped in a shrug, still unsure of the definite answer to that.

"She probably was just being a protective mom." Addie threw an arm around my shoulders, instantly soothing me. "Listen, whatever happened, happened. There's no point in dwelling in it anymore. Learn from me Sonia. When I lost Jaymin, it felt like my whole world went awry, like there was nothing for me if he wasn't there. And mind you, I only knew him for less than a year." I met her gaze, understanding exactly what she meant. "But you have history. Almost nine years of it."

"I tried, guys. I really did but he's not responding to me. There's nothing I can do anymore. I can't force him to talk to me." I alternated between them, observing both of their empathetic features as they took on my pain like it was theirs to harbor. "I'm not even mad at my mom. She told me she spoke to him about it too but ever since then, he hasn't said a word. He hasn't replied to anything nor has he returned any of my calls." I groaned, my head falling into my palms in frustration. "What if he doesn't want me anymore?"

"Oh shut it, Sonia." Jyoti placed both her hands on my cheeks, keeping my face steady towards her. "Listen to me loud and clear right now. If any man makes you feel unwanted he's a fucking fool. He'd be stupid to let you go right now. Especially after knowing how everything happened. You are possibly one of the most beautiful women he'd ever come in contact with and don't you ever forget it."

"I know, I know."

"You won't understand, Jyoti." Addie was smirking, her head shaking in disbelief. "When a man comes and flips your entire world around, you'll get it."

A bitter sound immediately left her, my mood positively changing in no time. "Yeah right. I would never let a man barge into my life and shake it off its surface."

"Just wait and see." Addie's hand extended for a high five and I met her halfway, holding onto her like the anchor she'd always been.

It felt good to finally let go of the position I'd always held as the *mom friend* and let them come cheer me up instead. The importance they'd give me held no candle to anyone else. They were the ones I'd always run to, always putting my hope in the fact that they'd be here for me.

Addie and Jyoti continued bickering regarding their opinions on how boys shaped our hearts, Jyoti promising to never fall into the patterns we had. "Why do you have that creepy smile on your face?" Jyoti halted her argument to glare at me in concern laced with fear.

"I'm just extremely thankful for you guys." Without another word, they both came across the kitchen island, pulling me into a huddle between them. "Guys stop, I'll cry."

"No more crying." Addie pulled away first, her eyes scanning my skin. "You already look so washed out. Kitni sukhi ho gayi." *You've become so dried out.* Rolling my eyes, I shoved her slightly although I knew she was right. I'd been non stop sobbing and even at the school, when people noticed, I'd equated the appearance to pollen allergies. "Really though, I want to ask something." Raising my brows, I waited, Jyoti holding on with anticipation as well. "How do you feel about him?"

It finally felt like the time to admit it, wanting to let the world do right by me. "I love him. I always have."

As if on cue, the doorbell rang, my body freezing on command.

After sharing a few looks, Addie treaded towards the door, opening it slowly as though an intruder could have walked in. Although the wood hid the other side, Addie bent down, picking something from the ground and made her way over.

Placing a box of Ferrero Rocher, my favorite chocolates, onto the counter, she grinned with all her might. "There's no name on it but maybe it's a sign that things might just work out."

CHAPTER 60
Kartik

Jenna brought out the drinks as usual, placing them onto the coasters of Bailey's, offering a sympathetic smile as if she could sense the tension around us. Even in the crowded bar, the air was eerily sad.

Kyle and Jaymin both remained silent, their stares raising goosebumps all across my body. "Ask." The bitter taste of the beer followed a trail down my throat, coating it to prepare for the plethora of questions I knew was coming.

That was the side of a friendship I'd missed.

Having people who cared enough to stand by your side and help you through the difficult parts of life.

It was also the only reason I agreed to meet them, knowing Addie had probably told her boyfriend everything she'd found out from the girl who stole my heart. Because there was no way Sonia hadn't opened up to her friends.

"What the hell is going on between you and Sonia?" Jaymin spoke first, Kyle patting his shoulder in encouragement.

"Nothing."

"Nuh uh." Kyle interrupted. "Don't give us that bullshit. I dealt with it enough when Jaymin over here was brooding over Addie. Get to the main point."

I couldn't help but chuckle, the casualty of the men always catching me by surprise. They both gulped through half their drinks, silently waiting in anticipation.

"Fine," I agreed. "It's just screwed up, man. We just found out there was a big misunderstanding between us that neither of us saw coming and it's just fucked with us. I thought we were good until I realized we never were."

"The hell does that mean?" Jaymin prompted, his hand shooting up to signal towards Jenna. "Listen, Kartik, when the heart is involved, you have to tread carefully. There's so many things that could go wrong especially when you refuse to back down."

"Look at my boy speaking true wisdom." Kyle chuckled at Jaymin's stern look, both of them relaxing me for the first time in days. I'd been so holed up about it all, the acknowledgment of all the pieces falling in place shaking me off my balance. "What?"

Jaymin smacked his chest before bringing his attention back towards me. "What actually happened? And get into the whole situation."

Summarizing the events of the past two weeks, I recounted every excruciating detail of my pain, masking it with a grin on my face. By the time I'd finished, we'd all downed two glasses of beer, waiting on a third to get to us and a boat full of fresh french fries.

"Damn." Kyle was the first to speak. "You both got yourself in some deep shit." He was moving his head in disappointment while reaching for the food between us.

"So have you talked to Sonia again?"

I shook my head, unable to meet his gaze. "She called and texted but I just couldn't do it then. It was still too fresh. Once her mom told me about the letter, it was like nothing made sense anymore. Before it, I convinced myself that we were just not meant to be, our story falling towards some sort of tragedy."

"Like Veer Zara?" Kyle's loud white accented words caused Jaymin and I to lock eyes, laughing in surprise. "What? I've been watching some bollywood movies."

"No, definitely not as dramatic as that," I said through my laughs. After we'd calmed down, I began again. "It just seemed so final, you know. Like we walked away from each other assuming we weren't good for one another, our hatred spewing every time we spoke. Like we would only argue and fight and in that, there would be no time for love. But after Sonia's mom came forward, I didn't know what to think. But then I realized while I needed the time, Sonia needed a talk. We never aligned, we never landed on the same page of the story. And then she stopped calling and texting after a week, which I don't blame her for. But even then, yesterday, I couldn't resist sending her favorite chocolates to her door hoping she'd call me again." Jaymin and Kyle had both been frozen, unmoving, the sight enticing discomfort. "What?"

Jaymin's lips curved as the words slipped through his lips. "You said love. Do you love her?"

"So much," I finally admitted. "I've loved her since the day I met her."

"You loved her since day one so why didn't you ever try to reach out to her or find her despite not hearing from her?"

It was a question I'd contemplated the answer to for years now. "I'm not really sure. I guess part of me wanted to let her make that decision. Part of me wanted her to choose me.

But I never realized that I had been the one to walk away." Empathetic smirks manifested on both their faces. "Even then, a year later, I tried texting her only to be met with a changed number. Plus everything with my mom, she'd made my life a walking hell. I never intended to stay away for so long. But for some reason seeing that she never replied ended up dragging me away. It was this fear of rejection, of knowing that if I was back, she might not even want me when I'd been so busy wishing for her."

"You've got to hop out of this delusion." Kyle chimed in, his palm hitting the table with a thud. "You literally know she wants you, and yet you're just both being so stubborn."

Jaymin grinned, nodding his head in agreement. "Yup, Kyle's seen it happen with me. You're better off not wasting any more time Kartik."

They were right.

I was simply scared.

But that was the definition of love.

Love was supposed to scare you, it was meant to make you feel like you'd handed the controls of your life to someone else, trusting them to keep you safe. And it wasn't even a question anymore. Sonia *was* my safe place.

She meticulously crafted me into the man I was today. The man who would do anything to finally let himself go in the name of love.

With one last gulp, I consumed the entirety of the rest of my beer, slamming it onto the wood while dialing a number onto my phone. "I'm gonna get my girl."

CHAPTER 61

Sonia

"What the hell is going on here?" The door to my mother's house had swung open, revealing an entire guest list of our friends. Jaymin and Addie were cuddled up in the corner, standing beside Kyle and Jenna while Jyoti stood beside my mother, urging me through the door. "Why is everyone here?" My brows pulled together, slowly stepping into the house to steer clear of any sign of an ongoing intervention.

"Shh." Jyoti latched onto my wrist pulling me into the house further as my mom shut the door behind me. "It's been seven days since we've seen you and we didn't want you to rot away in your bedroom playing that damn guitar. So we thought why not all of us just get together and have fun. Get your mind off things."

They'd all been staring expectantly, mimicking a scene from a horror movie.

It was slightly frightening.

It didn't help that as they stood as statues, the thunder crackled above them, adding to the eerie feeling.

"You guys are really freaking me out." My gaze traveled from person to person, trying to understand what exactly was going on through their robotic minds. "You sure you're not all going to kill me or?" All they did was continue to grin. "Something smells fishy."

"That might just be the Tandoori Salmon in the kitchen." My mother sidled up beside me, her joke making the entire room rumble in giggles. "Sonu, can you come to the kitchen with me really quick?"

Nodding, I followed her steps through the hallway, leaving everyone to watch Zindagi Na Milegi Dobara on the television.

"What's up, ma?" She began frantically pulling out plates from the cupboard, piling them up one after the other on the counter. Wordlessly making my way over, I began helping her arrange the cutlery for the guests.

"I just wanted to apologize again, Sonu."

With a *tsk* sound, I halted my motions, making sure to face her. "Ma—"

"Nahi, bolne do." *No, let me speak.* She sighed, placing a warm palm to rest against my cheek. "I may be your mother but that should never give me the right to mess with your life in the way that I did. I can never take what I did back but I just hope you have it in you to forgive me someday."

"Ma, I already forgive you." My hands shot up to her wrist, holding her there, soaking in the warmth of her skin.

"No," she shook her head immediately. "Not yet." Pulling my brows in, I attempted to read her face for any hint of her insinuation. "When I had taken that letter, I didn't intend to put you in an eight years' worth of pain. I thought I was being a good parent, keeping you focused on things that really mattered. But what I didn't come to terms with was that sometimes parents can mess up too. I hurt your right here," her finger pointed to the left side of my chest, "your heart. Which no one has the right to do. In the end, it is your life and I should have talked to you first before doing anything. I'm sorry for taking your choice away from you."

Pulling her into me, I wrapped my arms around my mother, wishing I could peel the guilt away from her.

I was no longer mad, no longer upset. I understood that sometimes, although it may not make you happy, certain things were meant to happen so that you could learn from them. But they never intended to stay.

I guess Kartik was just that. A mirage of fleeting moments that were never required to last long.

The doorbell rang loud through the corridor and my mother pulled away instantly, brushing a hand over both mine and her cheeks to wipe away any traces of tears. "Can you go get the door?" She carried the rest of the plates to the dining table, setting them down one at a time.

I nodded, strolling towards the door, still looking over my shoulder. "Were you expecting someone else?" The entire room went suddenly silent as I clicked the lock, exposing the only person that could cause me to collapse.

"Hi." Kartik stood before me, water droplets dripping down his jacket under the storm. His hair was floppy against his head, streams of liquid carving paths down his sharp face. No longer in his signature leather jacket, a black windbreaker hung from his arms loosely, coupled with black jeans and boots that still made him look deadly.

Even without seeing him for three weeks, he was still the most handsome man I'd ever laid my sights on.

"Shona?" His worried voice shook me out of my admiration, confirming that he was really standing in front of me.

Snapping back to reality, I hadn't realized I was gawking at him, an embarrassed smile making its way through. "Wha-" My eyes roamed anywhere but on him. "What are you doing here?" My brain refused to function, going numb at the sheer sight of him.

"I needed to talk to you." The lopsided grin he wore melted all coherent words from my mind, the only thing left for me to do was nod. "You look stunning, first of all. Yellow was always your color." I looked down at my sundress covered in daisies in an attempt to see what he was seeing, the memories of his words distantly playing in my head. We couldn't have been more different.

"Thank you," I managed, my voice still quiet. The only sound between us was the trickling of rain falling against the ground. It didn't miss me how the entire house had gone silent, everyone holding their breaths in response. Shuffling on my feet, my hand latched onto the doorknob tighter, willing him to speak. "Is that all?" My throat ached as it attempted to swallow dry gulps of air through the nervousness.

Kartik let out a breath before finally parting his lips, letting his thoughts take over. "You know, before I came here, I had a whole speech prepared. I knew exactly what I would say when you'd open the door and I'd even rehearsed it in front of the mirror a couple times. But here I am dumbfounded as always in your presence because beauty like yours deserves to be cherished and worshiped and fully attended towards. God, you look more exquisite every time I look at you"

My weight had entirely been shifted onto the door, hoping it'd be steady enough to hold me if my knees buckled.

Kartik took a step further, now only a foot away, my neck craning to watch him. The raindrops bounced off of him and made their way against my lids, drenching me in everything that had his name on it. "Shona, the day I left you was the worst day of my life. I don't care how many awful things have happened after, but nothing brought me the pain that losing you did. And look at the sick joke the world played on us. Because at the end of the day, what neither of us believed seemed to be proven true. At the end of the day, all we needed to do was talk to each other and we would've understood it.

"But being stubborn played a heavy hand on my life. I've never been one to back down, never one to just follow where I'm led. But if that's what you want, I'll happily tie a leash around my neck and place it in your hands. I'm not a good man and I'm not perfect, shona, and I don't think I ever will be. But what I do know is that *you're* perfect for me. I tried so hard these past three weeks to just leave you alone, to give you the space, but my heart won. I was readying myself to leave you alone, because being with me wouldn't be beneficial to you. I've done nothing but bring you pain, I've done nothing to even show you what you mean to me. But my stupid heart won't stop being selfish over you.

"I don't care if there have been eight years of distance between us. Because eight years is nothing compared to the rest of our lives. Which is why I'm here."

The ground beneath my feet shook with the force of thunder, my eyes blinking away the stray water drops that reached the entrance. "Kartik." His name tasted like chocolate the way it sweetly slipped between my lips.

"Sonia Desai, from the moment you walked into my life, you've given me a purpose to live. You've brought light to my darkness, illuminating every place you go. You've shown me time and time again that it doesn't matter if the cards you've been dealt are horrendous, there will always be someone to hold your hand through it all. Someone to make it all worth it.

"It's you, shona. You're the reason I live today. Your name is engraved in my soul and it doesn't matter how far life pulls us apart, I'll always crawl back to you. And even if you hate me right now, I'll accept it. I know I don't deserve you but having anything from you is better than nothing. Just allow me to be a part of your life while you hate me, baby.

"Because I love you, shona. I did eight years ago when I selfishly walked away without telling you. And I do now, standing here in the rain begging you to let me in again. I'll even get on my knees if that's what you need. And if you don't want me now, I'll wait as long as you want. I'd wait forever."

Every inch of me froze as he closed the distance between us, his cold hands coming around my neck, pushing it higher to meet his pleading black eyes.

"I love you."

CHAPTER 62
Kartik

She hadn't moved an inch. I was too late.

There were no emotions to be seen, her poker face stabbing me continuously, my heart contorting within seconds.

I was an idiot.

Disappointed, my arms fell to my sides, my feet shuffling backwards.

How could I expect her to simply fall into me after leaving her once again, albeit only for three weeks. But with us, every day mattered. Every minute of every hour mattered.

And I may have teetered the line between forever and never too often.

Sonia didn't owe me anything, she didn't need to say anything.

I knew it from the start. She was too good for me.

My soul crushed as I took another step back, the rain meddling with the water building behind my pupils. But I couldn't manage to turn away from her. I needed to look at her, needed to memorize her every feature so that I could live with the memory of her for the rest of my life.

But it was too painful standing there amongst all her loved ones, clawing at the remains of my heart and placing them in her doorway.

My face dropped, focusing on the cemented ground while my feet prepared to make their exit, only to be halted by the voice of my savior. "Kartik." My head immediately snapped up, spotting Sonia now standing out in the rain just mere inches away. The storm quickly soaked her, her beautiful blonde locks turning ashy and disheveled as they framed her shoulders. "You're leaving? You didn't even let me respond."

Scrambling to hold her, my palms clutched her face, my thumbs running circles on her cheeks. Her hands came up to hold onto my wrists, connecting us in more ways than one.

"Eight years, Kartik. You didn't say a word for eight whole years." Although it wasn't visible, the hiccups in her sentences made my chest quench with the realization that she had been crying. "You left me with a letter and although it may have just not been shown to me, it's a piece of paper. Eight years ago I broke apart because you thought it would be best to leave me with a small piece of paper." Her head shook under my hold. "How do I know you won't do that to me again?"

"Baby, I should have been selfish then. I should have stayed by you, by your side, even when I knew you were too good for me and I would only take you down with me. But I should have fought against it all. I should've been a better man, should've told you that I loved you. But I've found you again, shona. And I don't intend to let you go. Not now. Not ever again." Her eyes shut, clasping so tight the tears were now falling from the corners. "I understand if you can't forgive me now but I promise you, I'm not going anywhere. I'm made just for you, and if I can't win you back, I'll die trying."

Angrily, she peered up at me, her hand coming up to cover my mouth, as if the thought of dying had only hurt her further. "Don't say stuff like that." We stayed there, soaking in the weather as if time had stopped just for us. After what felt like five minutes of silence, she spoke timidly. "Okay."

"What?" Surprised, I stared at her, as if everything in my world was falling into place again.

"Okay, Kartik." Her upturned lips soothed me, the possibility of my love igniting once again, contrasting the shivers prompted by the rain between us.

I was clutching her tighter, my fingers tingling like if I had let go, she'd disappear into the sky. "Baby, I'm going to need you to tell me in clear words before I assume what you mean and do something you don't want me to."

The laugh she let out finally brought me peace for the first time in years. Knowing that I could make her laugh like she once did again was more than enough confirmation for me.

"I love you, Kartik Sharma. I never stopped."

Without another wasted second, my lips crashed against hers mixing with the clear salty rainwater that coated them. Her hands wrapped around my neck as I pulled her against me, snaking my hands across her waist, pulling her flesh against me. Even with her skin pressed into me, she still wasn't close enough.

She was mine.

Cheers roared behind us, Sonia breaking the kiss immediately to turn back in shock, watching all her loved ones standing and clapping at the door frame and glancing through the windows. She turned back to me with a huge grin and downturned eyebrows with a question loud in them.

"Your mom suggested I come and make things right today. She's the one who orchestrated it all. She hadn't stopped calling me and apologizing even when I told her she didn't need to."

Her eyes now welled up in happiness. "She knew?"

I nodded, pressing my forehead onto hers. "I love you, shona. With every fiber of my being I do."

"I love you, too, Kartik." With one final kiss, she laced her fingers with mine, intertwining them right where they always belonged. "Let's go inside now. You'll catch a cold."

"You're worth catching a cold for."

Throwing her head back, she giggled, pulling me towards the rest of my life.

EPILOGUE

Sonia

After witnessing my kindergarteners graduate, Kartik had driven me back to our home. The same home that he once wished to sell, but was now building it to be the place we'd fill with our cherished memories. I still kept my apartment, though, living there most days until Kartik had fully gotten the house renovated and updated. But that didn't stop us from spending most nights together for the past three months cuddled up in a bedroom that held remnants of an innocent life we once knew.

However, today, he'd been driving to the biggest surprise of his life.

"What the hell is going on, shona?" He attempted to break away as I tied a blindfold to his eyes from across the passenger seat. "Kya kar rahi ho?" *What are you doing?* His hands tried to shoo mine away, his eagerness always getting the best of him.

"Be quiet, would you? Always so impatient." I couldn't hold the laughter in any longer, his irritation only coming out in affection.

"Well maybe, if I was able to see, I wouldn't be asking so many questions." I didn't have to see his eyes to know he was rolling them behind the satiny cloth.

"Shush. I'm coming around to get you." Before he could say another word, I stepped out of the car and opened the driver side door, offering him a hand to pull him out. He stood tall in front of me, and I couldn't resist getting on my tip toes and pressing my lips against his for a quick peck.

He hummed in approval, mocking the scene he couldn't see. "Is this some new kink exploration thing you're doing? Cause if you wanted blindfolds you could have just told me."

"Shut. Up." I lightly smacked his chest as he feigned a scorned look, tugging and leading him towards the door and up the patio steps. "Okay, ready?"

"Sonia, how are you going to ask me if I'm ready when I have no idea what to be ready for?" Although his arguments were valid, it killed me to end the anticipation so soon. It was fun to see him turning screws in his brain to figure out what was going on.

"Okay wait." Swallowing a gulp, I faced him. "You have to promise me you won't be mad."

"Baby, whatever it is, I promise I won't be mad. I could never be mad at you. Just get this damn thing off my eyes."

His words should have been reassuring but there was still a doubt in my mind that the plan could go wrong any minute.

No longer wishing to torment either of us, I pressed my key into the lock, turning it to let the cool air hit us. One step in and I'd already felt better.

"Just remember, you said you won't be mad." Untying the blindfold, I let him blink a couple times before flashing on the lights.

"Surprise!" A unison of screams filled the air from everyone we knew. "Happy birthday, Kartik!"

I watched as he took in every face he could make out. Jaymin and Addie were grinning beside Kyle and Jenna, who had her arms interlocked with Jyoti. All our parents had been in another corner, standing next to Kartik's father, who looked equally as ecstatic as the rest of them. Mortada showed up as well, along with his girlfriend Alyssa. A few other mutual friends of Jaymin and Addie had been mingling with each other. And between them all, Trevor and Colt had stood right in front of us.

Kartik still hadn't moved, his expression unreadable.
I shouldn't have done this.

My heart thumped as I scrambled for words, pressing against the necklace I wore proudly now. "Listen, I know you say you don't celebrate your birthday but I thought maybe it's just because you haven't actually experienced what you should on your big day. And I wanted to bring that joy to you. When I told everyone they were really on board, your dad included who was surprisingly the most excited, and I know you haven't seen Colt or Trevor since high school when they were there for you and I've seen you looking at old pictures from your band days reminiscing and so it was kismet how a couple weeks ago I bumped into Trevor at the grocery store and he told me he's been in New Jersey this whole time and so had Colt and I thought what better way to reunite you guys than on your birthday." Kartik finally looked at me, his face displaying an expression so still it could freeze water. "I'm sorry, I know I shouldn't have. I can tell everyone to leave."

He took a step closer to me, his hand falling right into mine, his fingers fitting into the crevices of my knuckles. "You remembered my birthday?"

"I haven't forgotten a thing about you." My lips curved upward as I saw him release a decades long pain, letting go of the loneliness he learned to walk beside.

Our entire ensemble of friends hollered as he clasped his lips around mine, mixing our bodies together. Kissing him would never get old. With one final peck on my nose, he held me close to me, staking his claim. "I must have done something right in another life to deserve you in this one."

As his high school friends finally approached him, I let him catch up with them, admiring him off the sidelines with just one thought in my mind.

I'll find you in every lifetime.

Acknowledgements

Firstly, I'd like to thank my readers. Every single one who sat down and took time from their own lives to read my words and love (or hate) them. To all the readers who read the first book, messaging me your thoughts, loving it publicly, supporting me, you all are what make writing worth it.

To the girls who agreed to beta read this book for me, you have helped me mold this story into one I am proud of telling. Thank you for the dedication you had towards it, constantly replying with your thoughts and suggestions. This wouldn't have been the story it is now without you.

To my friends and family, for continuously cheering me on from the sidelines, for seeing all my drafted covers and excerpts and telling me the truth about them no matter how bitter. For supporting me tirelessly.

Thank you to the community I've built through my social media, including tiktok, instagram and twitter. You've all done unreal by me, boosting my posts and making them visible to new readers on the daily.

Lastly, I want to continue thanking my younger self for dreaming big, for shooting for the stars and never coming down no matter how many people tried to convince you to. I do this for specifically for you. I hope you're proud of who we've become.

About the author

Shivani Rana is a new Adult Romance and Contemporary author who loves to read, write and draw in her free time. She also loves anything fashion and loves photography and traveling. With a passion for all things art, she hopes to bring more equal representation for South Asians like herself.

If you want to know more about Shivani Rana and see news regrading upcoming releases, you could keep in touch at any of the places below.

Goodreads: www.goodreads.com/shivaniranaa
Instagram: www.instagram.com/shivaniranaa
Tiktok: @shivaniranaawrites & @shivaniranaa
Email: ranashivani218@gmail.com

Also by Shivani Rana

ARRANGED BY LOVE SERIES
interconnected standalones

The One I Want
I'd Wait Forever

OTHER BOOKS

Conversations With The Moon